SUSAN MALLERY

Praise for *Straight from the Hip*

"Mallery has penned an emotionally satisfying and thoroughly engaging story."
—*Booklist*, starred review

Praise for *Lip Service*

"Mallery breathes real life into these former lovers hoping for a secondchance."
—*RT Book Reviews*

Praise for *Under Her Skin*

"Bestseller Mallery's Lone Star Sisters series opener draws in readers with intriguing characters.... Their emotional journey makes for...satisfying reading."
—*Publishers Weekly*

Praise for *Sweet Spot*

"Mallery is in top-notch form as she takes troubled and stubborn individuals and portrays their emotional growth. Drama and trauma abound in this winner!"
—*RT Book Reviews*

"I strongly recommend *Sweet Spot*, especially to readers who like their family melodramas spiked with lots of laughter and hot romance."
—*The Romance Reader*

SUSAN MALLERY

HOT ON HER HEELS

HQN™

Recycling programs
for this product may
not exist in your area.

ISBN-13: 978-0-373-77384-8

HOT ON HER HEELS

Copyright © 2009 by Susan Macias Redmond

www.HQNBooks.com

Printed in U.S.A.

**Also available from
Susan Mallery and HQN Books**

Sweet Trouble
Sweet Spot
Sweet Talk
Accidentally Yours
Tempting
Sizzling
Irresistible
Delicious
Someone Like You
Falling for Gracie

**And don't miss the rest of the
Lone Star Sisters' adventures**

Under Her Skin
Lip Service
Straight from the Hip

Available now!

**Look for Susan Mallery's new series,
starting with**

Faking Perfect,
in May 2010

HOT ON
HER HEELS

CHAPTER ONE

IT HAD TAKEN FOUR MONTHS, calling in every favor ever owed her, a case of expensive Scotch and a date with a slimy private investigator who had made the mistake of thinking "date" meant "sex." A knee to the groin had cured him of that belief. In the end, Dana Birch had gotten her man.

Now, as she rode the elevator up to Garth Duncan's penthouse condo, she smiled at the paperwork in her hand. Paperwork that demanded he come talk to the good people at the Dallas Police Department. Paperwork that said Garth was going to have a very bad day. She, on the other hand, couldn't be happier.

"Rat bastard, weasel dog," she murmured as she stepped off the elevator and headed to his front door. "You thought you were so smart. You thought you could do whatever you wanted and get away with it. You thought you could hurt my friends."

If life were perfect, he would resist accompanying her and she could threaten him with her gun. Maybe even accidentally shoot him. If only he were the type of guy to cower in the face of authority, not to mention consequences. In her fantasies, he would tremble and beg. While it wasn't as good as watching him bleed, it would be a close second. Unfortunately Garth was more the type to have a thousand-dollar-an-hour attorney who lived to sue police departments. Not that his high-powered attorney would be much help today.

"You are so mine, Garth," she said, then knocked.

In the minute or so it took him to answer, she savored the victory. She'd worked hard to nail Garth and it had been worth every long hour of digging, following up clues and waiting for a lucky break. It was his own fault, she thought cheerfully. He'd messed with people she cared about. No one did that without having to face her.

The front door opened. She smiled as she saw Garth was half-concealed behind the door. Maybe he *was* afraid, she thought with a flicker of contempt.

She held out the papers. "Good morning. We're going to take a little ride downtown."

"Are we?" he asked as he opened the door wider, so she could see all of him. "Am I allowed to get dressed first?"

An unexpected twist, Dana thought grimly as she took in the towel draped around his neck, covering his chest, and the one around his waist. He was dripping, obviously just out of the shower. His dark hair stood in little spikes, his expression was far more amused than worried.

"At least you know I'm not armed," he said, his voice thick with humor.

"I wouldn't be afraid if you were."

"That's because you don't know what I'm capable of, Deputy Birch. So which is it? Are you prepared to parade me naked through the streets of Dallas or will I be putting on clothes?"

He sounded confident, as if he knew she wouldn't take him in a towel, which was true. Damn him. She liked situations where *she* was in charge.

"You can get dressed," she said grudgingly. "I'll need to be in the room, though, to make sure you don't try to escape."

He actually gave her a little wink. "Of course you will. That's as good an excuse as any."

Irritation coursed through her. Instinctively she rested her right hand on her sidearm. "You wish," she snapped. "Let me assure you I have no interest in seeing your bony backside. Or any other part of you."

One corner of his mouth turned up. "You can watch, Dana. I don't mind."

He was playing with her, trying to mess with her. She focused on the reason she was here.

"Joke all you want," she told him. "You're going to jail."

"If only wishing made it so."

"You're not getting out of this," she said. "I have the proof I need."

"No, you don't." His voice was low and deceptively

soft. "If you had what you needed, you'd be arresting me, not bringing me in for questioning. Admit it, Dana. You're not even close to charging me with anything. This is a fishing expedition."

While she knew in her head that reacting with violence only weakened her position and proved he was right, she really, really wanted to hit him.

"I'm officially bored," she said, dropping her arm to her side. "Let's get this over with."

"The part where you watch me naked?"

She stepped into his condo and rolled her eyes. "Yeah. Lucky, lucky me. Have you been featured in *Arrogance Monthly* yet?"

"I've been on the cover."

He shut the door, then led the way through the large penthouse.

The main room was huge—she was guessing she could fit her apartment and five others just like it in the space. There were floor-to-ceiling windows with a view of most of Dallas. Not that she cared about that sort of thing.

She returned her attention to the man in front of her, then frowned as sunlight caught his back, illuminating the scars crisscrossing his skin.

A few of them were thin lines, but most were thick and raised, as if the skin had been cut over and over again. Her stomach clenched slightly, not that she allowed her expression to change.

She knew the basic facts about Garth Duncan. He

was rich—scary rich, with dozens of companies and money flowing like water. He'd started in the oil business and while down in South America, no doubt raping and pillaging a pristine part of the world, he'd been captured and held prisoner by some angry locals. They'd kept him and a coworker blindfolded in the jungle for a month, torturing them both daily.

Her gaze dropped to his long, muscled legs. She could see faint scars there, too, but these had come from a surgeon. Both of Garth's legs had been broken during his captivity. His friend had carried him to safety.

If only Garth had died back then, Dana thought, but without a whole lot of energy. He wouldn't be hurting her friends. But he hadn't died. He'd come back home and flourished.

She followed a few steps behind as he entered a massive bedroom, then continued into a bathroom the size of a grocery store. That led into one of those fancy closets done in dark wood. All the clothes were perfectly organized by color. Shoes were lined up on racks.

She leaned against the doorway, never taking her eyes from him. "Anytime."

His dark gaze locked with hers. He seemed to be enjoying himself, which pissed her off. But once the investigation began, his attitude would change. She was bringing him in. For now, that was enough.

His smile returned. He pulled the towel off his

shoulders and let it fall to the floor. "If you don't have to be anywhere in the next couple of hours, we could take advantage of my lack of clothes."

"Hours? Oh, please. You'd be lucky to last six minutes. Quit playing, Garth. I have a full day ahead of me. Despite what you think, the world doesn't revolve around you."

"Yes, Deputy Birch."

He dropped the towel at his waist.

She kept her eyes on his face. Not only didn't he interest her in the least, but she was here in a professional capacity. She was proud of her job and what she did for the community. The good people of her town didn't pay her to ogle the likes of Garth Duncan.

"No?" he asked, completely naked and holding out his arms at his side. "I'm yours for the taking."

She faked a yawn.

He laughed. A rich, full laugh that spoke of amusement and perhaps grudging respect. For reasons she couldn't explain, she found herself wanting to smile back at him. As if they were sharing a connection. As if they had something in common. As if they almost liked each other and might even be almost friends.

Dana turned and walked out of the closet. "Get dressed," she called as she went.

"What if I have a gun in here?" he yelled after her.

"Then I get to shoot you."

She crossed to the window in the bedroom and stared out at the view. But she only saw her friends' faces. The three sisters Garth was trying to ruin. He hadn't been content to attempt to destroy Lexi's business or ruin Skye's foundation. He'd actually tried to kill Izzy. What the hell was she thinking, smiling at him?

Garth was the enemy. He was evil. She was going to put him in prison for a very long time.

Five minutes later he walked into the bedroom. He wore a suit she was sure cost more than she made in a couple of months.

"Let's go," she said. "We'll take my car."

"I'm calling my lawyer on the way. She'll meet us at the police station."

"You can call Congress and God for all I care." She pointed to the hallway. "Move."

Instead of heading toward the living room, he moved toward her. For a split second Dana wondered if he had really had a gun in the closet. She reached for her sidearm.

"I didn't try to kill her," Garth said. "I had nothing to do with what happened to Izzy."

"I'm not the one you have to convince," Dana told him.

"You're a cop. Look at me, Dana. Tell me if you think I'm lying." He stared into her eyes. "I didn't try to kill Izzy. I didn't cause the explosion. I never went after her at all."

He was standing too close, she thought suddenly. She wasn't worried about him coming after her, but she still felt uneasy. What was going on?

Hating to give up the power, she took a step back.

He was lying. He had to be lying. But the voice in her head that warned her when someone was trying to pull a fast one was oddly silent.

"I suppose you didn't do anything at all," she said, grabbing his arm and starting toward the hallway. "That you're completely innocent."

He only smiled.

He could have pulled away easily, but didn't, which left her in the uncomfortable position of hanging on to him. She could feel the heat of his skin, the muscles, the smooth fabric of his fancy suit.

"Don't mess with me," she growled.

"I didn't say a word."

So why did she feel so uncomfortable?

Weakness wasn't allowed, she reminded herself. Not with him, not with anyone.

"PLEASE TELL ME THEY threatened you before I got there," Mary Jo Sheffield said as she and Garth walked toward her car. "I'm itching to file a lawsuit."

His attorney—a fortysomething blonde who barely came to his shoulder—looked determined. She could scent blood with the efficiency of a shark, one of the reasons he'd hired her.

"Sorry to disappoint you," Garth told her as he waited for her to unlock her Mercedes. "They were polite and didn't notify the press."

Mary Jo wrinkled her nose. "Tell me someone hit

you or threatened to hit you. Tell me they manhandled your cat when they brought you in. I need something to work with here."

"I don't have a cat," Garth said.

"So few men do. Something I've never understood. Cats treat their owners with disdain and God knows your gender is constantly falling for women who treat them badly." Mary Jo grinned. "Sorry. Ignore the rant. So you're saying I can't sue the Dallas Police Department?"

"I'm saying I can't help you make your case."

"Damn."

She unlocked her car. Garth slid into the passenger seat.

He'd spent nearly six hours being questioned. Mary Jo had been present for all but the first thirty minutes. He'd been provided with coffee, sandwiches and plenty of breaks. It had been easy…too easy.

Deputy Dana Birch would be horrified if she found out, he thought, enjoying the thought of her screaming at some unsuspecting sergeant for not stringing Garth up by his thumbs and beating him with a pipe. If she had her way, he would be tortured into confessing all and then burned at the stake. Of course if she knew him, she would know torture wouldn't get him to talk. Fortunately for him, Dana wasn't in charge of the Texas criminal justice system.

"What about the deputy?" Mary Jo asked. "Deputy Birch. Can I go after her? What was she doing, bringing you in, anyway? She's not a member of the Dallas PD. She's from Titanville. There's something going on there. Maybe I can get her suspended."

"Leave Dana out of it," he said as they left the parking garage.

Mary Jo glanced at him, eyebrows raised. "Dana? You know her?"

"We've met."

"Tell me you're not sleeping with her, Garth. Tell me this isn't personal."

He chuckled. It was personal, but not in the way his attorney meant. "We're not involved or even friends. She's…"

Dana was his half sisters' friend. A deputy in the town where his mother lived. She was annoying, stubborn and determined to take him.

"She's a friend of the family," he said finally.

"I didn't know you had family."

"I'm more the type to have hatched?"

She sighed. "Fine. I won't sue Deputy Birch. But tell her to stay out of my way. She's trouble. I've had to deal with her in the past. I know the type. She's honest and loyal. You know how annoying those two traits can be."

He did. Once he'd believed in them. Lately though, he was more interested in results. An attitude that had cost him a lot but insured the win. And right now winning was all that mattered.

"I have the loan papers drawn up," Mary Jo said.

"Not to keep repeating myself, but you're totally insane. Jed Titan is never going to accept the terms of the loan. Even if he does need the money, he won't take it from you."

"He won't know it's me."

"He'll suspect."

"He won't have a choice. I'm continuing to buy up his company. The shareholders are getting nervous. They know I'm interested, but they don't know my end game, which is how I want it. Jed has had a lot of bad press lately. The possible treason charges alone cost his shareholders a lot of money as the price dipped."

Mary Jo glanced at him, then returned her attention to the road. "I find it interesting that the price of Jed's stock dropped right when you wanted to buy it."

"Funny how it all worked that way."

"Tell me you haven't broken the law."

"I have in no way violated Securities and Exchange Commissions guidelines or rules."

"Keep it in the gray area," his attorney advised.

He'd stepped far beyond that, but not in a way that could be traced to him. Most of his attacks on the Titan family had been more subtle. It kept things interesting.

"What happens now?" Mary Jo asked. "Or don't I want to know?"

"I go to work and start my day."

She glanced at him again. "You're not going to tell me what's really going on, are you?"

"No."

She didn't need to know about his plan to destroy Jed Titan or the fact that Jed was his father. Eventually word would get out. He would be branded the Titan bastard, but by the time that happened, he would own Jed's ass and everything else. He would have destroyed his father, taken possession of all the old man owned. He would have won.

She pulled up in front of his high-rise condo and parked. She looked at him. "You know you're my favorite client."

"I'm your only client." Mary Jo worked for him exclusively. It had cost several million to get her away from her high-powered law firm, but she had been worth every penny.

"I don't want to see you in jail," she said. "You're scaring me and you know I don't scare easily."

"There's nothing to be scared of."

She drew in a breath. "Dana's tough. Tenacious, driven. She's a lot like you. If she thinks she has something on you, she won't stop until she gets you. She's not someone to be taken lightly."

"She sounds like a worthy adversary."

"This isn't a game, Garth," Mary Jo told him.

He smiled and got out of her car. "Of course it is. Don't worry—I always come out on top."

DANA STUDIED THE BLUE fabric of her sofa, not that it interested her, but it seemed far easier to think about slipcovers than deal with the woman sitting across from her. But as the silence ticked on, she was forced to look at her friend.

"It didn't go well," Dana admitted, hating to say the words nearly as much as she hated failing. "I took him in and they questioned him for several hours."

"And?" Izzy prompted anxiously.

"And they got nothing. He was friendly, cooperative and didn't give up a thing."

Izzy grinned. "Yes!"

Dana stared at her. "You know this is the man responsible for the explosion that nearly killed you."

"He's not," Izzy insisted, leaning forward in her chair. "He didn't do it, Dana. I know he didn't do it."

"How? Because he told you?"

"Partially. And because Nick believes him."

Which was the problem, Dana thought, annoyed at the complication. Nick *was* one of the good guys. He also knew Garth better than anyone.

"I want more," Dana said stubbornly.

"I want to trust him."

"Wanting something doesn't make it so."

"Neither does denying it."

"I'll get him, I swear I will," Dana grumbled. "I don't know how, but I'll come up with something."

"If he's guilty," Izzy said, a warning in her voice, which annoyed Dana. "Only if he's guilty."

Izzy was the youngest of the Titan sisters. Lexi, the oldest, had gone through school with Dana, while Skye was a year older than Izzy. They had been raised in wealth and privilege, something Dana refused to hold against them. They were her family. They cared about her and she would do anything for them. Including taking down their half brother.

About nine months earlier, Lexi had encountered some financial difficulties with her day spa. After borrowing money to expand her business, the two-million-dollar note had been called, giving her only twenty-one days to come up with the amount owed. A few weeks later, Skye's charitable foundation had been accused of money laundering. Their father had faced trouble, as well. His racehorses had tested positive for doping. Through the spring and summer, the situation had only gotten worse, ending with an explosion on the oil platform where Izzy worked. She'd been temporarily blinded by the blast.

The person behind all of it? An angry Garth Duncan.

Dana didn't care if he went after Jed—the old man had been especially cruel to Garth—but the sisters were off-limits. Not that Garth saw it that way.

"I wish I could arrest him," Dana said, knowing that putting handcuffs on Garth would make her one happy camper. "Or shoot him."

"Hey." Izzy glared at her. "You're talking about my brother. I know he did a lot of bad stuff, but he swears he had nothing to do with the explosion and I believe him."

It wasn't Izzy's fault, Dana told herself. Izzy had been raised isolated from the real world. She didn't believe people could be truly bad. Although Dana's gut kind of agreed with her, which only pissed her off more. She didn't want shades of gray where Garth was concerned.

"You rich people do love to hang together," Dana muttered.

"I'm not rich."

"You will be as soon as your trust fund comes through." She leaned back on the sofa and closed her eyes. "I'm surrounded by rich people. How did that happen?"

"You love us," Izzy reminded her.

"True enough. You and your sisters are my best friends, which only goes to show what an incredibly understanding person I am."

Izzy laughed. "So was Garth surprised to see you?"

Dana opened her eyes and straightened. Better to deal with Izzy than remember Garth naked and dripping. "He handled the situation well."

Better than well. He'd been completely comfortable, not the least bit intimidated and almost...well, nearly...charming.

What was up with that? She didn't find men charming, certainly not men like him. He was an annoying, egotistical, determined bastard who had hurt the people she loved. Not charming. Never charming.

There was a knock at her front door.

She jumped up, grateful for the interruption, and crossed the small room. After flipping both locks, she let Lexi and Skye into her condo.

"It's actually cold out there," Skye said as she slipped off a light jacket. "I'm so ready for winter."

Dana grinned. "It's sixty-five."

Lexi rested her hand on her pregnancy bump. "Speaking as someone who is starting to swell professionally, I'm all for cooler weather." She grabbed Dana's arm. "Did you get him? Is he in jail, becoming Bubba's love slave?"

"No. He was questioned and released."

"Damn."

"It's fine," Izzy said, standing and hugging both her sisters. "I promise. Look, you need to sit down. There's something I have to tell you."

Both Skye and Lexi turned to Dana. "What has she done now?" Skye asked.

Dana held up her hands. "This is not my party. I'm simply a neutral location. But you might want to take a deep breath. It's going to be quite the ride."

Lexi and Skye exchanged wary looks before sitting on the sofa. Dana stayed by the door, thinking Izzy's announcement was going to cause an amazing explosion. She wanted to be able to see everything.

Izzy shook her head, then fluffed her curly hair. "I have an announcement," she began.

"We got that," Lexi said, keeping a protective hand on her stomach. "What is it?"

"It's about Garth. As you know, I talked to him right before Nick and I got back together. He took Nick's side and responsibility for what had happened."

"As he should have," Skye snapped. "The man goes out of his way to destroy everything you two had worked toward. It just makes me so mad."

"Excuse me." Izzy shook her head. "I was talking. While I was with Garth, I had an epiphany. I realized that he's our flesh and blood. Okay, I've known that for a while now, but they were just words. They didn't mean anything."

Lexi look at Dana. "Where is this going?"

"I am staying neutral here."

Lexi turned back to Izzy. "What's your point?"

Izzy smiled. "We've been trying to defeat him for months and it hasn't worked. The strategy is totally flawed. We shouldn't be fighting him. We should be protecting him from himself. That's what I wanted to tell you both. Garth is our brother and it's our job to bring him into the family. We're going to save him."

Skye and Lexi stared at their sister. They were both wide-eyed with shock. Their mouths fell open.

Dana folded her arms across her chest and shook her head. "Welcome to the show."

CHAPTER TWO

"SAVE HIM?" LEXI SHRIEKED, coming to her feet and glaring at Izzy. "Are you insane? Are you still on some kind of medication from your eye surgery, because you're talking crazy. We're not saving him. He tried to kill you. You were nearly left blind. That's not okay. That can never be okay. And he's still bent on ruining all of us. Save Garth? From what? *For* what?"

"You need to stay calm and sit down," Izzy told her sister. "Think of the baby."

"You leave my baby out of this. If you were so concerned about my baby, you wouldn't be worried about a man who is doing everything he can to make our lives hell." Lexi pushed her blond hair off her face. "Dammit, Izzy, I expect better of you."

Dana moved toward the sofa. If necessary, she would get between the sisters to make sure things didn't get too ugly.

Izzy stiffened. "You can expect all you want. What matters is I talked to Garth. He's family, Lexi. He's as biologically related to us as we are to each other. He's been hurt. Dad screwed him and you know it."

"Fine. Jed was horrible to both Garth and his mother. But that doesn't give him the right to come after us. We had nothing to do with it."

"He's not responsible for the oil rig exploding. I believe him and Nick believes him. Look, think of him like Darth Vader. He needs to be saved from himself."

"You really think that using movie examples will help your case?" Lexi asked.

Dana glanced at Skye who was listening intently, but not saying anything. Izzy's strategy was flawed. Skye was the more emotional of the sisters. If Izzy wanted the three of them to cooperate, she should have convinced Skye first. Then the two of them could have worked on Lexi.

"He's our brother," Izzy repeated stubbornly. "I saw something inside of him."

"The ravages of a black and empty heart," Lexi muttered.

"I saw who he was supposed to be." Izzy leaned forward. "I saw flashes of the fourteen-year-old boy who begged his own father, a man who had never acknowledged him, for the money to save his mother from a brain tumor. Jed turned him away. Jed threw him into the street. Jed is the reason he wants revenge."

"We all know this," Skye said quietly.

"But the person he should have been is still there. Imagine what Garth would be like if his mother had never gotten sick. Imagine if we'd met him when we were ten or fifteen. If we'd grown up together. We would have been a family."

"It's too late to go back," Lexi said flatly.

"But it's not too late to go forward. If you exclude the explosion, then he hasn't really hurt us."

"Not for lack of trying."

"He wanted me to get together with Nick," Izzy said.

"He's the reason you broke up in the first place," Lexi reminded her.

"Agreed, but he realized he was wrong. He came to me and pleaded Nick's case. Nick didn't know he was doing that. Garth had no reason to help us, but he did. He's not all bad."

Lexi and Skye looked at each other. Izzy saw the exchange and pounced.

"Why would he do that and lie about the explosion? He admitted to everything else." Izzy glanced at Dana. "Not in a way that can be used in court."

"I figured that."

Lexi sighed and turned to Dana. "You didn't try to talk her out of it?"

"I tried," Dana told her. "But she's very much her own person. Which is mostly your fault. She's your baby sister. You should have repressed her more as a child. But no. You had to nurture her. This is what you get as a thank-you."

"Very funny," Lexi said. "Do you have anything serious to add?"

Dana glanced at all of them. "Izzy's not an idiot and she has good instincts about people. Do I think she's right? I don't know. Am I willing to say she's totally and completely wrong?" She hesitated. "No."

Izzy grinned. "See. Dana believes me."

"That's not what I said," Dana told her.

"Close enough." Izzy smiled at her sisters. "We've got big-time pressure here. I want Garth in the family fold by Christmas. Then we can all celebrate together."

"I'm sorry I'm going to miss that," Dana said, almost meaning it. Talk about an uncomfortable day.

"You won't," Izzy told her, grinning.

"You're the one he tried to kill," Skye said, speaking for the first time. "You're totally sure he wasn't responsible?"

Izzy's smile faded. She leaned forward and stared into Skye's eyes. "I swear. I believe him. He's not innocent in this. But he had his reasons for acting against us *and* he's our brother. I know down to my soul that bringing him into the family is the only way to stop all this. To make it better."

"Jed will never accept him," Skye said.

"This isn't about Jed, it's about us. Jed has proven again and again that none of us matter to him. But that's okay because we have each other. And now we have Garth."

Skye was quiet for a moment, then nodded slowly. "Okay."

Izzy jumped to her feet. "I knew you'd understand."

"Maybe she does, but I don't," Lexi said. "Even if I accept he didn't try to kill you, which I don't, big deal. What about everything else? He still has a lot to answer for."

Skye nodded. "Lexi's right. We have to be sure. We all have to be sure this isn't a trick. That he hasn't come up with a new strategy. Maybe he wasn't responsible for the explosion. Maybe that was just bad timing or something. But there are other questions that still have to be answered."

Dana cleared her throat. "Technically this isn't Garth's strategy. It's Izzy's. I don't think he wants to be drawn into the family."

"Which will make the process even more unpleasant," Lexi murmured.

"We have to do this," Izzy said stubbornly. "We have to save him."

"If he's worth saving," Skye said. "How do we know for sure?"

There was a moment of silence as the women looked at each other. Suddenly Izzy grinned.

"Piss him off," she announced happily. "If I'm right and there's a nice guy just waiting to get out, he may be annoyed but he won't act out. If he's as horrible as you three think, he'll show his true colors. Stress brings out a person's real character."

"She's right," Skye said slowly. "If we can get in his face, we'll figure him out pretty quickly."

"We need to provoke him in an obvious way," Dana said, moving toward them, liking the idea of annoying Garth.

Skye smiled. "What about if one of us shadows him? Two birds with one stone—either we catch him being evil to someone else or he reacts to our personal surveillance."

Lexi nodded. "If he's everything Izzy claims, he'll understand. If not, maybe he'll get mad and show us what's underneath that tough facade. It's a win-win. I like it."

"I don't," Izzy said, "but I see the point of it. So which one of us should it be?"

Dana thought about everything that had happened in the past few months, how scared her friends had been and about Garth's ruthless actions. She thought about how Jed had ignored his own daughters, virtually leaving them on their own to handle a situation *he'd* created. She thought of how much each of the Titan sisters meant to her.

"I'll do it," she said, looking at them. "I'll take a leave of absence and stay on Garth full-time."

"You can't," Skye said.

"Sure I can. I won't have a problem getting the time. You need an objective third party, but also someone who knows what to look for. That's me."

"You have to let us pay you," Lexi said. "You won't have a paycheck."

"Not on your life."

Skye stood and faced her. She was a green-eyed redhead with a temper. It took her a while to get riled, but when it happened, it was impressive.

"Friends don't let friends work for free," Skye told her. "Either we pay you or we find someone else."

"It's not like they'll miss the money," Izzy pointed out. "They're rich."

"When you get your trust fund, you're kicking in your share," Skye told her.

Dana didn't want to take their money, but she also didn't want to trust anyone else with the investigation. There was too much on the line.

"Okay. But no more than my usual pay at the sheriff's office."

"Done," Lexi said, leveraging herself into a standing position. "You'll stay on Garth and find out everything you can. If he's becoming one of the good guys, then we'll all hold hands and sing 'Kumbaya.' If not, you get the pleasure of throwing his ass in jail."

Dana smiled. "I'd like that."

Izzy put her hands on her hips. "You be nice to him."

"I won't leave any scars," she promised instead.

"No bruises, either."

Dana sighed. "No one lets me have any fun."

GARTH'S PHONE BUZZED.

"There are two ladies here to see you," his assistant said through the speakerphone. "They don't have appointments, but said that you, and I quote, 'wouldn't mind taking time from your busy schedule to be with loved ones.'"

He only knew one person who talked like that. "Izzy and one of her sisters?"

"Ms. Skye Titan, sir."

"Send them in."

He rose and walked around his desk. Why would Skye and Izzy come to see him? Not to gloat. His time with the Dallas Police Department had hardly been a victory.

Seconds later Izzy breezed into his office. Her long, dark curly hair tumbled past her shoulders. She smiled as if they shared a delicious secret. Skye trailed behind her, looking less convinced this was where she wanted to be.

"An unexpected pleasure," he said, motioning to the sofas by the window. "Can I get you ladies anything?"

"No, thanks. We're here to talk," Izzy said as she plopped down on a sofa cushion. "Lexi had other obligations. That's what I'm supposed to say. Reality is, she's still not sure about you. I said you were fine, but only Skye really believes me."

He turned his attention to the curvy redhead in a tailored suit and pearls who had taken a seat near her sister. "You're sure about me?"

Cool, green eyes stared into his. "I said I was willing to consider you weren't completely evil. There's a difference."

"I agree." He turned his attention back to Izzy. "What are we talking about?"

"You. Saving you from yourself." She frowned. "You don't remember? We discussed this before."

Izzy had said some sentimental things about him being her brother and the sisters being his family—a fact that didn't change anything. He'd dismissed her comments as the babblings of a broken heart.

"You were upset about Nick," he said.

"Oh, please. That didn't affect my brain." She settled into a more comfortable position and patted the cushion next to hers. "Come on. Join the party. As I said the other day, you're family. This path of destruction you're on is just plain stupid. So we're going to save you."

"Against my will?"

"If necessary." She smiled. "We can be very persuasive."

"Izzy wants you to join the family," Skye said.

"By Christmas," Izzy added.

He remembered her saying something like that before. "Thanks, but no."

"You don't get a choice."

"Part of saving me against my will?"

"Uh-huh. Come on, Garth. We're your sisters. Didn't you ever wish you had someone to braid your hair?"

"I'll pass."

"Ignore him," Izzy told her sister. "He'll come around."

"And if he doesn't want to come around?" Skye asked. "This is not a well-thought-out plan."

"When has that stopped me before?"

Garth couldn't remember the last time he'd been so uncomfortable in the presence of two women. Just as strange, he couldn't define the cause of his unease.

He forced himself to walk closer and take a seat.

Skye turned to him. "While Izzy can be wild and impetuous, she's actually a fairly good judge of character. She says you're worth it."

"I'm not," he told her, knowing that the further the conversation went, the harder it would be to ruthlessly take over the Titan world.

Skye studied him, staring intently, as if she tried hard enough, she could read his mind.

"I understand why you went after Jed," she said after a few seconds. "What he did was horrific. I'm ashamed of his behavior and I apologize on his behalf. Not that my apology has any validity."

"None at all," he said easily.

"Fair enough. But why us? What did we do to deserve your contempt?"

He didn't like the word *contempt*. It implied emotion, not rationality. "You were easy targets," he said. "If I hurt you, I hurt Jed."

"By now you must be aware that Jed doesn't give a damn about any of us. He's not much of a father."

She said the words easily, but he heard the tight pain in her voice. She might have accepted the truth about her father, but it still had the power to wound.

Garth shrugged. "If it distracts him, that's enough for me."

"No, it's not," Izzy said. "Come on. You didn't mean for it to get this messy. That's not your style."

Her assessment annoyed him—probably because it was true. "You don't know my style."

"I can guess. You want a clean victory," Izzy told him. "When you started this, you thought we were one happy family. Cut one and we all bleed. You thought you could weaken Jed by going after those he loved most. Which was quite the miscalculation, big brother. Feeling a little foolish now, are we?"

"No." Foolish didn't exactly explain what emotions he'd experienced.

The ruthless side of him said that he should tell them the truth. That their father had come to him, offering him the chance to run Titan World on the condition that all three of Jed's daughters never get a penny.

But he didn't say the words. There was no reason to hurt them further. Jed would do that well enough without any help.

"We're not your enemy," Skye said. "We don't want anything from you." She glanced at Izzy, who was shaking her head, then sighed. "Izzy wants you to be part of the family, but that's different. We're not after power or money. We just want to live our lives in peace. Is it that you can't believe that, or you're in too deep to back off now?"

Before he could answer, Izzy moved from her sofa to his and sat next to him. She angled toward him and touched his arm.

"We're sorry about your mom. I don't understand how Jed could be so callous and cruel—which I guess are the same thing. Or maybe I do understand and it scares me. He's my father, too. Why does he have to be so bad?"

Garth didn't want to think about his mother or what had happened to her. He drew back. "This isn't going to work. I've made my decision. I know what I want and I'm going to get it."

Izzy only smiled. "You can't. We're your family. Not Jed. He deserves what he's going to get, but not us. You know we're innocent. You know we don't deserve what you're doing to us. Every time you act against one of us, you're becoming more and more like Jed, and that's not who you are."

He felt the truth of her statements but didn't say anything.

"You're pressuring him, Izzy," Skye said. "You have to stop. Enough with the emotional blackmail. Let's deal with facts. If you didn't arrange the explosion on the oil rig, who did? Or was it an accident?"

Garth appreciated the change in topic. "The preliminary reports all suggest a man-made cause. Someone did it on purpose."

"If not you, then who?" Skye asked.

"I'm working on that."

"Why do you care?" Izzy asked.

"I'll take responsibility for what I did, nothing else."

"With all you've been doing," Skye said, "you're a likely suspect."

He nodded. "I know, but it wasn't me. Explosions are too dangerous. There's no way to control all the outcomes. I always know the end game."

"I don't suppose you'd take a lie detector test," Skye said.

He chuckled. "No." Although he would be open to intense questioning by Deputy Dana, he thought humorously. She intrigued him with her determination and irreverence.

"When you find out who was responsible, will you tell us?" Skye asked.

"Be careful what you ask for. You may not like the answer."

She frowned. "Do you already know?"

"I suspect. There's a difference."

Skye looked stricken, as if she had thought of something impossible to believe. "Will you tell us?" she asked again softly.

"Yes."

"Just like that?"

"I'll tell you," he said firmly.

She stood. "Then I guess we'll wait to hear."

He and Izzy rose.

Izzy looked at him. "About the family thing. I'm not kidding. You're one of us now. Quit being mean."

Then, before he could stop her, she wrapped both her arms around him, leaning against him. The embrace was uncomfortable and unfamiliar. He was used to having women in his arms, but this was different.

She released him, then stared into his eyes. Her mouth curved into a slight smile.

"Next time you're going to hug me back," she whispered. "You need us, Garth. And we need you." Then she raised herself on her toes and kissed his cheek. "It's going to be okay."

As if she wanted to reassure him. But this was his game and he was winning. Didn't they get that?

Skye eyed him. "I'm not comfortable with the whole embracing thing just yet."

"Not a problem."

"I hope Izzy's right. I hope you are worth saving. We're about to find out." She smiled. "You may not like the process."

The women left.

He stared after them, wanting to call them back and say he wasn't worth saving. That they were ridiculous to waste their effort this way. At the same time, he had the strangest feeling that they had just won this round and that the unexpected victory had put him behind.

IT WAS NEARLY NINE that night when Garth rode the elevator from his condo building's parking garage. He was tired, not surprising after a nearly fifteen-hour day, but his weariness seemed to be deeper than usual. He'd brought home a briefcase full of work he had no intention of looking at and he was oddly reluctant to spend the evening by himself.

If he had to define his mood—something he rarely bothered doing—he would say he was lonely.

It wasn't as if he usually spent evenings playing poker with the guys, but lately the emptiness seemed more profound. Maybe it was because he'd lost his best friend. Or maybe all he needed was a drink and some TV time in front of a football game.

When the elevator stopped on the main floor, he got out and crossed to pick up his mail. On his way to the bank of locked boxes, he saw someone sitting in one of the overstuffed sofas. A familiar someone, watching him.

Dana Birch stood. "You're keeping late hours."

She wasn't in uniform. Instead she wore jeans, a leather jacket and boots. Nothing stylish or upscale, yet the no-nonsense clothes suited her.

Garth swung his attention to George, the evening doorman for the building. The older man shifted uncomfortably.

"You, ah, have a visitor, Mr. Duncan."

"So I see."

Dana moved toward him. "Don't blame George. His nephew is a new recruit in the Titanville sheriff's office. I've helped him out a couple of times. George owes me."

"Does he?"

Garth got his mail and tucked it under his arm. He had his briefcase in one hand and a bag of Chinese takeout in the other. "Why are you here?"

"Because you are."

Not that he minded—Garth wasn't intimidated by a powerful woman. In fact, he found the challenge appealing. There was something about Dana's mouth, though. The fullness of the bottom lip, the slight curve at the corners. It spoke of sensuality and promise. Or maybe that was wishful thinking on his part.

"Starting a fan club?" he asked.

"Not exactly. I've taken a leave of absence from work so I can follow you. I'll be on your ass until I figure out who and what you are."

"You already know who I am."

"Not really. Izzy thinks you're brother material. Skye and Lexi aren't so sure."

An unexpected twist. "You're the deciding vote?"

She smiled. "I'm here to test your character. Think of me as a trial by fire."

He would give the Titan sisters points for creativity. "You don't scare me, Dana."

"Give it time."

He chuckled and held up the bag of takeout. "You hungry? I have enough for two."

"Lucky me."

"Is that a yes?"

She paused for a second, before grabbing the bag. "Sure. Why not?"

They walked toward the elevator.

As they passed the main desk, George gave him a thumbs-up. Garth bit back a laugh. Given the fact that

Dana was both prickly and determined to see the worst in him, the odds of him getting lucky that night seemed close to zero. But he was a man who enjoyed a good challenge.

CHAPTER THREE

THEY RODE THE ELEVATOR in silence. Dana hadn't realized she was hungry until she inhaled the scent of the takeout and her stomach growled. Just as disconcerting was her awareness of the man standing next to her. Garth hadn't bothered to look even slightly concerned about her showing up for the second time in two days. Why couldn't he at least pretend to be nervous?

They exited on the top floor and she followed him to his penthouse. He unlocked the door, then waited for her to go first.

She walked into the dark space. Seconds later Garth flipped on lights.

Yesterday morning she'd been more interested in the man than his home and hadn't noticed much beyond the open floor plan and killer view. Now she ignored the display of city lights and instead concentrated on the surroundings.

The condo had been built in a loft style, with a huge open room. The living area was in front, a dining area to the right. A half wall separated a restaurant-sized kitchen with sleek cabinets and gleaming granite from the rest of the room. The furniture was large, the colors subdued and masculine, the carpeting plush. The space looked expensive and comfortable, a rare combination.

"You had a good decorator," she said.

Garth tossed his leather briefcase and mail onto a table by the door and shrugged out of his suit jacket. "Thanks. He did a nice job."

"Not a woman? Color me surprised."

"I appreciate talent in either gender."

"Aren't you Mr. Open-minded?"

He came up beside her and pointed to the large, wood dining room table. "Shall we?"

She walked to the table and set down the bag. He crossed to a built-in wine cellar tucked in the wet bar between the dining and living rooms.

"Wine?" he asked. "Or are you on duty?"

"Wine is fine."

He returned with two glasses and a bottle of red. Dana didn't recognize the label, which wasn't a huge surprise. She was more of a beer drinker.

"Plates are in the kitchen," he said, walking to a buffet, opening a drawer and pulling out a corkscrew.

She walked into the big kitchen and hit the lights. There was counter space for twenty, double sinks, double ovens and a warming drawer.

"Your caterer must love working here. All you need are minions."

"I have minions. It's their night off."

She turned away so he couldn't see her smile, then opened cupboards until she found plates. The flatware was in the drawer below. After grabbing a couple of paper towels for napkins, she returned to the dining room.

He'd put the now-full wineglasses at one end of the table, across from each other. While she set out the plates, he put containers of Chinese food in front of them.

"It's a historic occasion," he said as they sat. "Did you want to say a few words?"

"None would be fit for polite society."

He winked. "I'm not that polite."

"True."

He offered her what looked like kung pao chicken. "You're serious about the leave of absence?"

She scooped the spicy chicken onto her plate. "Absolutely. My new job is you. I know that makes your heart all quivery."

Instead of serving himself, he rolled up the sleeves of his white shirt and took a sip of wine.

"I wouldn't describe any part of me as quivery, but I *am* curious as to your plan."

"I told you. Watch, follow, catch you being bad."

He gave her a slow, sexy smile. "There will be so many opportunities."

"You think you're all that, don't you?"

"I know I am."

The man had balls, Dana thought as she reached for

the egg rolls. Really big ones. And an ego the size of the *Titanic*. Both of which could work in her favor. If he didn't think she was a threat, he would be careless. And that's when she would see the real Garth Duncan.

He served himself from the containers. The overhead lights flattered his dark good looks and his easygoing personality made him an appealing dinner companion. He must have women lining up five deep to get a shot at him and his fortune. Fortunately, she was immune. She could certainly appreciate what she saw, but she wasn't interested. He wasn't her type.

"You must be disappointed," he said. "My interview with the Dallas Police Department didn't include questionable practices. They were polite and didn't once beat me with a pipe."

"Another hope crushed. I'll get over it. There's always tomorrow." She sipped her wine. It was a smooth red that would probably be described as saucy or impatient or something else equally stupid. She just thought it was good.

"Izzy and Skye came to see me today," he said. "Izzy's determined to save me from myself."

"She has more heart than sense."

"Not a fault you share?"

"I'm heartless," she said cheerfully.

"Then we have that in common."

"Lucky us. You might have snowed Izzy, but the rest of the sisters won't be so easy."

"I wasn't trying to snow anyone. Izzy's decided this

on her own." He leaned toward her. "How do you play into all this? If Izzy's convinced I'm to be brought into the arms of the family, why are you so determined to throw me in jail?"

"I've always liked sports. Besides, Izzy hasn't convinced me or Lexi that you're interested in changing your plan. The theory is if you're really who Izzy thinks, you'll understand my need to protect my friends. If you're not, you deserve what you get."

"You're not a big believer in gray area, are you?"

"No. I'm not. And neither are you."

He raised his glass to her. "Be careful, Deputy Dana. If we have much more in common, we'll have to be friends, and neither of us would be happy with that news."

"Don't worry. I'll never like you."

He smiled. "Is that a promise?"

"Sure."

"Good. A challenge. And here I thought it was going to be a dull evening. My mistake."

There was something in his eyes. Something predatory that made her want to squirm in her seat. She had to remember Garth was just a guy. He put his pants on one leg at a time.

"You expect to get away with things because of your position and your wealth," she said. "That won't work with me."

"Are you saying you've never used the fact that you're a deputy to get out of a ticket?"

"That's different."

"No, it's not. Everyone likes to feel powerful and to feel that they have a certain amount of control in life. The need to be unique and recognized lives in all of us."

She reached for her wine. "Don't tell me you're going to be insightful about the lives of ordinary people."

"I'm ordinary."

She rolled her eyes.

He shrugged. "I was. I've been there."

"Remind your cell mate of that when you're in prison."

He smiled. "That's not going to happen and you know it. I've done nothing wrong. Not legally."

"If we exclude the explosion, you're still guilty of plenty. You've started rumors to drive down stock prices, including telling some reporter that executives at Titan World were stealing."

He passed her a shrimp-and-vegetable dish that smelled delicious.

"How do you know they weren't?" he asked. "Your assumption is I've created the situation from thin air. What if it was there all the time?"

Something she didn't want to think about. Jed might be a mean old bastard who didn't give a rat about his daughters, but she'd never thought of him as a crook.

"You're saying he *did* export illegal weapons to terrorists?"

"I'm saying you should check out the possibility before you assume anything."

From everything she knew about Garth, he didn't bluff. "If you had proof, you'd take it to the Feds."

"Maybe I'm collecting data. I do my homework, Dana. You should do yours."

She pushed away her plate. She was here to make things better for her friends, not worse. If Jed was involved with all that Garth had accused him of, there was going to be one big mess to clean up.

"Let's change the subject," he said, pouring her more wine. "How's your father? Florida is a great place, this time of year."

If she'd been swallowing, she would have choked.

How much did he know about her? And there were variations on the question—who had told him and why? How had he known to go digging? And was he just playing the odds or did he have actual information?

"I wouldn't know," she said coolly. "We don't keep in touch."

"I'm not surprised. You never confronted him. Some children do—go back as an adult. Face the devil, so to speak. You just wanted to put it all behind you."

She didn't know if he was asking or telling and she didn't care. She could go the rest of her life without seeing her dad and be very happy. There had been too much one-on-one time when she'd been younger.

Her mother had died when Dana had been young— too young to remember her. Dana's father hadn't been all that interested in his baby daughter and a series of girlfriends had offered indifferent care. Later, when she'd been six or seven, she'd become a liability. The women who came and went didn't like a "brat like her" hanging around. Annoyed with Dana for making trouble, her father had started hitting her.

Or maybe he'd just hit her because he liked it.

The beatings had dominated her young life. There were always bruises she had to hide, sprains she couldn't explain. Maybe her teachers had known, maybe they'd simply looked the other way, but no one ever asked questions.

He'd left one day, without saying a word. She'd been sixteen and so grateful, she hadn't told anyone. She'd practically moved in with Lexi and her sisters who might have suspected the truth but had never discussed it.

Eventually she heard the old man had settled in Florida. She'd gone to college and never looked back. But how had Garth known?

"You did something with the fear," he said. "I respect that."

"I have no idea what you're talking about."

They stared at each other. There was no judgment in his eyes, nothing to make her uncomfortable, save the fact that he'd obviously uncovered her deepest, darkest secret. Which meant she had to learn his.

She remembered the scars on his body, scars he'd gotten while a prisoner, blindfolded constantly and tortured on a daily basis. Maybe Garth didn't have any secrets. Maybe he wore the truth on his body every day.

"I would recommend revenge," he said, "but you're not the type."

"I believe in that old Chinese saying. The one that says before you begin a journey of revenge, first dig two graves."

"Not a problem. I'm sure there's a Titan mausoleum somewhere."

Jed had created this enemy, Dana thought, almost able to feel sorry for the old man. He had earned whatever happened to him.

After getting Kathy, Garth's mother, pregnant, he'd set her up with enough money to take care of her and her baby. It beat marrying her, at least from Jed's perspective.

Everything had been fine until Kathy developed a brain tumor. Aggressive treatment and surgery burned through her insurance and Jed's money. Fourteen-year-old Garth had been desperate to save his mother and had gone to Jed to beg for enough to cover a last-chance surgery. Jed had refused and had thrown his bastard son out on the street.

That fourteen-year-old boy had grown up into the man sitting across from her. A man determined to exact painful vengeance. Garth had finally found a doctor willing to do the surgery for free, but by then it had been too late. While Kathy had survived, she'd been left mentally challenged. A friendly, simple woman who adored Garth but in no way realized she was his mother.

"What happens if you win?" Dana asked. "What do you want? The company? Your name on the letterhead? Are you going to run Titan World?"

"No. I'll break it up and sell it off. When I'm done, nothing Jed worked for will exist anymore."

"It's not about the glory?"

"I was never in it for that. I want Jed to pay for what he did, nothing more. You should respect that. It's all black and white. You like absolutes. It's why you're a cop."

A lucky guess on his part, she told herself. He didn't really know her that well.

"You're breaking the law to get what you want," she told him. "That makes it gray. And going after the sisters is pretty sad. Come on. They're girls."

He laughed. "Would you let them hear you say that? They think of themselves as powerful women."

"They're powerful in ways you can't understand, but what you're doing is wrong." She eyed him over her glass. "And you know it."

"Now you're reading minds?"

"You claim to know me. Why can't it work both ways?"

"Because I've been studying you. Can you say the same?"

"You're not that interesting."

"Now you're lying. You find me very interesting."

Was it hot in here or was it her? Dana put her wine back on the table and grabbed her fork. Only she wasn't that hungry anymore and the sensations in her stomach had little to do with the food she'd eaten.

She knew he was playing her. He was good at it and she wasn't. She didn't do the game thing. She was direct, maybe too direct. In her personal relationships she said what she wanted. If the guy didn't want to hear it, he was gone.

But being with Garth was anything but straightforward. Like a perpetual game of cat and mouse.

"Are you in for the night?" she asked as she came to her feet.

He stood. "Yes."

"Then I'm going. I'll be on your tail tomorrow, annoying you. You're heading to the office at the usual time?"

"Yes."

His dark eyes seemed to see more than they should. Talk about unnerving.

She reached in her jeans pocket for her keys and turned to leave.

"Or you could stay."

Four little words. Four syllables. Taken apart, they meant almost nothing, but together…

Or you could stay.

Was he asking what she thought he was asking?

Stupid question.

It was a joke, she told herself quickly. It had to be a joke. He wanted her to say yes, so he could laugh at her. He wanted her to consider for even a second that he wanted her. Because men like him were never interested in women like her. It was one of life's rules and didn't bother her a bit.

She turned back and met his dark gaze, then raised her eyebrows. "I don't think so. But thanks for asking."

Nothing about his expression changed. "If you're sure."

Sure that she didn't want to have sex with him? Oh, yeah. She was beyond sure. She had very specific rules and one of them said she was always in control. He would never allow that and she would never accept anything else.

There was also the issue of not being sure if he'd tried to blow up Izzy and knowing he was doing his best to ruin his sisters, which she probably should have thought of first, damn him.

"I'm sure," she said.

"Another time, then."

"Again, I don't think so."

He gave her a slow, sexy smile. One that spoke of confidence. It was the smile of a man who knew women.

"I do."

He was trying to rattle her. He wanted her to react, to question herself, to engage. That so wasn't going to happen.

She walked to the front door and let herself out without saying anything. But all the way down the elevator, through the lobby and out to her truck, she had the feeling that he was still with her. Not in a scary, stalker kind of way, but almost as if the essence of him lingered.

"He's just a guy," she muttered as she started the engine. "Nothing special."

The good news was there was no one else around to point out it was very possible that she was lying.

GARTH HAD ARRANGED THE meeting for ten. At thirty seconds before the hour, Agnes buzzed to let him know Dana had arrived. Garth stood, interested in seeing her again. If he didn't know better, he would say she'd been disconcerted the night before. Or maybe that was wishful thinking on his part. Dana was a strong woman—she wouldn't let herself be vulnerable for any man. Not an unexpected reaction, considering her past.

She walked into his office, her head held high, the set of her shoulders determined. She wore a plain blue shirt tucked into jeans, and boots.

"No uniform?" he asked by way of greeting.

"I wasn't kidding about taking a leave of absence."

She didn't wear makeup or earrings or anything remotely feminine. There was a toughness about her. A wariness. He wondered if she knew her determination to never show a soft side only made him more aware that there was something she was trying to hide.

She was the kind of woman who gave as good as she got. Which made him think about her naked. Not just because he was intrigued by the concealed curves, but because she would expect to take charge. It would be a battle of wills…which was the kind of battle he most enjoyed.

"I hope the Titan sisters appreciate all you're doing for them," he said, leading her to the sofas by the corner of the large office.

"We look out for each other. That's what friends do. Not that you would know anything about that."

"Speaking of which…" He glanced at his watch. "Nick should be here soon."

Something flashed in her brown eyes and was gone before he could read it. "Nick's not coming. Izzy called me while I was driving over. Something came up."

Garth knew nothing showed on his face. He was a master at keeping his thoughts to himself, so she couldn't know he was disappointed. Nick had every reason to be pissed as hell at him, but Garth had hoped to lure his former friend to his office with news about Izzy. He'd thought they would have a chance to talk. Apparently Nick wasn't ready to move on.

Garth knew he only had himself to blame. He'd crossed the line and betrayed a friend. He might regret what he'd done, but he couldn't change what had happened.

"Then it's just the two of us," he said, motioning to one of the sofas.

Dana sat down. He settled next to her and reached for the folder on the glass coffee table.

"I've been investigating the explosion on the oil rig," he said, passing Dana the latest report from his private investigator. "I don't have proof yet, but I suspect that Jed is at the heart of this. The guy who set the explosion is Cuban—a known expert. Currently he's working out of Mexico. My people are tracing the payments. He didn't use a Swiss bank, so that's in our favor. We should be able to get information on who paid, but it's taking time."

Dana stared at him. "Meaning you couldn't hack into a Swiss bank, but you can get into a different one? Can you give me the name so I don't put my money there?"

"We don't hack in," he told her. "We get information."

"A subtle difference."

"Life is nuance."

"Thanks for the tip, but you're not the Zen master and I'm not your little grasshopper."

He stared at her, noting the flecks of gold in her irises. "Someone didn't get her coffee this morning. Should I order some?"

"I'm not an idiot."

"Since when does coffee imply stupid?"

She glared at him. "You know what I mean."

"I haven't got a clue."

The muscles in her jaw tensed. He'd annoyed her, which was fun on many levels.

"You take yourself too seriously," he told her.

"You're getting on my last nerve. I'm armed. Don't mess with me."

The thought of her with a gun didn't bother him in the least.

"We could wrestle for it," he suggested.

For a second he thought she was going to actually spit in rage. Instead she drew in a breath and picked up the folder.

"Is there anything else?" she asked, her voice tight with suppressed annoyance.

"Yes." He tapped the second folder. "Some interesting information on Jed. A friend of his does work for the government. Mostly experimental military weapons. Some of the prototypes go missing for months at a time, then they reappear in inventory. Coincidentally, a few months after that, a dozen or so exactly like the prototype appear on the black market, usually in the Middle East. I haven't connected all the dots, but so far everything leads to Jed."

Dana's bravado faded, as did her color. Her eyes widened. "That's not possible. You're saying he really is guilty of treason."

"I'm saying there's a possibility it's real. When I have what I need, I'll turn it over to the Feds."

Dana still looked stunned. "I've known Jed all my life. I can't believe this. I'll accept he's a bastard and treats his daughters like crap, but this is on a totally different level. It's beyond wrong. Why would he sell out his country?"

Garth no longer cared about why Jed did anything. He simply wanted the old man ruined in every way possible. Having Jed make it easy almost took away from the sweet taste of victory, but it was a disappointment Garth would live with.

"I want to take this to Lexi," Dana said.

"Those are your copies."

She picked up the second folder, but didn't open it. "You shouldn't have gone after your sisters. They weren't a part of any of this."

"A Titan is a Titan," he told her. It was how he'd started the game—believing they were all the same. Now he wasn't so sure. Not that he would tell her that.

"You're a Titan."

"Only technically. Besides, they'll be fine. They have you to protect them."

She raised her chin, as if facing a challenge. "I'm more than ready to take you down."

"So you keep telling me. Talk is cheap."

Annoyance tightened her face and he knew she was searching for some scathing comeback. Or something heavy to throw at him.

Dana took her responsibilities very seriously. She *would* worry about her friends and do anything in her power to protect them. But who looked after her?

She would say she didn't need protecting, that she was fine. But was it true? Or were there vulnerabilities she hid from the world?

"Is there anything else?" she asked.

"That's all I have, unless you'd like to arm wrestle for dominance."

She ignored that and stood. He rose and stepped beside her as she walked to the door. Instinctively, he put his hand on the small of her back, as if to guide her out of the office.

He hadn't planned the touch. It was something a man did in the presence of a woman. A polite gesture, nothing more.

But as he felt the warmth of her skin through her shirt, it seemed like more. It seemed…intimate.

She glanced up at him, her brown eyes clouded with emotions he couldn't read but could guess. Wariness. Maybe fear. Which made him want to tell her that everything was going to be all right. As if he could predict the outcome of any of this.

"I can make it to the door on my own," she said, moving away. "But thanks for trying to help."

"You're prickly."

"Part of my charm."

Part of the way she protected herself.

He wanted to tell her that she could trust him—that he wasn't her enemy. But that wasn't true. He was exactly who she should be wary of—he was her worst nightmare. A man willing to do anything to win.

"Until tonight," he said.

"It's not a date. I'm there to watch you. My ultimate goal is to see you in jail for the rest of your life."

He tapped the folders she held. "Maybe it was, but it's not anymore. I'm not the bad guy and you know it. But you're welcome to watch anytime you want."

Her jaw clenched and then she was gone. Garth smiled as he returned to his desk. Dana made things interesting and he liked that in a woman.

DANA PACED IN LEXI'S office. The fountain and the spa music in the background were supposed to be soothing. Instead it made her want to climb the walls. Or shoot something.

After she was done here, she would go work out for a couple of hours. Maybe take out her frustrations on a punching bag.

Lexi glanced up from the folders. Her normally pale skin had gone white, her eyes were wide.

"Did you read this?" she asked.

Dana nodded. "Scary stuff."

"I can't believe it, but even as I say that, there's a part of me that isn't surprised. Jed's ruthless. He's always been that way. He pretties it up when he has to, but it's there. Still, he could have killed his own daughter. Did he even care that Izzy was on the oil rig? What about the other lives? But hey, winning is all that matters, right?" Her voice rose as she spoke, her tone got more shrill.

Dana moved to the desk and looked at her. "Deep breaths. Baby on board and all that. Try to stay calm."

Lexi nodded and exhaled slowly. "I know. I'll be okay. I'm just in shock. Jed doing all this. Treason." She sighed. "I need to think about this. We need a plan. The next step. I'm going to need a little time."

Dana settled across from her desk. "Take all the time you need. You have a lot going on."

Lexi leaned back in her chair. "I'm having a baby. Women do it every day."

"I don't care about them, I care about you. You're my friend."

"Thank you. I'm doing okay. This is a stunner, but I'll get through it. We're working together and that makes me feel better."

Dana eyed Lexi's growing belly. "Just remember what's important. We can go after Jed anytime."

"We're not stopping because I'm pregnant. I'm taking excellent care of myself and Cruz practically hovers."

"Skye mentioned something about a baby shower." Dana managed to get the sentence out without shuddering. She wasn't really a baby-wedding shower kind of person. What was up with the strange games? And why did the food have to be cute?

Lexi grinned. "You'll be there, honey, if we have to drag you. Don't think you're getting out of it."

"Oh, joy."

"It could be worse."

"How?"

"There could be balloon animals."

"I happen to like balloon animals."

Lexi laughed. "It won't be too horrible, I promise. No color-coordinated mints."

"Is Skye planning the shower?" Skye might run a nonprofit foundation but she was also an expert party planner. Her system of organization rivaled any battle plan the Pentagon put out.

"Yes. Okay. You're right. The mints might match. But it will still be fun."

"If you define the word very loosely."

"Poor Dana," Lexi teased. "My baby shower is only the start. Skye's talking about getting married."

"We all knew that was going to happen," Dana grumbled. Skye was madly in love. No one would be surprised when she and Mitch set the date. "You'll be next."

"After the baby is born," Lexi said. "I never planned to be unconventional, but here I am, having a baby and then getting married. I'm sure my mother is horrified. Cruz and I are talking about late spring. So you'll have time to recover."

Which she would need, Dana thought. "At least Izzy is more the type to simply run off some weekend and show up Monday with a wedding ring and a new last name. She was always my favorite."

Lexi laughed again. "How you suffer for us all."

"I know. That's me. The suffering friend."

"Maybe you'll meet someone you want to marry."

"No, thanks."

"Not ever?"

"When pigs fly."

The next words were spoken softly, hesitantly, as if Lexi were treading carefully. "Not all men are like your dad."

She and her friend had never talked about what it

had been like, but Dana also wasn't surprised that Lexi had figured it out. What did startle her was having the subject brought up twice in two days.

"Garth knows about my father," she said. "I don't know if he put the pieces together and got lucky or if he'd spoken to someone."

"You talked about it?"

"He did mostly. Last night. I think he was making a point—that he knew a whole lot more than I'd realized. I hate it when men are insightful. It upsets the balance of power."

"What do you think of him?" Lexi asked. "A card-carrying member of the evil empire?"

Dana shook her head. "Nothing that simple. He's so damn sure of himself. Confident he's going to win. And just when I think he's barely human, I remember those scars."

Izzy had told them both about Nick and Garth's time in the jungle. Lexi could only imagine what the scars looked like, but Dana had seen them for herself.

"What does he think of Izzy's plan to bring him into the family?" Lexi asked.

"It confuses him. Of course that's just a guess on my part. We aren't exactly sharing secrets."

"Do you like him?"

Dana glanced at her. "I don't hate him."

"Izzy would say that's progress."

"It depends on how you look at the situation. I still don't trust him. But he's not the devil."

There was more. He made her uneasy. His casual touch on her back had seared her down to her bones. She'd felt each of his fingers, the pressure of his palm. She'd wanted to move toward him.

Garth made her aware of her weaknesses and that terrified her.

"What happens now?" Lexi asked.

"I wait for him to make a mistake."

"What if he's no longer our enemy?"

"Then everything changes."

CHAPTER FOUR

JED TITAN HAD KNOWN Brock Lyman since college. Nowadays they were both tall men with graying hair and a taste for the good life. They'd played football together and Brock had introduced Jed to his first wife. Something Jed never held against him. Now some thirty-plus years later, Brock was the chief financial officer at Titan World and the only person Jed was willing to trust.

Which didn't mean he had to like what his friend said.

"He's bought even more stock," Brock said from his place across the conference table.

Jed and Brock were having their morning meeting. In the past, the time had been more about sports scores than any real business, but in the past few months, they'd been scrambling to manage what seemed like a new crisis every other week.

"Did he file with the SEC?" Jed asked, even though he already knew the answer. Damn Garth Duncan. He was always careful to follow the rules. Once he'd crossed the threshold of stock purchases, he'd done all the paperwork required. Just once Jed wanted him to make a mistake.

Brock nodded. "Filed on time and correctly. He's up to fifteen percent ownership in Titan World. More in a few of the subsidiaries. So far we've been able to keep the news out of the media, but I don't know how long that will go on. A few major stockholders have taken notice."

Which was Garth's plan, Jed thought, annoyed by how well he was being played.

By buying large blocks of stock and holding on to them, a case could be made that Garth was planning to take over the company. That made other stockholders nervous. SEC rules required public filings when a shareholder reached a certain amount of ownership, which Garth had done. He wasn't hiding what he was doing, and that made Jed uncomfortable. He couldn't go after someone who wasn't breaking the law.

"If he wants to buy the company, why doesn't he approach us?" Brock asked, obviously frustrated.

"It's not his way. He's waiting until the time is right."

It was all a game and whoever had the most at the end won. Jed could almost be proud of Garth. After all, the man was his son. But things had gone too far. Garth had to be stopped.

"What about the investigation of the oil rig explosion?" Brock asked. "Why hasn't Garth been arrested for his involvement in that?"

"I don't know." Jed couldn't figure it out, either.

Enough evidence had been planted to indict Garth. What had gone wrong? "He's smart. Maybe smarter than we gave him credit for. We have to find his vulnerable spot. No target is off-limits."

"First we have to find one," Brock grumbled.

"We will. In the meantime, we have to buy back shares. He owns too much of the company."

"There's no money."

"We'll find it. Borrow it, whatever. I want to start buying back shares from anyone who will sell."

"If word gets out," Brock began, then shook his head. "No one can know, Jed. People will think the company's in trouble and that'll start a stampede of shareholders trying to sell. Any panic will drive down the price of stock."

"Then we'll keep it to ourselves."

"We'll need a bunch of cash. I don't know where we're going to get it. Unless you're willing to start selling some of your assets."

Something Jed had always refused in the past. There were dozens of choices but only a few worth tens of millions. His racehorse farm, the shipping company and Glory's Gate, the family home.

It was all about winning. Defeating the upstart bastard who was trying to take him down.

"This is war," Jed said at last. "Sacrifices have to be made. Start making discreet inquires about potential buyers. But remember, this isn't a fire sale. I want top dollar."

Brock stared at him for a long time. "It may not be enough."

"Then we'll figure out something else. I don't care what it takes to beat Garth. I want him crushed and swept up with the trash."

DANA DID HER BEST to sit quietly in the lobby of Garth's condo. Usually she enjoyed a good stakeout. She found it relaxing. It gave her time to think. But today her brain was not her friend, not when it kept racing from subject to subject, the most annoying of which was the anticipation she felt at the thought of seeing Garth again.

She was actually worried about what she was wearing. She'd thought about changing her clothes. Worse, she'd gone home and put on mascara, which happened to be the only makeup she owned. Mascara. Like she was a sniveling teenaged girl nervous about a date.

This wasn't a date—it was surveillance, dammit.

She shifted on the comfortable bench, thought about leaving, then tensed when the elevator doors slid open and Garth stepped into the foyer of his condo building to pick up his mail.

He looked good. The stubble on his jaw, the slightly loosened tie all suited him. There was a weariness in his eyes, as if it had been a long day. She felt a definite quiver low in her belly and did her best to ignore it. She wasn't the type of woman to quiver for any man and if she pretended it wasn't happening, eventually it would go away. At least that was the plan.

"Hope you like Italian," he said, holding up two shopping bags.

He'd stopped for dinner. One part of her brain said it was no big deal. He wasn't the kind of man to cook for himself and he'd known she would be here. The other part of her brain wanted to know if he'd bought dinner with her in mind. If he'd thought about what she might like. As if this were...

Nothing. It was nothing. He was nothing, they were nothing. That's the way it was going to be.

She stood and walked toward him without saying anything. Garth collected his mail, then walked back to the elevator. She took the food from him and followed. George wished them a good night.

The elevator ride was silent. When they reached his floor, he pulled out his keys and they stepped into his condo. She collected plates while he chose a bottle of wine. She set the table, he flipped on a CD. Their actions were familiar, which should have been comfortable but instead made her nervous. It was only the second night. There was no way she could be comfortable around Garth.

Finally they sat across from each other. He poured the wine, then toasted her silently before taking a sip.

He watched her, as if assessing her. She felt the weight of the mascara on her lashes and wondered if he'd noticed. If he thought it was about him, which it was, but she would rather die than have him know. Which made her feel like a girl. Time to get the attention back on him.

"Where's your girlfriend?" she asked. "I've been here two nights in a row. Aren't I getting in the way of something?"

"If you've done your homework, you know there isn't a girlfriend."

"Just a string of willing beauties," she said, remembering what she'd read. "You favor smart and pretty, but if you have to pick just one, you go with pretty. Typical and a little disappointing."

He pulled out covered containers from the bags and passed her one. "Be careful, Dana. Do you really want to talk about our personal lives? I'm not the only one with a string of easy conquests. What about the men you date?"

Touché, she thought, refusing to apologize for her romantic choices. Maybe she did like men who weren't especially powerful or challenging. Maybe she did find them just a little boring. But that was her business, not his.

"I gave the information to Lexi," she said, to change the subject. "She wasn't happy."

"Neither is Jed, if that's any help," he said as he opened a carton of salad and passed it to her.

He'd brought lasagna and salad. The delicious scent made her stomach growl.

"I've been buying up stock," he continued. "Large blocks of stock. It's all legal."

"Are you sure? You love the gray area."

He smiled. "More than most, but not this time. I've

filed the paperwork. The only thing I haven't done is announce what's going on. But word will get out and the other stockholders will get nervous."

"Is that your plan?"

"Yes. I'm going to back Jed into a corner and force him to do something stupid."

"He's a dangerous man when cornered."

"I'm dangerous all the time."

"You forgot modest," she said before taking a bite of the lasagna. It was so good, she nearly moaned.

"I don't care what people think of me. I want to win."

This wasn't a moment she could have predicted— having dinner with Garth in his penthouse. She could see all the lights of Dallas glittering around them. The meal was excellent, the man more interesting than she could have imagined. If his dark eyes seemed to see too much, she would just have to learn to keep herself disguised.

"What happens if Jed starts to buy back stock himself?" she asked.

"To do that, he'll need cash and right now he doesn't have any."

"Do I want to ask how you know that?"

"Not really."

"Okay. So he'll sell something to raise…" She got the big picture. "That's what you want. Him selling off assets. Then you'll buy them, one by one."

"A Titan yard sale."

She thought about Jed Titan's holdings. Which would Garth covet most? The shipyards? The oil field? "You want Glory's Gate," she said. "It's been in the family for generations."

"I'm family."

His sisters had grown up there. It was home to them. Well over a thousand acres of prime pasture and cattle. A huge house and all the prestige that went with owning it.

"Jed will never risk Glory's Gate."

"You may be right."

Garth didn't sound worried.

"You think he will?" she asked.

"It depends on how much he wants to win."

"How much do you want to win?"

"You really want me to answer that?"

He didn't have to. She knew. She could feel it. Garth would do anything to settle the score. Lethal and ruthless—a dangerous combination.

"I'm surprised all this talk doesn't scare off your women," she said. "Or do they like this side of you?"

"They don't see it."

"Because they can't handle it? But it's who you are." She picked up her wineglass. "Is that the trick? Don't let them inside?"

"Do your conquests see the real you?"

"We weren't talking about me."

"We are now."

His gaze was predatory, his expression knowing.

She shivered, then did her best to conceal it by shifting in her seat. She knew she could hold her own with him, as long as he didn't touch her.

Something happened when she had felt his skin on hers, even through a protective layer of clothes. She didn't like it and couldn't explain it. Therefore the only logical solution was to avoid it. Not that Garth was begging for a little one-on-one time. But caution was always smart.

The CD ended. He got up and walked over to the player concealed in the buffet. He moved stiffly, as if his leg bothered him.

"Are you all right?" she asked before she could stop herself.

"Old war wound," he said, putting in another CD.

Not exactly. She remembered the scars she'd seen and that both his legs had been broken while he'd been held hostage all those months.

"Did you have to have surgery on your legs after you and Nick escaped?"

"Some. The breaks had started to heal badly, so they re-broke my legs and set them."

"What did they do for the knife wounds?"

"Treated the ones that were infected and left the others alone to heal."

"A big price to pay for oil."

"Nick would tell you it was the price we paid for being wrong." He returned to the table and sat across from her. "Did Izzy tell you what happened?"

"Some," she said. Izzy had told her pretty much everything but she wanted to hear Garth tell the story.

"We knew there was oil in the jungle, but it was nearly impossible to extract. That's always the bitch of it. People think it's hard to find, but it's a whole lot harder to get it out of the ground. Nick had some ideas on new ways we could drill."

"Did it involve raping and pillaging?"

Garth grinned. "Not my style. I prefer a nice, quiet seduction."

Her throat seemed to close in a little. "Back to the story, please."

"You're the one who changed the subject."

"I won't do it again."

For a second, she thought he might continue to challenge her. Instead he started talking.

"The land was owned by a guy named Francisco. He was the head of the village and while he told his people and family he would never negotiate with us, he really wanted the money. He had a fair idea of the value and pushed for every penny. Local legend said not to take the oil, but Francisco dismissed that as bull and cashed the check. We started work. A few weeks later, we realized we were poisoning the water. By then it was too late—three people had died."

"Does that bother you?" she asked. Izzy had said Nick had been emotionally devastated by what had happened and blamed himself. Did Garth?

"I didn't set out to kill them, if that's what you mean.

I'm sorry it happened. We made an honest mistake. Knowing what I know now…" he hesitated "…it would be different, but life isn't that tidy. We don't get a do-over."

"Do you want a do-over with Nick?"

His gaze sharpened. "The question of the day."

Garth had used his best friend to get to Izzy. Nick hadn't known what was going on and when he figured out he was being played, he had been furious.

"You have to have regrets," she said. "Nick was your best friend."

"I made a tactical error."

"Stop being such a guy," she snapped. "It wasn't an error. You set up Nick to hurt Izzy. Then you completely miscalculated the fact that they were falling in love with each other. You expected Nick to side with you instead of Izzy and when he didn't, you got angry. You lost a friend. A good friend."

"You don't need me here to have this conversation," he told her. "You're doing fine all on your own."

"More guy-speak. You lost Nick and now you're sorry. Was it worth it?"

"What do you think?"

His expression was unreadable, but she could feel his pain as if it were her own. He was strong, powerful and dangerous. But he was also alone. He had no one. His mother was as much of a responsibility as a small child. He'd set himself on a course to destroy his father and alienate his sisters. It was a battle of one against the world.

A battle he could never win, because even in winning he would lose.

Oddly enough, that made her want to go to him. Part of her wanted to tell him that everything would be all right. Which made her stupid, or at the very least confused.

"I suppose you'll ignore me if I tell you to apologize," she said. "That saying you regret what happened might go a long way to healing things with Nick."

"I might listen if you tell me naked."

She rolled her eyes. "Do you really think a comment like that will distract me?"

"It's worth a try."

"You need a better game plan. I'm not your average bimbo."

"I don't date bimbos. Marly was a Rhodes Scholar."

"Then what was she doing with you?"

"Use your imagination."

"Doesn't being on the defense all the time get exhausting?" she asked.

"I'll answer that question when you do."

Oh. Right. That was kind of her thing.

They looked at each other. He'd taken off his jacket when he'd first walked into the penthouse. Before dinner he'd rolled up the sleeves of his white dress shirt. Now he pulled off his tie and tossed it onto the table next to him.

The act was nothing. His fingers unfastened the knot at his throat, then he pulled the length of fabric free and threw it to the side. Yet the movement was unbelievably sexy and masculine. It made her think about undoing buttons and hands on bare skin. It made her want to squirm and reach and get lost in whatever magic Garth possessed. It made her want to be taken—an ironic longing considering she never allowed herself to lose control. To be taken, one had to surrender. Something she would never do.

"Dana?"

She blinked slowly. Time for another subject change. Dining with the man was not particularly restful.

"Izzy's serious about her plan," she said. "Whether you're willing or not, she's determined to have you in the family."

"Let me guess. They're going to love me into submission."

"If that's what it takes."

"Is that what happened with you?"

"They're my friends and my family. They have been for years. There are worse places to be."

"I'm not a family kind of guy."

"You don't know that. You've been on your own since you were fourteen. Maybe you should give this a try."

He poured her more wine. "Because you're so concerned about my well-being?"

"Not really, but if you do start to think about them as your sisters, you'll stop attacking them. And that's what I want. You know they're innocent in all this. Admit it. Move on."

"They're lucky to have you."

"And I'm lucky to have them."

And with those words once again came the reminder that Garth had no one. He faced his demons alone. Fate and Jed Titan had conspired against him, leaving him solitary and angry.

"I should go," she said, pushing away from the table and standing.

She expected him to make a joke about her staying again, but he didn't. Which was how she wanted things—at least that's what she told herself.

He followed her to the front door, then shifted so he was between her and the handle. She found herself staring into his eyes.

He was taller than her, with broader shoulders and plenty of muscle. Intensely male. If she had to overpower him, she would need surprise on her side, and possibly a solid two-by-four.

"I, ah, thanks for dinner," she murmured, feeling uncomfortable. This felt *way* too much like a date, which it wasn't.

"You're welcome. Tex-Mex next time?"

"Sure."

She tried to inch around him, but he wasn't moving. And she couldn't seem to push him out of the way. Well, she could, of course, but it would be awkward, especially if he resisted. She should just say good-night then stand there looking expectant. He would figure it out and move aside.

But as she opened her mouth to speak, he took a step toward her. Before she could move back, he reached up and lightly stroked the side of her face with the back of his fingers.

The unexpected contact glued her to the floor. She couldn't run, couldn't turn, couldn't do anything but stand there feeling helpless and exposed. As if he had the power to control her.

She told herself he didn't. He would never hurt her and should he try, she could nail him in the balls, draw her gun and change him from a stallion to a gelding in two seconds.

If she had to.

His dark eyes stared into hers. She had no idea what he saw there, but she hoped it wasn't anything he could use against her. Despite his slow, gentle touch, she felt tense inside. What was he doing and why?

She told herself to step away, to push past him and get the hell out. But her body didn't respond to the command and then he said the most extraordinary thing.

"Your mouth drives me crazy."

She'd barely had time to absorb the words before he lowered his head and pressed his mouth against hers.

The good news was he stopped touching her face. The bad news was they were kissing.

The second she felt his lips on hers, it was as if

someone had set the world on fire. There was heat and need and fiery sparks she could see even with her eyes closed. There was no contact anywhere else, which was fine with her. This was enough. Actually it was too much.

Her skin practically sizzled. She would swear she could hear music and feel the floor tilting. She wanted to throw her arms around him, pull him against her and shove her tongue in his mouth. She wanted to be naked, pressed up against the wall, being taken hard and fast until she screamed her surrender.

Dana reached out both hands, shoved him back and sucked in a breath. She'd never screamed in her life. She barely allowed herself to breathe hard. What the hell was going on?

Not that she planned to find out. She ducked around him, heading for the door, only Garth got there first. He grabbed her arm and held her still. She could have broken free easily, only she didn't and that scared her more than anything else.

"Wait," he said.

"No."

Something hot flared in his eyes. "You felt it, too."

"I didn't feel anything. It's late. I need to go."

"It's barely eight and you need to be here."

She hated the fear. It reminded her of being young and terrified of what her father would do next. It made her feel powerless and that was the worst thing of all.

Her emotions must have shown on her face or Garth

was a hell of a guesser because he dropped her arm and moved away from the door.

"I'm sorry," he said. "You're right. It's late."

He picked up her hand and kissed her palm. It was as if he branded her. She knew in her gut she would carry the feel of his lips on her skin with her forever. When he released her, she curled her fingers closed.

She hesitated for a second, then turned to leave.

This time he didn't stop her. She walked out into the hallway and the door closed behind her. She stood there, alone, aching with desire for the one man she could never have. Life, as always, had a killer sense of humor.

THE NEXT MORNING DANA followed Garth to work, but didn't try to speak with him. She hadn't slept much the night before and wasn't up to one of their cryptic exchanges. Once she knew he was at the office, she returned to Titanville, thinking she would either try for a nap, or a really jumbo coffee to go.

But on her way to Starbucks, she passed the Titanville Pet Palace and saw Kathy Duncan entering the store.

Fifteen minutes later, Dana parked in front of the Pet Palace with her own coffee and a latte for Kathy, then went inside. She nodded to the young woman at the cash register and made her way to the rear where Kathy was talking softly to a large white bird.

"Good morning," Dana said, handing over the coffee.

Kathy, a pretty woman in her late fifties, smiled broadly. "Dana. You came to see me. Thank you for the coffee."

There was delight in her voice, along with a studied slowness. As if every word had to be considered before it was spoken and the act of speech itself was vaguely unfamiliar.

"You're welcome." Dana passed over the paper cup. "Extra foam. Just the way you like it."

"I do like it." Kathy tilted her head, her soft brown hair falling over her shoulder. "You need a pet. Not today. You're not ready. But soon. Maybe a puppy, but you need a yard first. Don't worry. You'll get one."

Dana did her best not to run screaming into the morning. Kathy was known to have an extraordinary sense about people and pets, putting unlikely pairs together. She'd insisted Lexi take home a kitten. Lexi had agreed with the idea, thinking she would give the animal away. But somehow that hadn't happened and C.C. was as much a member of her family as Izzy or Skye.

"I'm not really a dog person," Dana said. "I'm not home very much."

"You will be," Kathy said calmly. "When you have children."

Dana resisted the need to make the sign of the cross and instead took a step back.

"Okay, then," Dana muttered. "Ah, how are things?"

"Good. We have new birds. Not that you want one." Kathy smiled. "But they're very pretty."

Dana smiled back, searching Kathy's face for a hint of the woman who had existed before the tumor that had stolen her intellect. She looked for whispers of Garth. What had he inherited from his mother? If those echoes had left her, were they still in her son?

How could this all have been different? If Jed had agreed to pay for the surgery back before the need was so desperate, would Kathy still be herself? And if she was, how would Garth be a different man? Dana knew the need for revenge had changed him. Once he had won, would he change back? Or was he forever trapped by the need to exact compensation for a debt that could never be repaid?

CHAPTER FIVE

DANA SPENT ANOTHER NIGHT doing more tossing than sleeping. Shortly after five, she gave up the pretense and got in the shower. Twenty minutes later, she'd driven to Garth's condo, mostly to pass the time. She had to follow him to work, anyway. Maybe a couple of quiet hours in her car would relax her.

She parked where she could see the exit from the underground parking garage, tuned into her favorite talk radio and leaned back in her seat. She'd just gotten comfortable and was talking back to the radio host when a familiar BMW pulled out of the garage. A BMW that Garth had only purchased a couple of weeks ago.

Even as she started the engine and began to follow him, she checked her watch. It was barely six. He didn't leave for his office until seven. What the hell? He *knew* she would be escorting him to and from work, as she had all week. He'd never complained, never tried to avoid her. Until today. So where exactly was he going so early in the morning?

Not work, she thought a few minutes later as he

ignored his usual turn and headed for the freeway. Bastard, she thought grimly, following him close enough that he could easily see her. Just let him try to shake her.

But he didn't try, nor did he acknowledge her. Instead he drove to a private airfield and parked. She pulled in next to him.

"Where are you going?" she asked as she got out of her car. She got a look at him and nearly lost her train of thought.

Instead of the usual custom suit, he wore jeans, boots and a white shirt, all of which looked really good on him.

"I have to take a trip," he said. "I'll be back this afternoon."

"Don't for a second think I'm not coming with you."

He looked her up and down, as if he really imagined he had a choice in the matter.

She knew he'd left an hour early deliberately to give her the slip. She wanted to complain that he should play by the rules, but there weren't any. She was tailing him to annoy him. That hardly made them friends.

The complication was Garth wasn't quite as horrible as she'd first thought. There was also the issue of the kiss, but this wasn't the time to bring that up.

"You'll need a passport," he said. "Sorry, that's not my rule. It's a government thing. I'd offer to wait while you go home and get it, but we both know I'd be lying."

She opened her purse, unzipped the concealed compartment in the back and pulled out her passport. "Anything else?"

His expression didn't change, so she couldn't tell if he was pissed or not. As her understanding of him was confused by her reaction to him, she couldn't make a guess, either.

"You'll need a gun."

She didn't doubt he was very aware that her jurisdiction ended at the border. Did she want to be armed in a foreign country?

"I assume you have an extra," she said.

"Only if you're prepared to use it."

"To protect myself or you?"

"Either. I'm not expecting things to go that far, but I'm going in armed and if you're coming, you should be, too."

"Where are we going?"

"Mexico."

Across the border could be a fun and friendly place or it could be a war zone. It depended on their destination. Based on how serious Garth looked and his insistence that she be armed, she was going to guess they weren't heading for a resort.

"I'm prepared to use it," she said.

He motioned to the steps of the private jet.

Five minutes later they were airborne.

Garth watched Dana buckle herself into a leather seat. She didn't look happy, not even when he passed her a case filled with handguns.

"You can pick first," he told her.

"Don't do me any favors." She picked up three different guns before picking a .45 caliber Glock. "You have extra magazines?"

"Underneath the gun."

She raised the false bottom of the case and pulled out the extra magazine for the Glock. After checking the gun to make sure that magazine was full, she put both on the seat beside her.

She looked annoyed. He wasn't sure if she was pissed that he'd tried to leave without her or that he was handing out weapons. Maybe both.

"You want some coffee?" he asked, walking toward the small galley in front. "Breakfast?"

She followed him and peered over his shoulder at the pot of coffee heating and the insulated boxes of food.

"There's no flight attendant, so we'll have to serve ourselves," he told her. "I didn't want anyone along who wasn't necessary."

"I must have been an unwelcome arrival," she said, pushing him out of the way and opening the box.

There were containers of scrambled eggs, bacon and sausage. Hash browns, toast and a warm fruit compote. In a separate insulated container was milk, juice, sliced fruit and several Danish.

"You do know how to travel in style," she murmured. "Are there plates?"

He pointed to a cupboard above the tiny counter.

"Do the pilots eat?" she asked.

"Not usually. They'll come back and get coffee when they want it."

She pulled out all the food and set it on the counter. They each filled their plates, then carried them back to the leather seats.

"You were up early," he said. "How'd you know I was leaving?"

"I didn't. I got lucky." She glared at him over her breakfast. "You tried to leave without me."

"Yes."

"We have rules."

"No, we don't."

Her brown eyes were bright with annoyance, her skin flushed. She looked like a woman ready to take him on. Normally he would welcome the challenge, but this morning he had a lot on his mind.

"We do now," she snapped. "You don't go anywhere without telling me."

That made him chuckle. "Because you're going to make me?"

"I'll do what I have to."

He was letting her hang around because she was a conduit to his sisters. Information flowed both ways, whether Dana recognized that or not. If he needed to set them up, she would be the method. Although that seemed less and less likely. He also allowed Dana to stay close because he enjoyed her company.

She was tough and strong, but still relatively naive.

He would guess for all her bravado, she didn't have the instinct to go for the cheap shot. His instincts had been honed while being held and tortured in a South American jungle. He knew he would kill to survive. She hadn't been tested yet. Neither of them could know how she would react.

Oddly, a part of him wanted to make sure that didn't change. He wanted to ensure she was never that scared, that up against a wall. He wanted to keep her safe.

Travel light, he reminded himself. Caring only brought trouble. Nick had been an easy friend. Nick had understood and could take care of himself. But Dana would require things he didn't have to give.

"Dana, I'm cooperating because it suits me, nothing else. The day you get to be too big a pain in the ass is the day it all ends."

"You don't scare me."

"I'm not trying to. I'm making a point. I don't owe you or my sisters anything."

Her mouth twisted. "You're wrong. You do owe them and you know it. You hurt them because of something Jed did. That isn't right. Now you have to make up for that."

She sounded sincere. Did she actually believe that?

He looked at her. "Have we met? I'm Garth Duncan, ruthless bastard."

She dug into her breakfast. "You're not all that."

"Sure I am."

The corners of her mouth tilted up in an almost-smile. "Oh, please. I'm so not impressed."

She was lying, but he could live with that.

Once again she was dressed for comfort, not style. Jeans, a pullover shirt shapeless enough to hide every curve. Her boots looked worn and she wasn't wearing any makeup.

He was used to women who understood the power of a well-fitting skirt and just a flash of breast. Women who smelled like exotic flowers and sparkled with expensive jewelry. He guessed Dana didn't understand the appeal and if she did, she didn't care. He should have been able to dismiss her.

But he couldn't. Maybe before he'd kissed her, but not since. There had been an instant connection, a compelling heat. He enjoyed sex and took his pleasure easily. This wasn't about getting laid. It was about what he felt when she was in his arms. Hungry. Desperate.

Uncomfortable sensations for a man used to being in charge. Which meant he would have to tread carefully. He would have Dana, but on *his* terms.

They ate in silence. Dana finished first, then went and got a sticky Danish.

"Not counting calories?" he asked.

She licked frosting off her fingers. "Do I look like I need to?"

"No, but that is rarely why women do it."

"I'm not that typical."

"Yet my sisters are. How did you become friends with them?"

He thought she might avoid the question, but she finished her Danish, then picked up her coffee.

"I met Lexi first. We were in school together. I mostly played with the boys, but when I was ten or so, they stopped letting me hang out with them. The girls all got on my nerves. Too silly, I guess. I hated playing with dolls. But Lexi was different. Mostly she was by herself. Maybe it was being a Titan. The other kids thought she was different and she didn't know how to convince them otherwise. We both liked horses and reading. It was just the two of us until Skye and Izzy got older."

There was more to the story, but he didn't press. He could fill in the details. How she would hate to go home because her father beat her. How Glory's Gate was big enough to hide in. How being friends with Jed Titan's daughter would be a measure of protection at home.

"Now they're my family," she continued.

"Is that a warning?"

"It's a threat."

He grinned. "Want to tie me up and punish me?"

"You wish."

He glanced at his watch. "We'll be there in less than an hour. We should talk about the meeting and what to expect. Things should go smoothly, but if they don't we'll need a plan. Before I forget, there's a bulletproof vest in the back. Put it on."

DANA FOLLOWED GARTH OUT of the jet onto the tarmac. The airport was little more than a strip of road in the middle of nowhere. There were mountains in the distance, trees and grass nearby and the only sign of civilization was a small building a hundred yards away.

The structure was more shack than house, weather-worn. The wood had once been painted red and blue but most of the paint had flaked away. There were holes where windows had been, and several lizards scampered across the uneven boards.

The heat was oppressive, especially for November. She'd dressed for an overcast, cool day in Dallas. The vest she'd put on under her sweatshirt added a layer of heat that made her sweat. She had her gun in her hand and an extra magazine in her left front pocket.

She had no idea where they were, what they might be facing, and there was a chance she might have to shoot someone. That wasn't her favorite way to start a day.

She wasn't afraid, exactly, but she was on edge. Her senses were heightened. She knew exactly how many steps it would take to get back to the plane and how fast she could move at a dead run. Based on what she'd seen of his body, Garth would move faster, which was good for both of them. Of course, if they were running and someone was shooting at them, the person running behind was more likely to be shot. Something she didn't want to think about.

He checked his watch, then walked toward the building. There were no cars or trucks around, no signs of people, but she had the feeling they were being watched.

"You realize we're prime targets," she said, keeping pace with him. "Out here in the open."

"Where do you suggest we hide?"

His point was a good one. There was nothing but cement and grass between the jet and the building. Nowhere to crouch or take cover.

"Don't worry," he added, waving the paper-wrapped package in his left hand. "This is a financial transaction. We'll be fine."

"If that's an attempt to reassure me, it's not a good one. We're wearing bulletproof vests. That implies a certain amount of concern."

"I'm a good customer. They have no reason to kill us."

"So you've done this before?"

"Not so directly, but yes, I've used unconventional means to get information."

She was carrying a damn gun and they were both wearing bulletproof vests and he considered this unconventional? She would have worded that a little more strongly.

"There's something wrong with you," she told him.

"You're not the first person to mention that. Now be quiet. I'll be doing the talking."

For once she didn't argue. She had no idea what they were facing and would prefer to spend her energy on staying alive. Garth could talk all he wanted.

They entered the small structure.

It was dark and at first she couldn't see anything.

After a few seconds, she made out a battered table and several chairs. Other than that, the room was empty.

She quickly figured out the best defensive position and stood there. She could see out the front door and two of the three windows. Which left them only one blind side. Garth shifted so he could see anyone coming from that direction, then nodded at her.

"Now we wait," he said.

This was very different from the low-key stakeouts she was used to. No talk radio, no relaxing time with her own thoughts. Adrenaline pumped through her, as her back prickled with sweat. The building smelled musty and unused. Something rustled in the leaves on the floor, but she refused to react until she saw what it was. Seconds later, a small lizard scurried through the front door.

"Three men," Garth said quietly. "They're armed. Stay relaxed. We're here to do business."

This was so not her world, she thought as her heart rate doubled. She stayed where she was, her gun in her hand, not prepared to start anything but more than ready to finish it.

Two of the men walked into the building. They glanced around, taking in her and the room, but not acknowledging her. She moved between them and the door. The meaning was clear—if anything went wrong, they would have to get through her to get out.

"Duncan," the first man said. He was of average height, muscular and tanned.

Cuban rather than Mexican, Dana thought, remembering the report Garth had showed her. His source of damning information.

Here was the bastard who had set up the explosion that had nearly killed Izzy. He'd been paid for that job and was being paid again for sharing the details. Asshole, she thought angrily, wishing she could shoot him.

Something must have shown on her face or in her body language, because Garth gave her a warning glance. Which only made her want to shoot him, too.

"Ramon." Garth nodded.

They spoke in Spanish. Dana caught a few words. From what she could tell, they were asking about each other's family and how business was going.

Garth set his package on the rickety table. Ramon did the same with a box the size of a business file.

"Always good doing business with you," the man said as he picked up what Garth had left. "Have a good flight home."

Garth nodded.

The men turned to leave. Dana kept her gun trained on them. Ramon walked past her without acknowledging her, but the second man hesitated before hurrying out the door.

Dana stayed where she was until Garth said, "They're disappearing into the trees. Come on."

He picked up the box and started for the plane.

Less than two minutes later, they were on the jet.

Even as Garth pulled the door shut, the engines started. They taxied to the end of the runway and took off.

"You okay?" Garth asked, unbuttoning his shirt and tossing it onto the leather seat.

For a second, she thought he was getting naked for her. But before she could tell him off, he was unfastening his bulletproof vest.

Right. Because he didn't need it anymore. They were done.

She ducked into the bathroom at the back of the plane and leaned against the closed door. She shut her eyes and deliberately slowed her breathing. It was finished. They were safely on the plane. She could relax. In and out.

It took a few minutes for her heart to slow. Her hands stayed steady, which was a point of pride. She pulled up her sweatshirt, then shrugged out of the vest. She slipped the sweatshirt back on, then splashed water on her face.

Garth was waiting for her by the leather chairs. As she approached, he handed her a glass of something clear over ice.

"I'm not thirsty," she told him.

"It's not water. Straight vodka. It'll be the easiest to get down. I have Scotch if you prefer."

It wasn't even noon, but she felt as if she'd lived through three days already. After taking the glass, she downed the contents in two gulps, then gasped as the alcohol burned the back of her throat.

She moved to her seat and saw the package sitting on the small table.

"Go ahead," he said. "I already know what's in it."

"Ramon told you?"

"I guessed."

She unwrapped the package, then opened the box.

There were receipts, some original, some copies. Photos, notes, checks and lists of materials. There was also a timeline that went back several months.

Dana looked through everything. With each new piece of paper, the knot in her stomach grew. She recognized Jed's handwriting on a few pages, a call log with a Dallas area code listed and a diagram of an explosive device.

Individually there wasn't all that much, but together, it was enough to convince her of what she'd been desperately trying to avoid accepting.

"Jed arranged for the oil rig explosion," she said, barely able to form the words. "It wasn't you."

Garth sat in the seat across from hers and watched her. "It wasn't me."

"He knew everyone would think it was you. That must have been part of his plan."

"Escalation."

"Izzy could have been killed." She couldn't wrap her mind around that fact. Jed could have killed his own daughter. How was that possible?

"She was lucky, as was everyone else on the rig. There weren't any fatalities."

Dana felt sick inside. "There's no way to make this right. There's no way to explain it. How am I going to tell them?"

"You're not," he said. "I am. I'm meeting with Cruz later."

Cruz. Right. Cruz would know what to do. He would protect Lexi and Mitch would protect Skye and Izzy had Nick, now. They would be fine.

Dana pushed the box away and closed her eyes. It was Jed, not Garth. Jed, whom she'd known for years. She might not have liked him too much, but she'd trusted him. She believed he had a moral code.

"This has to stop," she whispered.

"That's the plan."

"You think you can defeat him? He's ruthless."

Garth gave her a cold smile that made her shiver.

"He hasn't got a chance. I'll destroy him. When I'm finished, he won't have anything and there'll be no coming back."

Dana swallowed. There was a promise in Garth's words, but that wasn't what made her uneasy. It was the knowledge that he would do anything to win. How far was this deadly game going to go?

"NICK'S HERE TO SEE YOU," Agnes said through the intercom.

Garth looked up from the report he'd been reviewing. He hadn't talked to Nick in weeks, not since Garth had sacrificed their years of friendship in the name of winning. He had nothing but regrets but didn't know if Nick would want to hear them.

"Send him in."

Nick walked through the door and into the office. Garth stood. They met in the middle of the big room.

"Cruz sent me to pick up the information you have for him," Nick said by way of greeting.

Information Cruz could have collected himself, Garth thought. Or sent an assistant.

Garth pointed to the large envelope on the corner of his desk. "It's copies of everything I picked up in Mexico. I have the originals in my safe. If anyone needs to see them, they can, but I want to keep them for now."

"You're not turning them over to the police?"

"Papers I bought from a Cuban in a foreign country? No. I'm not turning them over to the police. If we're going to get Jed, we'll have to do it another way. Besides, this is insurance. If he gets out of hand, then I can threaten him."

"He already tried to kill Izzy. I would say that's out of hand."

"You can't change the past."

Nick stared at him. "You got that right."

At one time they'd been friends—even brothers. They'd nearly died together. Garth would have thought they would be there for each other no matter what. Until he'd played to win and lost one of the few relationships that mattered.

"You're still going after Jed." It was a statement from Nick, not a question.

"With everything I have. It's what he deserves."

Garth glanced at the envelope, then back at Nick. "There's a tape recording inside. Cruz might want to listen to it before playing it for Lexi and her sisters."

Nick frowned. "What is it?"

"Jed offering me Titan World on the condition I cut out his daughters."

"When did that happen?"

"A while back. Before Izzy had her surgery."

"That bastard."

Nick walked to the desk. Garth waited until he had the envelope before saying, "I'm sorry. I know it's too late, but I want you to know I'm sorry. For what I did, for what happened. I was wrong to assume you didn't care about Izzy. I was wrong to risk our friendship. You saved my life and I owed you. I should have remembered that."

Nick's expression remained unreadable. They were both good at hiding their feelings.

"I came between you and Izzy. I could have destroyed what you had."

Nick looked at the papers he held. "Maybe not. I'm not the kind of guy women let go of so easily."

Humor? It was a good sign. "If I had it to do over again, I wouldn't."

His former friend walked to the door. "I heard what you said, Garth. I'm going to need some time to figure out if I think you mean it."

THAT AFTERNOON Garth arrived for his meeting with Cruz. By the number of cars in the driveway, he could tell it wasn't going to be just the two of them. Nick's SUV was parked behind a truck, making Garth think all three Titan sisters were waiting for him on the other side of the door.

Not only was he hesitant to see them, he wasn't excited to be the one to inform them that their father didn't give a rat's ass about them. He would rather that kind of news came from someone else.

Nick answered the door, but didn't speak to him. Garth followed him into a large living room where Garth's three sisters, Cruz and Mitch, Skye's fiancé, waited.

No one said anything. Garth could feel the anger in the room and had a bad feeling it was directed at him. A case could be made that he'd earned it. He'd hurt everyone standing in front of him.

He'd loaned Lexi a couple million dollars, only to call the note when she was most vulnerable. That had been the opening shot of his campaign. He'd messed with one of Cruz's drivers, had tried to turn Mitch against Skye, gone after Skye's foundation more than once and played Nick to hurt Izzy. It wasn't a body of work to be proud of.

"You need a hug," Izzy said unexpectedly, coming up to him and wrapping her arms around him. "Don't let them mess with you."

She hugged him fiercely, as if trying to give him strength. He wanted to tell her he didn't need it, that he would be fine on his own, but the warm embrace was oddly comforting. Without meaning to, he found himself hugging her back.

When Izzy stepped away, Cruz motioned to the sofas. "We should sit down and discuss this."

Garth noticed Cruz waited until a very pregnant Lexi had settled on a cushion before sitting next to her. Izzy curled up next to Nick and Mitch stood behind the club chair Skye had chosen. Only Garth was alone.

Cruz nodded at him, as if telling him to start. Garth was unprepared, not sure what he should say. Which annoyed him. He would tell the truth. If people were hurt by that, it wasn't his problem.

"I've been following several leads on the explosion," he began. "The last few pieces came together yesterday morning. Dana and I flew to Mexico and picked up some information. I gave Cruz copies of it."

"Nick and I went over it," Cruz continued. "It's pretty damning."

Lexi wrapped her arms protectively over her belly. "What does it say? What do you know?"

Nick reached for Izzy's hand. Mitch put his hand on Skye's shoulder. Cruz hesitated.

"It was Jed," Garth said, figuring they all hated him anyway. They might as well stay on that road. "He arranged for the bomb to be put on the oil rig. He paid the money and he set the date."

The sisters looked at each other. Garth could read the shock in their eyes, the pain. Izzy went pale.

"My father did this to me?" she asked, sounding

breathless and stunned. "He knew I was going to be there and he…"

Cruz held Lexi's hand. "He wanted to set up Garth to take the fall for the explosion. Maybe he didn't know you'd gone back to work…"

"He knew," Lexi said fiercely. "He knew and he didn't care." She crossed to Izzy and embraced her. "I'm so sorry."

Skye joined them. They held on to each other, whispering things Garth couldn't hear, which was fine with him. This wasn't his thing. He wanted out.

But there was more. Nick got out a small tape recorder and played the recording Garth had made of Jed's visit to his office a few months before. The one where he offered Garth control of Titan World, with no strings. He could run everything on two conditions. That Jed got to remain CEO and that the Titan sisters never got a penny.

The ugly words sounded especially loud in the quiet room. Cruz, Mitch and Nick walked over to the sisters and separated them, then pulled each of them close. They clung to each other—their love obvious. Garth shifted uncomfortably, wanting to be anywhere but here. He should have brought Dana.

"Are we taking this to the police?" Skye asked. "They have to do something."

"We can't," Lexi said, wiping her eyes. "Garth didn't obtain any of it legally."

"At least we know," Izzy said, sounding surprisingly strong. "We know our real enemy is Jed."

The sisters all turned to Garth.

"Are you done?" Skye asked, her green eyes filled with tears. "Is the fight with us over? Or do we have to deal with you disappointing us, too?"

He hadn't come here with a plan. His goal had always been to take down Jed Titan. Messing with the sisters had just been for sport. But somewhere along the way it had all gotten out of hand. He'd lost his best friend because of it. He'd also given Jed a chance to hurt Izzy.

"He's done," Izzy said with a sniff. "He won't hurt us."

"While that sounds really nice," Lexi said, "I want to hear it from him."

Garth had faced greater odds before and stronger adversaries. But he'd never felt so overwhelmed. Not by numbers, but by the damage he could do. Looking at them, he realized it was a power he didn't want, and he usually wanted it all.

"I won't hurt you," he said awkwardly. "I want Jed to crawl, but the rest of you…" He cleared his throat. "I'm sorry about what happened before."

"See," Izzy said. "I told you."

"That wasn't the most eloquent apology," Lexi said.

"Maybe not," Skye told her. "But I think it came from the heart. Nick? Can we believe him?"

They all turned to Nick.

"What do you think?" Skye asked.

Garth stood in the center of the living room while

the man he'd wronged carried his fate in his scarred hands.

Nick stared at him. "He's broken our trust. He'll have to earn that back. For what it's worth, I'd give him the chance."

CHAPTER SIX

DANA ARRIVED AT CRUZ'S house late in the afternoon. Her three friends sat together, looking shell-shocked. There was evidence of tears and despair, which made Dana uncomfortable. It wasn't that she didn't care about her friends' suffering, it was that she didn't know how to fix it.

The normally perfectly groomed Lexi looked rumpled. Mascara blackened the skin under her eyes. Izzy looked smaller somehow, as if the pain had caused her to shrink. Skye's red hair was an even bigger contrast against her especially pale skin. All the color had faded from her face, leaving her looking defeated.

"I'm sorry," Dana said lamely as she walked into the living room.

"There's nothing to be sorry about," Lexi told her. She stood and walked toward Dana. "You did everything we asked and now we know the truth."

The two women embraced, hanging on to each other, as much as they could with Lexi's large belly between them.

Izzy and Skye joined them before they all sat on two couches and faced each other.

"Where are the guys?" Dana asked.

"We sent them away," Skye told her. "This is our problem and we have to figure out a solution together."

"Then why did you call me?"

Lexi was next to Dana. She smiled and put her hand on Dana's arm. "Because you're practically a Titan. Like it or not, you're stuck with us."

"I can live with that." Dana drew in a breath. "I'm sorry about all this. I never thought…"

"Us, either," Izzy said.

"Are you okay?" Dana asked.

"No, but I will be. I wanted to be right about Garth, but not like this. I suppose I shouldn't be surprised to learn Jed doesn't care if I live or die, but I am."

Skye put her arm around Izzy. "Don't go there. It only makes it worse. You have us and Nick and we all love you. We'll always be here for you."

Izzy nodded, but didn't look convinced.

"You went over the material?" Dana asked.

Lexi nodded. "Garth played us the recording of Jed offering him everything. So we're totally convinced."

Dana winced. It was probably better that they knew everything their father had done, but she hated having them hurt. She fought guilt, telling herself she didn't have any part in this.

"It shouldn't be a surprise," Skye murmured, pulling Izzy close and stroking her hair. "We all knew what Jed was, but I don't think any of us wanted to believe it. Now we have proof, which makes denial more difficult."

"I could probably swing it, but I don't want to," Izzy said, blinking back tears. "We have to remember this. It changes everything."

"She's right," Lexi told Dana. "Garth is determined to bring Jed down. It appears our father is a lost cause. We've been talking about it and our larger concern now is Garth."

"We don't want him to end up like Jed," Skye said.

"How are you going to make sure that doesn't happen?" Dana asked. Garth was a determined and powerful man. "You're not going to get him to change his mind. He's been focused on this for years."

"It will take time," Lexi said. "Part of our plan is that we'll work *with* him to stop Jed. Hopefully he'll see that being a part of something is better than going it alone."

"Have you met Garth?" Dana asked. "He's not likely to be swayed by hot chocolate and pictures of the family tree."

"That's where you come in," Skye said. "We want you to keep working with him. Be our emissary, so to speak."

Dana nodded because the alternative was to admit that Garth scared her. Not just with his ruthless ability to get everything he wanted, but because of how she reacted when she was around him. He made her feel things she didn't want to feel. And she knew better than most the danger of letting a person have emotional power. Better to be alone and strong, than weak with someone else.

"You're also going to help him get Jed," Izzy said quietly.

Dana stared at the youngest Titan sister. Izzy's normally bright eyes were dull and swollen. There were red blotches on her skin, probably from crying.

"Izzy, you're upset," she began.

Skye shook her head. "We've talked about it, Dana. Jed has gone too far."

"He's your father. You don't want to do this. Once you start down this path, there's no going back. Jed is already in trouble and facing charges. Do you really want to pile it on? Can you handle being the reason he goes to jail for the rest of his life?"

The sisters looked at each other, then at her.

"It isn't us," Lexi told her. "Jed did this himself. He claimed his destiny when he refused to help Kathy and Garth all those years ago. Maybe it wasn't his responsibility, but the money would have meant nothing to him. When Garth first came after all of us, Jed could have told us what was going on. We could have worked together. Instead he lied about some things and misrepresented others. Then he arranged for the oil rig explosion. He could have killed his own daughter, not to mention everyone else on the rig. Jed deserves what he gets."

The words all made sense, but Dana wasn't willing to let it go. "He's your father. I don't want you to have regrets."

"We want you to help Garth bring him down," Izzy said quietly. "Legally. We won't create the problem. Jed can do that all on his own. We want to find the paper trail legitimately and take it to the police."

"Unless you don't want to get involved," Lexi added. "We'll understand if you're uncomfortable."

Dana looked at all of them. "You're my family. I love all of you. Of course I want to help."

UNSURE OF THE NEXT step, Dana drove back to her condo to figure it out. Instead of tailing Garth and hoping to catch him doing something wrong, she was supposed to work with him now. Talk about changing the rules. She wondered how he would react to the news that the sisters now considered him one of the good guys.

She pulled into her covered parking space, then walked to her apartment. As she approached the door, she saw someone standing there. He moved into the light. It was Garth, and for reasons she couldn't explain, she was almost not surprised.

"You spoke to them?" he asked.

"Yes. I was just there."

"Are they all right?"

She unlocked the door and stepped inside. He followed her.

"Be careful," she told him. "Someone could inter-
pret that to mean you care what happens to them."

"Maybe I do."

He wore a suit—no surprise there. As they stood in
her small living room, he shrugged out of the jacket and
draped it over the club chair she'd bought on sale at a
furniture liquidator with a storefront by the freeway.
Her sofa had seen better days and the entire square
footage of her apartment could probably fit into Garth's
penthouse bathroom.

The small space made her want to back away from
him, but there was nowhere to go. Besides, she didn't
back away from a challenge. She faced it head-on.

She motioned to the sofa. After he'd taken a seat, she
slid out of her leather coat, then hung it on a chair in
the dinette. She took the club chair because she didn't
want to sit next to him. Caution, she reminded herself.

"You're actually interested in the welfare of your
sisters?" she asked. "The same women you have been
going after for months? Color me surprised."

His dark gaze settled on her face. "You don't
believe me?"

"I'm not sure. Why the change?"

He stood and crossed to the window that looked out
on the courtyard. "I didn't like what I saw earlier today.
Them. When they found out about Jed it was like…"
He cleared his throat. "I didn't like it."

It was like they were broken. At least that would be
her interpretation of what had happened. She knew

that Garth had a heart—she just wasn't sure she believed it was so easily touched.

"What about Jed?" she asked.

He turned back to her. "He's finished. I'll make sure of that."

"So you end up with three loving sisters and you still get to face your paternal demons. A win-win for you."

He shoved his hands into his pockets and walked toward her. "The situation is a little more complicated than that, but you have the basics right."

She stood so she wasn't looking up at him. "They want me to help you bring down Jed. It's a two-pronged attack. Your financial assault, along with a campaign to make sure he goes to jail for all he's done."

"I don't have a problem with that."

Jed going to jail or them working together? She decided to assume he meant both.

"There have to be some ground rules," she told him.

He smiled. "Of course. You like rules."

Was it her, or had he just moved closer? She'd always really liked her apartment, but right now it seemed tiny. They needed more space, or at least she did.

She cleared her throat. "Nothing illegal. We'll find what we find through legal channels. If we're building a case to send Jed to jail then it has to stand up in court."

"Agreed."

She looked at him. "I thought you'd want to keep up your little covert operations."

"I wasn't looking to play spy. My way is faster, but you're right. If we want to be able to use it against Jed in court then we'll do everything legally."

"Okay. The sisters are off-limits."

"I've already said I'm not going after them."

"I'm just checking. You haven't exactly been brother of the year through all this."

He nodded. "I give you my word that I will do nothing to hurt any of my sisters. Now or in the future."

Now came the hard part. She squared her shoulders and looked him in the eye. "This is strictly business. We're helping people we care about, nothing more."

One corner of his mouth turned up. "Meaning?"

"Nothing personal between us."

The words just kind of hung there in the silence. She braced herself for his laughter because this was where he pointed out she was nothing he would ever want.

"Haven't you figured out it's all personal?" he asked right before he kissed her.

She was caught off guard, something she never allowed to happen. One second he was speaking, the next he had his hands on her upper arms and was drawing her close to him. At the same time his mouth claimed hers with an intensity that left her breathless.

This wasn't an exploring, getting-to-know-you kind of contact. This was hot and demanding. He kissed her as if he didn't have a choice.

Heat swept through her. It burned away any conflicted feelings, so that she could feel nothing but his hands on her arms and his mouth on hers. She couldn't think, either. There was only the sensation of skin on skin and the fact that she needed so much more than this.

She shook off his touch so she could hang on to him. He wrapped both arms around her, drawing her nearer still. They touched everywhere and it wasn't enough.

The intensity of the flaring passion frightened her, but it also intoxicated her so that resisting wasn't possible. She tilted her head, then parted her lips before he even asked. He swept inside and she met him stroke for stroke. They kissed deeply, taking and giving, straining for more.

His hands moved up and down her back, then to her sides. She broke the kiss long enough to nip his lower lip. He dropped his head so he could nibble the length of her neck.

Everywhere he touched burned. Her breath came in gasps. She ran her fingers through his hair, in part to touch him, in part to hold him in place. His breath was hot on her skin, his mouth warm and teasing.

Without thinking, she reached for his shirt. She told herself to stop, that this was insanity, but there she was, unfastening the small white buttons. He pushed her back and grabbed the hem of her sweater. With a single, swift movement, he pulled it up and over her head. Then they were in each other's arms, mouths clinging, tongues teasing.

She felt fire on her skin and a quivering that began

low in her belly. The wanting was beyond powerful. It was greater than her need to breathe. She knew she would die if they stopped—that her heart would cease beating.

He touched her bare arms, then her bare back. Every inch of contact was heaven. She wanted his hands everywhere.

Her bra was suddenly loose. She hadn't felt him unfasten it, but was grateful that he had. She tossed the sensible white undergarment away and reached for his hands. She placed them on her breasts and moaned softly as he cupped her curves.

His thumbs and forefingers found her aching nipples. He squeezed them, sending ribbons of liquid need pouring through her. She was ready, so ready. She wanted to be taken until she was weak with surrender.

Surrender. The word was nearly enough to stop her. While she enjoyed sex, she never gave in completely. There was always a part of her that she kept to herself. A place no man went.

A problem for another time, she thought frantically, trying to tug off Garth's shirt so she could touch him.

He drew back enough to shrug out of it. While they were separated, he kicked off his shoes. She pulled off her boots. His pants went flying, as did her jeans. Socks followed and soon his briefs and her panties were puddles on the floor.

She had a brief impression of toned muscles under scarred skin. He was already hard and thick. Just the sight of his arousal made her thighs tremble. The intensity of her desire made it difficult to catch her breath. They reached for each other again.

Even as they kissed deeply, he was urging her backward. She took several steps, then felt the sofa behind her. He pushed lightly on her shoulders, urging her to sit. Unsure of what he wanted, she hesitated, then he pressed a little harder and she sank down.

Before she could figure what was going on, he'd dropped to his knees on the carpet and leaned in to kiss her breasts. His mouth sucked deeply, pulling satisfaction from her. His hands explored her thighs before dipping between them. She knew she was already wet and swollen and waited breathlessly for his fingers to discover all her secrets.

He didn't disappoint. He parted her curls and went directly to that one spot designed to bring her pleasure. He circled it, then rubbed it lightly, making every muscle in her body tremble. It wouldn't take long, she thought. She was so close, so fast. A few minutes of concentrated attention and she would be flying.

He shifted to her other breast. She closed her eyes and leaned back, torn between the sensations he evoked. His mouth and tongue against her nipple, the steady movement of his hand between her legs. All of it made her strain for more. Then he shifted his hands to her hips, where he pulled her forward, so she was nearly hanging on the sofa. He lowered his head.

She knew exactly what he planned to do.

"No," she said, trying to move back.

He didn't bother looking up. "Yes."

"No. I mean it. Not like that."

He straightened and stared into her eyes. There were questions there, questions she didn't want to answer. Fortunately men were easily distracted.

She reached for him. "Be inside of me," she said, guiding him toward her. "I'll come that way." She rubbed the length of him, then stroked her thumb against the tip.

She shifted so she could take him inside, but instead of going along with the suggestion, he pulled out of reach.

"Why?" he asked.

"It's not my thing."

"Maybe it's mine. Talk to me."

Words no normal male ever said on purpose, she thought, annoyed and feeling the passion fade away.

"Does there have to be a complicated story about everything?" she snapped. "I don't like it. So let's move on or forget it."

Actually moving on was no longer an option. She stood and stepped around him. There were clothes everywhere, a testament to their uncontrolled desire. Or at least it had been uncontrolled until he'd insisted on getting bossy.

This was exactly why she didn't have anything to do with men like Garth. They were too used to getting their own way every damn time.

Instead of grabbing her clothes, she stalked out of the living room, down the short hallway and into her bedroom. She picked up her robe off the bed and pulled it on. But before she could tie the sash, let alone return to the living room, she felt him reaching for her from behind.

She started to turn toward him, but he held her with both arms around her waist. His powerful body nearly dwarfed hers and she wasn't especially tiny. Only one more wildly annoying thing about the man.

"You should get dressed," she said. "This isn't going to happen."

She braced herself for the temper tantrum sure to follow, but all she got was a soft kiss on her temple.

"Why does it frighten you?"

"It doesn't. Just because I don't happen to like something doesn't mean there's a problem. It's a personal preference. Now it's getting late. You should go."

"It's barely six in the evening."

"It'll be late soon."

He turned her so they were facing each other. He was still completely naked and mostly aroused, which was a little disconcerting. She shifted her gaze to his face. He looked curious and a little determined. Not a good combination.

"Did someone hurt you?"

She tied the sash on her robe. "No. Why do you have to assume that just because it's not something I like that I must have a problem? Maybe it's you. Maybe you're obsessed. You should consider therapy."

He gave her a slow smile. "Are you done?"

"No, but you can talk if you want."

"I'm not obsessed. I like that part of sex because the feedback is easy to understand. Plus it practically guarantees my partner is satisfied."

She rolled her eyes. "And you're all into a job well done. Aren't you a giver?"

"Do you always tell guys no?"

"Yes, and most of them are fine with it."

He put his hands on her shoulders, easing her backward. She only resisted moving a little.

"I'm not like most men," he told her.

"As I've pointed out before, you're not all that."

"Sure I am." He unfastened the tie and slipped off her robe.

"We're not doing this," she said, but without a whole lot of force.

"Sure we are."

He moved closer and kissed the side of her neck. A shiver rippled through her. His hands skimmed her back before finding her breasts. Okay, maybe she wasn't as out of the mood as she'd thought.

He eased one hand down her belly, then between her legs. He immediately found where she wanted him to be and rubbed her swollen center.

"We wouldn't want all this going to waste," he murmured against her skin. "One more step back and then you'll be on the bed."

"Right where you want me," she said, taking the step, then letting herself fall onto the mattress.

He settled next to her, touching her, kissing her mouth, then her breasts. He worked his magic, sucking on her tight nipples until the heat was back, as was the frantic need. She was more than ready. It wouldn't take but a second.

But instead of kneeling between her thighs or touching her with his hand, he shifted on the bed, moving lower and lower until they were back where they started. She slammed her legs together and half rose on her elbows.

"Look, there's no way we're going to—"

"Trust me."

Two words. Meaningless, really. Because she had no reason to trust him. He was the enemy. At least he had been until today. This was all about winning. He wanted to defeat her, to make her surrender and she wouldn't.

"Why do you have to go and spoil a perfectly good moment?" she asked, furious with him for insisting and herself for being tempted.

"Trust me."

She should throw him out. If the need didn't go away on its own, she had a very nice shower massager that would take care of business. Didn't he understand? She didn't like oral sex. Not that she'd ever actually allowed anyone to do that to her, but what was the point? One orgasm was as good as another.

"Five minutes," he said. "If you want me to stop after that, I will."

"Can I hold a gun to your head while you do it?" she asked.

"I'd be worried what you'd do when you lost control."

"I won't."

"Want to bet? Come on, Dana. What's the worst that could happen?"

The answer to that question was vague at best, but full of dark fear. If she allowed that, if she gave in, then... What? What would happen? Did she actually think Garth would physically hurt her?

The idea was ridiculous and because she never let fear win, she grudgingly relaxed back onto the bed.

"Five minutes," she said, bracing herself for something hideous. "Then you'll stop."

"If you tell me to."

"I will."

Instead of answering, he stretched out between her legs. When he was comfortable, he reached for her hands and brought them in so she could use her fingers to hold herself open for him.

The feeling of being wildly exposed nearly made her blush. She wanted to jump up and announce that she'd changed her mind, but she reminded herself it was only for a short time and then they could be done with this nonsense.

At first there was nothing. Just a whisper of breath. Then she felt a single, slow stroke of his tongue, as if he were getting the feel of her.

The warm, soft, wet contact nearly made her jump. It was…different. Nothing like she'd thought. If she had to assign a single-word description it would be delicious.

He licked her again and her insides clenched. A third stroke of his tongue had her tingling. Then he focused all of his attention on that one swollen, hungry part of her.

He shifted his tongue up and down, moving steadily, but not too fast. There was just the right amount of pressure. The sensations were unlike anything she'd experienced before. Incredibly intense. Amazing and wonderful.

She drew back her knees and pulsed her hips in time with his movements. Pressure built inside of her, pushing her toward the edge, making her rock her head from side to side. Every part of her tensed. Her toes curled against the sheets. More. She needed more. He must have read her mind because he moved faster and faster until she couldn't hold it all.

She came with a cry as her body shattered. Ripples of pleasure cascaded through her, making her shudder and moan and hang on to every ounce of release. He continued to please her with his tongue, moving exactly in time with her release, drawing it out until she was drained and boneless.

When he finally drew back, Dana could barely open her eyes. She knew she should say something, but she couldn't bring herself to speak. Nothing had ever felt like that.

But as good as it had been, she felt strange inside.

Twisted up and confused, as if she'd exposed a part of herself and didn't know how to cover back up. What was he thinking? Vulnerability wasn't her best feature and it was one she fought to keep to herself.

As Garth sat up, she opened her eyes. His expression was tense and hungry.

"Condoms?" he asked, his voice raw with need.

She pointed to the nightstand drawer. As he opened it and pulled out the small box, she saw his hands were shaking slightly. His swollen erection throbbed slightly.

He fumbled with the condom, finally siding it in place, then without any style at all, he pushed into her, filling her.

He was still a moment, his breath coming through clenched teeth. When she started to move, he groaned, then grabbed her hips.

"Give me a second," he muttered.

If she'd been standing, the shock of it would have caused her to fall over. Just to be sure, she pulsed her hips and he swore. His eyes were glazed with passion, his muscles rigid as he struggled for control. He was a man on the edge.

She hadn't been the only one to enjoy what he'd done to her, she thought happily, raising her legs and wrapping them around his hips. From the looks of things, he'd been caught up in the experience nearly to the point of losing it.

Suddenly surrendering didn't seem too bad. Not when it brought a man like Garth to his knees. She shifted again, drawing him in deeper. She stroked his arms and his back, feeling thick scars and warm skin.

"Anytime, big guy," she whispered.

He gave a short laugh. "My goal is to make it last longer than it would have when I was eighteen."

"All flash and no substance. I should have guessed."

He pushed into her and hissed out a breath. "It's your fault."

"Sure. Blame it on the woman."

He pushed in again. He was thick and long and filled all of her. If he had five or ten minutes in him, she would have enjoyed the ride, but judging from the way he shook, that wasn't going to happen. Which was fine with her. She'd had her turn and watching him fight for control was about the best part of her day.

"Next time," he promised. "Is that okay?"

She smiled slowly, feeling intense female power, possibly for the first time in her life. "Absolutely."

"I think I'll struggle a few seconds longer. For pride's sake."

"I don't think so." She tightened her muscles around him, then pulsed again.

He tensed, pushed into her and two thrusts later, was done.

Still inside of her, he stared into her eyes. "I can do better."

She smiled. "It was great. Better than great. It's been a long time since I was with a teenaged boy."

"Gee, thanks."

"You're welcome."

He kissed her. "Let's get some dinner."

Dinner as in eating together? As in going out?

"I, ah, don't think that's a good idea. I meant what I said. I don't want anything personal between us."

He chuckled. "Dana, we're naked. My penis is still inside of you. We passed personal a long time ago."

"I know, but we're going to be working together and we should…"

She didn't know what, exactly, but there should be rules and clarification and didn't he want to leave? Guys always wanted to leave after sex.

He kissed her again. "You just had an orgasm. Be quiet and bask like every other woman."

"That's not me."

"I know. Which is why I offered dinner."

"What would you have done otherwise?"

"Offered to cuddle."

Oh, please. "On what planet?"

"Okay, maybe I'm not much of a cuddler, but I can fake it the same as every other guy." He nipped her bottom lip. "Which is it to be? Dinner or cuddling?"

"Dinner."

He withdrew and sat up. "That's my girl."

"Let's get this straight. I'm not your girl and after dinner, you're not getting any again. And don't for a moment think you're spending the night."

"Of course not. I'm not the type."

"Neither am I."

CHAPTER SEVEN

"WHAT DO YOU MEAN you want breakfast?" Dana asked, sounding suspicious. She stood with her hands on her hips, her short brown hair still wet because she would never bother to blow it dry.

She'd pulled on jeans and a long-sleeved purple T-shirt with a designer logo. Must have been a gift, Garth thought, doing his best not to smile at her obvious annoyance. Dana wasn't the designer type.

"You kept me up most of the night with your demands," he said calmly. "I'm hungry."

"Stop for fast food on your way to work. Millions do it every day. It's practically a tradition."

"I don't like fast food."

She narrowed her gaze. "You're doing this on purpose, aren't you? You're just screwing with me because you think it's fun."

Which was true, but not something he would admit. Pissing her off was a great way to spend an hour. Besides, he liked her company.

Last night they'd gone to dinner. Afterward, she'd done her best to show him the door and he'd done his best to get her back into bed. He'd won. Not that she'd resisted too strongly. Afterward there hadn't been any talk of him leaving. They'd fallen asleep in a tangle of arms and legs, which surprised him. He usually preferred to sleep alone.

"You're supposed to be running your own money-hungry corporation, not to mention devising a plan to take down Jed Titan. You don't have time for breakfast."

"I'll make the time. I worked up an appetite last night, Dana. The least you can do is feed me."

She scrunched up her face as if trying desperately to come up with a better argument. But the underlying message was clear. She wanted him gone because she was scared.

He'd figured that out the first time they'd made love and she resisted an easy road to pleasing her. She'd succumbed, but her reticence made him wonder who had hurt her so badly that she felt the constant need to protect herself. Did the fear go back to being a small child who'd been beaten by the one person who was supposed to take care of her? Or was the wound more recent?

He knew he shouldn't care. He shouldn't want to find whoever was responsible and beat the shit out of him. But he did. Something he would deal with another time. For now, he wanted to go to breakfast with Dana because he wasn't willing to leave her just yet.

"After breakfast, you'll leave?" she asked with a sigh. "You give me your word?"

"Unless you try to seduce me again."

"I never seduced you in the first place."

"You do it with every move you make."

Garth was good, Dana thought, doing her best not to react to the words. He was playing with her. Teasing because it was fun. He knew the exact line to get to her. The trick was to make sure she didn't start believing him.

"Then I get to pick the place," she said, knowing that the quickest road to getting him gone was to eat and then watch him drive away.

"Sure," he said easily.

She gave him her first smile of the morning. "You ever been to the Calico Café?"

"No."

The smile turned into a grin. "You're going to love it."

They walked because the restaurant was only about two blocks away, one of the things Dana liked about living in Titanville. It had a small-town feel right on the edge of Dallas.

"Your great, great, I don't know how many greats, grandfather founded this town," she said as they left her small apartment. "During the eighteen hundreds. He was something of a gambling man who liked his women. Apparently he didn't care who he slept with. He left a lot of women disgraced. You would have liked him."

He glanced at her. "I'm very nice to the women in my life."

"Are you? Mind if I take a small survey?"

"Not at all. They'll speak well of me."

Damn him, they probably would, she thought glumly. He was just that kind of guy. Good in bed. Too good. She was still experiencing sensual aftershocks. Little tingles that came out of nowhere. They zoomed to life, pinged her privates, then disappeared, leaving her slightly aroused and a little flustered.

"Not all of them," Dana said. "There have to be at least a couple who hate your guts."

He chuckled. "Want to meet them and form a club?"

"I don't hate you."

"Now you're just talking sweet to flatter me."

He was teasing. She knew that. But knowing didn't make it easier to respond. She'd never been the type who knew how to flirt with a guy. She hadn't been born with the skill. Or maybe it was a confidence issue. Either way, it was a whole lot easier to be crabby. Unfortunately, she couldn't think of a reason.

They walked toward the café. Seeing the familiar big windows and calico curtains lifted her spirits. She couldn't wait until Garth got a look at the inside.

He held open the door. She went in and he followed. She turned and waited.

He glanced around the small space. She followed his gaze, anticipating his reaction. There were dozens of tables with glass tops. Underneath, long tablecloths hung down nearly to the floor. Wallpaper added color on color. There were shelves of china figures, bowls, cloth-covered books in stacks and every single item was done in calico.

It was an explosion of the pattern. The tiny floral print bred in the night and grew. The menus were calico, as were the seat cushions and the plates. It was calico heaven…or hell—depending on one's perspective.

Men rarely survived more than a few minutes without visibly withering. Most begged for mercy and ran. The problem was, the Calico Café had the best food in ten counties. Their motto, clearly printed on their menus, stated they served breakfast all day and if you wanted something else, go away. It was an attitude Dana could respect.

Garth barely reacted at all. "It's nice," he said. "Is the food good?"

She frowned. "That's it? You don't want to talk about all the calico?"

He shrugged. "Somebody must like it. I've eaten in worse."

Where?

Renee, one of the regular servers, bustled out of the kitchen. Her ample hips brushed against chairs as she moved. She barely glanced at them.

"Get yourself a table," she called, carrying a heavy tray to the west side of the café. "We don't stand on ceremony here."

Garth put his hand on the small of Dana's back. "Wherever you'd like," he told her.

Her usual choice was up front, by the window. She liked to keep an eye on the sleepy town. But maybe today that wasn't such a good idea. She could see but she could also be seen.

"How about there?" she asked, pointing to a table in the back.

"Fine."

They were barely seated, her with her back to the wall, facing the room, when Renee hurried over with two menus.

"There's no special," the fiftysomething waitress snapped, turning their coffee cups over and pouring. "The cook wasn't in the mood. If you want…"

Renee finished pouring the coffee and actually looked at her customers. Dana braced herself, hoped desperately that nothing was going to happen, then wanted to bolt for freedom when the woman she'd known most of her life said, "Dana. A man? I'm so proud."

Why? Why did it have to be like this? Why did Renee have to look so happy in an uncomfortably maternal way, as if Dana were a baby turtle who had finally found her way to the sea?

The red-haired waitress looked over her half-glasses, studying Garth intently.

"And you are?"

"Garth. I'm a friend of Dana's."

"Uh-huh." She patted Dana's shoulder. "I'll let you two decide on breakfast. Take your time." She winked, then left.

Dana did her best to think cool, restful thoughts. She was calm. She was one with the universe. She'd forgotten this wasn't Renee's morning off.

Garth's dark eyes sparkled with humor. "I'm guessing you don't bring a lot of guys here."

"Not only could I shoot you, I would know how to hide the body so no one could find it. Ever."

He patted her hand. "It's all right, Dana. Your secret is safe with me."

While they were on the subject...

"Look," she said, leaning toward him. "No one can know. About last night." She'd almost said "us" but there wasn't an us. One night of hot monkey sex did not an *us* make. "Especially your sisters. We're not going to talk about it or even think about it."

He reached for his coffee. "I plan to think about it, Dana. A lot. You're incredibly passionate. Do you know how rare that is? No pretense, no games, just one-on-one pleasure." He sipped his coffee.

Her well-honed sense of control seemed to crumble to dust. She wasn't passionate. She was difficult and crabby and she didn't let anyone in. She was restrained.

She opened her mouth to tell him so, only to realize that when she thought about this morning, Renee would barely be a footnote when compared with everything else that had happened.

The front door of the café opened and in walked all three Titan sisters. They were talking to each other and hadn't looked around the place, but in a few seconds they would. They would look and they would see her with Garth.

He turned around and laughed.

"It's not funny," she snapped.

"As this place was your pick, it is. You'd better stop looking so guilty, or they'll guess in a second."

"I don't look guilty." She cleared her throat and forced her expression to something she hoped was neutral. "If they ask, this is a working breakfast. We're discussing strategy. Nothing else."

She wanted to say more, maybe even threaten him if she could figure out how, but just then Lexi looked up and saw them. She looked puzzled for a second, then Izzy turned and spotted them.

"What are you two doing here?" she asked as she walked over. "Never mind. I already know. Do you ever sleep? Work, work, work. Dana, when this is over, you have to swear you'll take a vacation. Hey, big brother."

Izzy bent down and hugged Garth from behind. He smiled at her.

"You're all up early," he said. "A sisterly tradition?"

"We still have a lot to talk about and this is the best breakfast in town."

Skye and Lexi joined them.

"How's the plan coming?" Skye asked. "Are we interrupting? Should we go away?"

"No. Of course not." Dana rose and reached for a larger table. "Let's pull this over and we can all have breakfast together. Garth and I were working out the details. There are actually a few things we need to discuss with all of you, so this is perfect timing."

Skye and Lexi grabbed the other side of the table and dragged it close.

"You're just going to sit there?" she asked Garth.

"I like watching women work."

"I'll just bet."

She had hoped in the confusion that someone would take her seat, allowing her to settle a little farther from Garth, but the sisters took other chairs, forcing her back across from him. It wasn't that she minded the view, it was that she was terrified of what she might say or do. Rational thought was more challenging when there were still tingles going on.

Renee returned to the table. Dana started to panic, but the waitress simply raised her eyebrows then passed out menus.

"Big crowd this morning," she said, giving Dana a knowing wink, then announcing there wasn't a special.

"But I love the special," Izzy whined.

"You're always the difficult one. I'm bringing you coffee. By the time I get back, I want you to all know what you're ordering. And no, Lexi, we don't have organic butter, eggs, juice or anything else. So get over it."

Lexi laughed. "I didn't say a word."

"You were going to." Renee looked at Lexi's impressive belly. "You're due to pop soon, and speaking as the person who's heard the organic lecture fourteen thousand times, I can't wait."

"I have two months," Lexi told her with a grin. "Plenty of time for us to talk about renewable farming."

"Gotta go." Renee scurried away.

"I'll need herbal tea," Lexi yelled after her.

Skye shook her head. "You should give Renee a break. She's old-school."

"She loves the attention," Izzy said. She turned to Garth. "So you're in Titanville early."

"There's a lot going on," Dana said, hoping she looked and sounded casual. "I'm going to be speaking with some guys I know at the Dallas Police Department. While a lot of their investigation is confidential, I'll be able to get a sense of what they have and what they need. There's no point in duplicating work. But before I do that, I want each of you to be sure about this. Once it's done, it can't be undone. If Jed is charged, it sets a course in motion."

There was a lot more she could say—like no matter what, he was their father. She might think he was a class A asshole, but that was because he'd nearly killed a close friend. But she wasn't family.

Skye, ever elegant in a tailored suit, shook her head. "We don't have any second thoughts. Garth said nearly the same thing yesterday. We talked for hours and we know this is what we want."

Lexi put her arm around Izzy. "He crossed the line. We want him taken down."

Izzy, normally so full of life, was oddly silent. Her face was pale, a stark contrast to her dark, curly hair.

Dana had a small idea of what her friend was feeling. She'd had to deal with a father who was abusive. But she'd known what he was all her life, while Izzy had to deal with the shock of learning her own father had been willing to consider her a casualty of war.

Renee returned and they ordered breakfast. When they were alone again, Skye said, "If he hadn't arranged for the explosion, we would have backed off. But that changed everything. We have to protect ourselves against him. He needs to be prosecuted for everything he's done."

The sisters were so different, Dana thought. Lexi, the cool blonde, with her holistic view on life. Pregnant and glowing, she looked radiant enough to make even the most cynical woman long for motherhood. Skye, with her fiery red hair, had the appearance of the wild child of the group, while she was the most maternal. The quietest and most caring.

Izzy, always ready for adventure, had nearly been defeated by the aftermath of the blast that had left her blind. Not permanently, but it had been a scare. She'd changed, but was still the one who led with her heart.

These women were her family, Dana thought. She would die for them, if necessary.

"If that's what you want, I'll move forward," she said. "We'll get him."

Renee returned with a pot of hot water, a teacup and a tray of teas. "The kitchen's backed up. It'll be a couple of minutes."

"No problem," Skye said.

Lexi sniffed. "Oh, Renee. Look." She pointed at the tray of tea bags.

"So?" Renee's eyes narrowed. "What's your point?"

Lexi stood and hugged her, her big belly getting in the way. "They're organic."

Renee shook her off. "Yeah, yeah, so what? I slipped when I placed my order. Checked the wrong box. Now I'm stuck with them, so you'd better drink them all."

Lexi sniffed as she sat. "I will. I promise."

"Cheap talk," Renee muttered as she walked off.

Izzy grinned at Garth. "See what we do to people."

"It's terrifying," he said as he picked up his coffee. "I don't stand a chance."

"If only that were true," Izzy said. "But I have high hopes. Especially with Dana's help."

Had Dana been drinking she would have choked. "You're on your own," she said, hoping she wasn't blushing.

"While we're talking about changes," Skye said, then paused.

Lexi leaned toward her. "Tell them."

"Maybe it's not the time."

"It's the perfect time."

Garth looked at Dana, as if asking what they were talking about. She shrugged, not sure what Skye meant.

Skye shifted in her seat, then smiled shyly. "It's probably a ridiculous thing to say or even think about, with everything going on," she began.

Izzy rolled her eyes. "Would you get to the point? It's wonderful. Come on. Tell them."

Skye looked from Dana to Garth and back. "As you know, Mitch and I are engaged. We've been talking about the wedding and, well, it was Erin's idea, really."

Izzy dropped her head to the table. "Will you get on with it?" she said, her voice muffled.

Skye cleared her throat. "We're talking about a Christmas Eve wedding. Erin thinks it would be romantic and I know Mitch is excited that he'll never have to worry about remembering our anniversary."

"I don't think that's what has him excited," Dana said with a laugh. A holiday wedding. Skye's daughter was right…it was very romantic. "It sounds perfect. And very you. Imagine the party you can plan."

Skye looked more worried than happy. She stared at Garth. "Is it a bad idea? I'm thinking about all the things going on with Jed. Should we wait?"

"No. Getting enough on Jed could take weeks, months or even years. Don't put your life on hold. A Christmas Eve wedding sounds very…nice."

"Nice?" Izzy straightened. "You are such a guy."

"Thank you."

"It would be a small wedding," Skye said. "Family and a few close friends."

"Don't compromise," Dana told her. She might not

be a "fancy party" kind of person herself, but she cared about her friend. "Have the wedding you want."

Skye smiled at her. "I appreciate that and I know you're right. We've talked and we want something intimate. Special. Just the people we love, at the house. But there isn't much time."

"If anyone can do it, you can," Izzy said. "You're gifted at the party thing. And I'll help." She held up her hands, palms out. "I know, I know. I'm a giver. I can't help it."

"I'll help, too," Lexi said, resting her hand on her stomach. "As long as I can do it sitting down."

"I'll be busy," Dana muttered, thinking she would rather tackle Jed in a gun battle than address invitations or fold napkins.

Everyone laughed.

Lexi started to say something, then frowned at Garth. "Didn't you have on that exact shirt and tie yesterday?"

The table went silent. Dana's first thought was complete panic. Oh God, oh God, oh God! Now what? Everyone would know. What would they think? What would *she* think? She didn't know what to say, where to look, how to breathe.

Garth calmly sipped his coffee. "No."

Lexi squinted at him. "I guess you're right. They look the same."

"All men's clothes look the same," Izzy complained. "Have you seen their shoes? All those identical loafers. The big question is tassels."

Just then Renee showed up with breakfast. Dana accepted her plate with a sense of being handed a reprieve. Slowly, carefully, she glanced at Garth, who was watching her. He winked.

AFTER BREAKFAST, EVERYONE went their separate ways. Lexi and Dana walked to Lexi's car. Dana hovered as her very pregnant friend waddled more than walked.

"How are you going to survive the last two months?" Dana asked.

"I'll manage," Lexi said cheerfully. She paused by her car, then said, "He's not your usual type. Garth, I mean."

Dana opened her mouth, then closed it. "I have no idea what you're talking about."

Lexi raised her eyebrows. "I noticed the tie yesterday specifically because Cruz has the same one. I thought it was interesting. Men don't wear the same tie two days in a row unless they haven't gone home to change."

"Right," Dana said, struggling to stay calm. "But maybe he wasn't with me."

Lexi watched her without saying anything.

Dana collapsed like overcooked pasta. "Okay, it was me. I don't know how it happened, but it did. And then he wouldn't leave. He spent the night."

"Fascinating," Lexi said slowly. She smiled. "I know we've been after you to try someone new, but Garth?"

"I can't explain it," Dana muttered. "He's your brother. Is it too weird?"

"Of course not. Just…" She hesitated. "Be careful. We don't know that much about him. I don't want you to get hurt."

"Hey, this is me we're talking about. I don't get that involved."

"He's different."

"I'm not. I take care of myself."

"Then go for it. Enjoy the ride, so to speak. And if you want any advice…" She shook her head. "Never mind."

"Advice? On guys? You're the one with a ten-year dry spell."

"That was before Cruz and not what I'm talking about. I meant clothes and makeup."

Dana glanced down at the shirt she'd pulled on. Izzy had given it to her for her birthday last year. "What about my clothes?"

"Just that he moves in different circles. He'll probably ask you to some events that require something more dressy."

Events? As in a date? "We're not dating."

Lexi's blue eyes brightened with laughter. "You're just having sex?"

"Yes. I would never date him." She held up her hand. "I'll admit sleeping with someone you wouldn't date is probably bad, but I'll accept the consequences. We don't actually have a relationship."

Lexi studied her. "Or so you think. You might want to ask Garth his thoughts on the subject."

"I'd rather be shot."

"I'm sure that's true."

THAT AFTERNOON Garth found his weekly staff meeting interrupted by the arrival of his three sisters. As they'd just had breakfast together less than six hours earlier, he didn't know what was so important, but he knew better than to keep them waiting.

He excused himself from the staff meeting, then returned to his office to find them "exploring" everything from the coat closet to several of his drawers.

"Ladies," he said as he walked in.

Izzy was bent over, looking into drawers in his credenza, Lexi was on his computer and Skye smoothed the coat in his closet before closing it.

They looked at him without a trace of guilt.

"We were making ourselves at home," Izzy said, closing a drawer.

"So I see. Lexi, would you like my password?"

She smiled and stood. "No, thank you. I was just… checking my e-mail."

He motioned to the sofas by the window and waited until they were seated before joining them.

"An unexpected pleasure," he said. "And the reason for your visit?"

"We want to know your intentions toward Dana," Skye said, watching him intently. "She's our friend."

"News travels fast." He doubted Dana had coughed up the information, so apparently Lexi hadn't bought the similar tie story.

"She's a very close friend," Izzy said. "Practically a sister."

"You're not known for having serious relationships," Lexi added. "You have a broken engagement and a string of abandoned women."

"Abandoned," he said. "As bad as all that?"

Skye drew in a breath. "Not that we don't care about you, too."

"I can see that. Your concern for me is overwhelming."

While he found their meddling irritating, a part of him was pleased that Dana had these women looking out for her.

"We don't want Dana hurt," Lexi said.

"Neither do I," he told her. "It's been less than twenty-four hours. Can you give me a week to figure all this out?"

"We're not asking if you're planning to propose," Skye said. "Just be careful. We love her and we don't want you playing with her emotions."

"I wouldn't do that. I respect Dana."

"Then we won't have a problem," Lexi said.

"Good. Anything else?"

When they all shook their heads, he stood. "I have a meeting to get back to. If you'll excuse me."

"You're angry," Skye said, coming to her feet.

"No, just not sure I'd want any of you at my back during a fight."

Skye moved toward him and touched his arm. "We'll love you, too. It'll just take a little time."

The words stunned him and burned away any lingering annoyance. He wanted to tell her that he didn't want their love. He preferred to go it alone. But he couldn't find the words and by the time he did, she and Lexi had left. Only Izzy stayed behind.

He turned to her. "You have something else?"

She tilted her head. "Maybe we're worried about the wrong person. Maybe we should be worried about you."

No one worried about him. "I'm fine. I'm the powerhouse here."

She smiled. "Okay. But just so you know, Dana usually gets involved with men she can push around. Then she gets bored and leaves. She's never taken a chance romantically. You're not her type and I don't think she's your type, either. So you might want to think about protecting yourself."

"Thanks, but I'll be fine."

She walked to the door, then faced him again. "It's funny. That's exactly what everyone thinks right before they fall."

CHAPTER EIGHT

"THIS IS RIDICULOUS," Dana grumbled to no one in particular. Which was a good thing. No one was listening. She didn't know where the idea had come from, but it was totally stupid.

"Where do you want these?" Leonard, Skye's key IT guy, asked as he walked in with three laptops still in their boxes.

"On the desks," Dana told him, pointing to where the furniture guys were moving desks into place.

Lexi looked up and smiled. "Oh, you have the computers. Thank you, Leonard. You'll stay to set them up, won't you? I'm so not in the mood."

His gaze dropped to her belly. "Um, sure, ma'am. Shouldn't you be sitting down?"

Lexi rubbed the small of her back. "Probably." She sank into a rolling chair and motioned to the boxes the furniture guys had brought in first. "If you bring those to me, I'll start opening them," she told Dana.

"Right. And then I'll be in trouble for making the pregnant lady do the hard work." Dana crossed to the boxes and pulled out her pocket knife. "I'll do it."

"You are so crabby," Lexi told her.

"We don't need an office. We're not selling sandwiches."

"We need an easy way to coordinate what we're doing. Garth and I think it's better to have one central location."

"As long as *you* and *Garth* think it's the right thing to do."

Lexi blew her bangs off her face. "Don't make me roll my eyes. It makes me feel like I'm twelve. With the office, all the information is kept in one place. Leonard is going to put in a fancy firewall so Jed can't get into our system. If he wants to come after our information, it's not in someone's house."

An excellent point, Dana thought, still wanting to grumble. Opening an office was too official. This was a private investigation. It should be kept private.

"As soon as Leonard gets us up and running, I'll see if I can access Jed's private computer," Lexi said. "I know several of his passwords, or at least I did. Plus I have a few passwords from my ex-assistant."

Before Dana could remind her how she felt about anyone breaking the law, the front door opened and a petite, well-dressed blonde swept into the room.

"Just so we're clear," she announced as she set a black leather briefcase on a desk. "I'm in charge."

Lexi looked at Dana who was staring at the woman. She recognized the piercing blue eyes, the determined mouth, the flashy diamond cocktail ring.

"Mary Jo?"

"Good morning, Dana. I'd heard you were involved in this mess. What was Garth thinking?"

Dana hadn't seen the other woman in years. Not since Dana had arrested a bank officer and Mary Jo Sheffield had been his attorney.

Lexi stood. "Who are you?" she asked coolly.

Her tone was "Who the hell are you, bitch?" but Lexi would never say that. Not at a first meeting.

"Mary Jo Sheffield. Garth's attorney. He told me what you all were planning and I came by to make sure I approve."

It was the battle of the blue-eyed blondes, Dana thought, not sure if she should back away or pull up a chair.

"Your approval isn't required," Lexi told her. "But thanks so much for stopping by."

Mary Jo didn't even blink. "I'm Garth's representative. I'm here to look after his interests."

"He's being protected by a girl?" Dana said with a grin. She couldn't wait to mention that to him.

Mary Jo raised her eyebrows. "Dana, you of all people know what I'm capable of."

That was true. She'd been in court and watched Mary Jo in action. It had been damned impressive.

"How do you know her?" Lexi asked, turning to Dana. "Who is she?"

"We were on opposite sides of a case. Mary Jo used to work for a big law firm."

"Now I work for Garth," Mary Jo said with a smile. "Exclusively for Garth. He has a lot to lose."

Dana had always liked Mary Jo, but family came first. She moved between the lawyer and Lexi. "The Titan sisters have discovered that not only is their father willing to sell them out to the highest bidder, he arranged for an explosion that nearly killed Izzy. I would say they have a whole lot more to lose than Garth."

Mary Jo smiled. "That's my girl. I'm looking forward to working with you, Dana. I know how formidable you can be."

Dana cocked her head. "Right back at you, Mary Jo."

"Okay." Lexi looked concerned. "Can we trust her?"

"I'm standing in the room," Mary Jo pointed out.

Dana ignored her. "Yes. But she's not kidding about working for Garth. Don't for a second think she's neutral."

"There shouldn't be sides," Lexi said with a sigh. "There should be a single goal."

"In a perfect world." Mary Jo smiled. "But we're in this one. Now where are we?"

Dana let Lexi bring her up to speed. She went to help Leonard with the computers, doing the unpacking while he set them up. Next she tackled office supplies, which she quickly put away. Mary Jo had a heated conversation with the phone company. Fifteen minutes later, all their lines were working, including their high-speed Internet.

Mary Jo and Lexi seemed to have established an uneasy peace. Dana figured there would be trouble later, but she was willing to accept the calm while it lasted.

About eleven, Garth breezed in.

Dana didn't have to look up from the notes she was making. She could tell he was there by a subtle shifting inside her body. Her chest got tight and anticipation filled her. Talk about acting like a girl, she thought in disgust. This was why she never got involved with anyone like him. She hated that he was on her mind, that she was aware of him in the room. That she noticed he greeted Lexi and Mary Jo before coming over to her.

"How's it going?" he asked.

"It's not. There's too much activity. It will be better when the setup is done and everyone gets out of here."

He laughed. "You're such a people person."

"Bite me."

"All right. I'll tell you something you'll like. I'm about to piss off Jed Titan."

"By doing what?"

"That would be my question," Mary Jo said, hurrying over to them. "Nothing illegal. We've talked about that."

"Several times," he agreed, settling on the corner of Dana's desk. "I'm backing him into a corner. I want him pissed and panicked. Both will cause him to act without thinking. That's to our advantage."

Dana glanced at Lexi, who was listening from her desk. "You okay with this?" she asked.

Lexi nodded. "Perfectly. He has to be stopped and

this is the only way. It's not just for us, but for Erin and my baby. We can't trust him. He's proven that."

"What are you doing?" Mary Jo asked.

"I don't want to spoil the surprise," Garth told her. "It'll be in the papers soon enough."

"I hate it when you do things behind my back," his attorney said. "It usually means trouble."

"That's why you get the big bucks."

"I might need a raise."

Dana listened to the exchange with interest. Garth could have hired any lawyer in the city. Or the state. Why had he chosen an opinionated woman who wouldn't be afraid to tell him he was wrong? Did he want the truth? If so, it was an unusual characteristic for a man used to being in charge. Jed had never liked dissenting voices.

"Do any of you need anything?" he asked. "Except for Mary Jo and her raise."

"We're good," Lexi said, returning her attention to her computer.

Dana nodded.

"That's what I like to hear." He stood. "Dana, want to walk me out?"

"It will make my day complete," she muttered, but rose and followed him. Once they were outside, she faced him and folded her arms across her chest. "What?"

He smiled. "You're kind of prickly."

"Part of my charm."

"It's subtle. I need to talk to you."

She braced herself for bad news. He didn't want to see her again socially. Not that they were dating. They weren't. They were working together and they'd spent the night together. Big whoop. So he wasn't interested in sleeping with her again. She didn't care. She wasn't sure she even liked him.

He leaned in and kissed her. "Tomorrow's Saturday. Want to do something?"

Huh? "What do you mean, something?"

"Go out. Have lunch or dinner or both. Help me pick out drapes."

"You need drapes?"

"No. I'm saying let's spend some time together."

On purpose? It wasn't a date. It wasn't that specific. It was…

"All right," she said cautiously.

"Good. I'll pick you up at ten."

"I'll come to your place."

He chuckled. "Sure. If that's better."

"It is."

"I'll see you then." He walked to his car and opened the driver's door. "Oh, I wanted to tell you. Lexi and her sisters know. About us. They came to see me and asked me my intentions. See you tomorrow."

He got in the car and drove away.

She stared after him, unable to believe the words. Lexi had told her sisters and they'd gone to see Garth? Obviously she needed to have a very serious talk with all three Titan girls. Starting with Lexi.

"WE HAD TO TALK to him," Lexi said later as she propped her feet up on a box.

Dana had waited a very long forty-five minutes until Leonard and Mary Jo had both finished and left. Now she stared at her friend, unable to believe she wasn't sorry.

"He's not your usual type," Lexi added, sipping on bottled water. "Come on, Dana. He's very successful with women. He has a reputation. We love you and want you safe."

"You're saying I couldn't handle him? I can so handle him. I don't need you protecting me."

Lexi sighed. "Yes, you do."

Just then Izzy breezed in, a bag of sandwiches in her arms. "Hi. I brought lunch." She looked from Lexi to Dana and back. "What happened?"

"I just found out Lexi told everyone about me sleeping with Garth and that you went to see him." Dana's voice rose with each word. "What is wrong with all of you?"

Izzy's eyes widened. "I've never heard you shrill before. Careful, Dana. You're acting like a girl."

"Not funny. None of this is funny. Why would you do that? Why would you get involved?"

Izzy put the sandwiches on the desk and sat next to them. "If it makes you feel any better, I also told Garth he needs to be careful, too. After all, he's in as much danger of getting his heart broken."

Apparently aliens had swooped down and taken

over the world. Or they'd all fallen into an alternative universe. None of this made sense.

"Seriously?" Lexi asked. "You're worried about Garth?"

"Dana's different for him, too. I'm not saying if I had to pick, I'd take his side, but Dana has all of us and he doesn't have anyone. He thinks he knows the rules of the game and I think he's wrong."

"I hadn't thought of that," Lexi said slowly. "Maybe you're right."

Dana glared at them both. "You two will stop it right now. We're not having this conversation. Is that clear? You will stay out of my life. You won't discuss this anymore, not even among yourselves. It's my life and my business. Not yours. And leave Garth alone. He can take care of himself."

Izzy grinned. "Have you met us? We get involved. We give advice and we talk. A lot. So sue us."

Lexi nodded. "She's right and you know it. We love you, Dana."

Dana wanted to scream with frustration. When had she lost control of the situation? "I can take care of myself. I'm perfectly capable of protecting my heart. As for Garth, I'm not sure he has one."

The idea that he might be at risk of falling for her was laughable. As if. He would never care about her that way, she thought wistfully.

Izzy dug in the bag and held out a sandwich to each of them. "He has one. We'll see what happens there.

As for you, Deputy Dana, you've been protecting your heart your whole life. Maybe it's time to let go and see what happens."

"When pigs fly."

Lexi smiled. "I saw a flying pig just the other day."

"You make me insane. Both of you."

Izzy handed over chips. "You're getting shrill again. You need to watch that. Next you'll be buying fashion magazines and talking about shoes."

"I'd rather be dead."

Lexi unwrapped her sandwich. "Don't be dramatic."

"She's probably close to her period."

Dana gritted her teeth.

Lexi held up her water. Izzy grabbed a can of soda. They toasted, as if they'd just won.

"We're good," Izzy said.

"The best," Lexi agreed.

It was all Dana could do not to scream.

GARTH'S CALL TO CHINA was interrupted when his office door burst open and Jed stalked in. Garth excused himself just as Jed reached his desk, braced his hands on the edge and leaned in.

"I don't know what you think you're playing at, you little fucker, but this is going to stop."

Garth leaned back in his chair, letting his satisfaction show on his face. "Hey, Dad. Nice to see you. What brings you by?"

"You know exactly what." Jed's usually tanned face was flushed with anger. "You bought my horses."

"The race team? Yes. The deal closed today. I was surprised you were selling them, especially at that price. It was a bargain." He feigned concern. "Are you having a cash problem, Dad? Do you need a loan?"

Jed straightened. "You won't get away with this. Any of it. I swear, I'll make you regret ever taking me on."

The last few months had not been kind to Jed. His face was lined and there were bags under his eyes. He'd put on twenty or thirty pounds but hadn't bought new clothes, so everything pulled and gapped. He looked like what he was—a washed-up loser.

Garth stood. "You should know better than to threaten someone who is kicking your ass, old man. You're hemorrhaging money and I'm cleaning up. Soon I'll own your soul."

"Never." Jed practically spit the word. "You're not as smart as you think."

"I only have to be smarter than you and that's not a very high bar. I'm buying up your company piece by piece."

"I'll take that information to the shareholders."

Garth smiled. "And tell them what? That a very successful businessman is interested in their well-being? They'll be happy to hear the news. Ever since you were taken in for questioning, your investors have been nervous. It's not going to take very much for them to start leaving in droves. Your problem is, there are so many ways you've screwed up. Which one is going to come out first?"

Fury blazed in Jed's dark eyes. "I'll kill you before I let you win."

"Did I mention I record many of the conversations I have in this room?" Garth asked casually.

Jed glanced around. Worry replaced anger for a moment, then he shook it off. "The police can't use an illegally recorded conversation."

"True, but it gives them a place to start looking."

Jed's hands curled into fists. "I'll stop you. You think I don't know about your games with my daughters? Your office and how you plan to hack into my computer system? It won't happen. Any of it."

Garth moved toward him and lowered his voice. "Let me be clear. You touch anyone working with me and you'll be the one feeling the pain."

Jed scoffed. "What do you care about your sisters? You want to win."

"There are many ways to define victory."

"Not for you."

"Don't test me on this," Garth told him. "You won't like how it ends."

Jed turned and left. Garth watched him go.

Would the old man listen or had things just escalated to the next level? He couldn't be sure, so precautions would have to be taken. The Titan women weren't going to like it, but their annoyance would be nothing when compared with what Dana was going to say.

DANA TOOK THE EXIT for Titanville. There were two miles of open road between the crowded freeway and the slower speed limit of the city limits. Normally she enjoyed the quiet, but this afternoon she felt restless.

She couldn't stop thinking about what Lexi and Izzy had said. That she needed to protect herself against the likes of Garth. While her friends were well-meaning, they could also be idiots when it came to men. She wasn't at any risk. She could take care of herself.

So what if he was different? She could handle any situation that came up. She was strong and she knew how to stay safe. Years of surviving her father's beatings had taught her that. She knew better than to care too much when it came to men. Showing a vulnerable side just meant a stronger possibility of getting hurt. There were—

The skin on the back of her neck prickled, interrupting her thoughts. She immediately glanced in her rearview mirror, then out the side windows. Nothing had changed. The black Suburban was still behind her. The F-250 truck that had been in front of her had gone into the other lane, which would have been fine, if it hadn't suddenly slowed. Something was wrong.

She sped up. Both vehicles paced her. The speed

limit was forty-five. She punched it to sixty, then seventy. They stayed with her. Dark, tinted windows meant she couldn't get a look at either driver.

If she braked suddenly, the Suburban would rear-end her. Not an outcome to be hoped for. She needed another plan.

Without warning, the truck swerved toward her, slamming into the side of her smaller truck. Her whole body crashed against the door. She struggled to keep control, but weight was against her. In a battle of sheer tonnage, the larger truck would win. Slowly she was pushed off the road.

If the embankment had been steep, she would have rolled for sure. As it was, she simply drove off onto the dirt. The two other vehicles sped away.

Dana slowed, then came to a stop. She reached for the notebook she kept in her glove box and wrote down both license plates. The plates or the vehicles were probably stolen, but the information would be a start. She got out of her truck and was pleased that her legs weren't shaking at all. Her left arm hurt and she'd banged the hell out of her knee, but otherwise she was fine.

After drawing in a few deep breaths to chase away the adrenaline, she circled her truck to survey the damage. The whole passenger side was smashed in. It wasn't pretty.

Someone had sent her a warning to back off. A very clear warning that would cost a few thousand dollars to fix. Had circumstances been different, she could have been seriously hurt. Someone else might have taken the admonition to heart, but not her. If Jed Titan thought this was enough to scare her away, he didn't know her at all.

CHAPTER NINE

GARTH MET WITH MITCH, Cruz and Nick shortly before five in the afternoon. They'd picked a quiet bar by the freeway. It was the sort of place that didn't get much action before nine or ten, which suited them just fine. They only needed an out-of-the-way place to talk.

The other three men were already there when Garth arrived. He'd left his suit jacket in the car, but was still the only guy wearing a tie. They were all successful, but completely different. Under normal circumstances, they were unlikely allies, but Jed and the Titan sisters had brought them together.

Four beers sat on the table. Garth took the one in front of his chair and swallowed.

"Jed came by to see me," he said.

Mitch's mouth twisted. "Lucky you."

"He's having a bit of a cash flow problem. He put his racing horses up for sale. I bought them."

Nick looked at him. "He found out?"

Garth shrugged. "He wasn't happy about it. He threatened to take my plan to buy him out to the share-holders, not that they would mind."

"You think he will?" Cruz asked.

"Maybe. It won't change anything. I'm more concerned about the other things he said. He didn't come out and threaten the women, but it was implied. I would say he didn't have it in him, but after what happened with Izzy…" He shook his head. "He's dangerous."

The other men exchanged glances.

Country music played in the background. A couple of guys were playing pool at the table in the center of the room. A few other customers were talking or already so drunk they could barely stay seated.

"We'll have to take precautions," Nick said flatly. "Izzy's at the ranch most of the time, so there's some distance between her and Jed."

Cruz drew in a breath. "I worry about Lexi. She's living with me, so she's safe at night, but what about during the day?"

Garth knew Cruz was also concerned about Lexi's advancing pregnancy. "I know a couple of good bodyguards. They're discreet. She wouldn't necessarily have to know they were watching her."

"And when she finds out?" Cruz asked. "Hell, I'll take the fight. It would be worth it. Sure. Give me the names."

"Me, too," Mitch said. "Skye and Erin are vulnerable when they're away from the ranch."

Garth wanted to say even Jed wouldn't hurt his own granddaughter, but he didn't know that for sure. Not anymore.

"What about Dana?" Mitch asked. "You think she's safe?"

Garth didn't have an answer for that. Dana was more capable of taking care of herself than any of the sisters. She was a cop. But she'd also known Jed all her life—she'd stayed in his house, spent holidays with him. Would she be willing to take him on or would she hesitate? Indecision could be fatal.

"I'll talk to her," he said. "If I explain the situation, she'll take precautions. Maybe move in for a while."

All three men stared at him.

"You want Dana living with you?" Nick asked, sounding stunned.

"It would keep her safe."

"Dana? Seriously?" Cruz shrugged. "Whatever floats your boat."

"Hey, back off," Garth said, a warning tone to his voice.

Cruz raised both his hands. "Sorry, man. She's great. Not my type, but great."

Mitch looked at him with a combination of curiosity and pity. "You're going to ask her to move in with you so you can protect her?"

Why did everyone keep saying Dana wasn't his type? What did they know about his type? He shook off the question and turned to Mitch.

"She's smart. She'll agree."

Mitch grinned. "Sorry I'm going to miss the explosion. Dana's not big on being told what to do and she's always had a problem with men trying to run her life." He glanced around the table. "I went to high school with her. She's pretty damned intimidating."

Garth wanted to get more details. How well had Mitch known Dana in high school? Did they have a history?

"I can handle her," Garth said. "Don't worry about it."

Conversation shifted to their next move. Cruz was working with some of his ATF friends. Mitch had been talking to the FBI.

"That's going to take too long," Garth grumbled. "I'm still going after him financially. That's faster. Once he's backed into a corner, he'll do something stupid. Then we'll get him."

"You have to be careful," Mitch warned. "I've known Jed all my life. Back him into a corner and there's no telling how he'll react. He could hurt someone."

"Which is why we want the women protected," Nick said. "I'm with Garth. Taking everything he's worked for is quick and legal. We're in control."

Garth appreciated Nick's support. Not just because he believed in his plan but because it could be a sign that Nick was willing to if not forgive, then at least give Garth another opportunity to make up for what he'd done.

The men discussed various options for a few more minutes, then Cruz and Mitch left. Nick stayed behind.

"What else did Jed say?" Nick asked.

"He threatened me. I've got the conversation recorded."

Nick nodded. "He's dangerous, mostly because he's too arrogant to believe he can be caught or he can lose. That'll make him unpredictable."

"Agreed. We'll plan for what we can and take the rest as it comes."

Nick finished his beer and set the bottle on the table. "Izzy thinks you're coming along just fine. A few more weeks and you'll be domesticated. That true?"

"Izzy's determined."

"Must be a family trait."

"Maybe." Garth still had trouble thinking of the Titan sisters as family. He knew he was related to them, but that was different. There was more distance when one spoke of "relations" than family.

"I'm sorry," Garth told him. "About everything."

Nick's gaze was steady. "I believe you. Izzy is convinced this is all going to work out. Is she right?"

"Maybe. I'm not sure of what it means to have them in my life."

"They're going to help you figure that out."

Garth chuckled. "Whether I want them to or not."

Nick grinned. "You gotta love 'em." He picked up his empty beer bottle. "Want another one?"

"Sure."

DANA ARRIVED AT GARTH'S place at ten Saturday morning. She'd already taken her truck in for an estimate and had winced at the high price of the repairs. Not that she had a choice. Her insurance would cover most of it, but there was still the deductible, not to mention the pain and suffering of her truck. Damn Jed and whoever was working for him.

She parked her rental—a nondescript pale gold sedan—and hoped Garth would offer to take his car. She didn't plan to tell him what had happened. Not yet, anyway. Maybe it had been a one-time thing. Maybe Jed was stupid enough to think she would be too scared to continue investigating him.

As she walked toward his condo building, she fought down some fairly serious guilt. In the spirit of everyone working together, they deserved to know what had happened. But she believed that everyone, including Garth, would overreact. The last thing she wanted was her friends worrying about her. She was a big girl—she could take care of herself.

The elevator rose swiftly to the top floor. She crossed to his door and braced herself for the impact of seeing him. Chemistry, she thought as she knocked. Nothing but great sex and chemistry. Garth was little more than a new ice cream flavor. After a few more tastes, she would get tired of him. At least that was the plan.

"Right on time," he said as he opened the door.

All the bracing in the world didn't stop her stomach from doing a little hula at the sight of him in jeans and a Texas A&M sweatshirt. The worn boots were a nice masculine touch that made her feel all gooey inside.

"I believe in being prompt," she said, pushing past

him, then wishing she hadn't as they touched. She took a deep breath. "So what's the plan?"

"First we talk."

"Because you're turning into a girl?"

"Nice," he said, leading the way into the living room. "Very nice. Jed paid me a visit yesterday. He's miffed because I bought his racehorse farm."

She stood in the center of the room and raised her eyebrows. "I'm thinking 'miffed' doesn't completely describe his mood."

"Probably not. He threatened me—all of us, really. Last night I met with the guys. We're worried about everyone staying safe."

She assumed "the guys" meant Cruz, Mitch and Nick and that "everyone" meant the women.

"Did you come up with a plan?" she asked.

"That's what I want to talk about."

She patted her purse, which was more small backpack than fashion statement. "I'm armed, so you don't have to worry about me."

"I'm not the only one who's worried, Dana. This is serious. I want you to move in with me. Temporarily. Until Jed is under control."

Move in with him? Was he serious? She opened her mouth to yell her displeasure, then saw by the look on his face that he was expecting that.

"What do you think you can do that I can't do myself?" she asked instead. "I'm the trained professional in the room."

"Safety in numbers."

"Or a really convenient booty call."

He actually looked amused. "I don't have to trick you into my bed."

Maybe not, but she would like to pretend he did.

"This is a whole egotistical male thing, isn't it?" she snapped. "You're going to go all macho and protect the poor helpless women. Worry about Lexi and Skye and Izzy, but I'm fine. I can more than take care of myself."

"No one questions that," he said reasonably. "But you should consider there are other people involved. Lexi's pregnant. Do you think it's good for her to worry about you? What about Skye? Isn't she already dealing with enough?"

"Guilt won't work on me," she told him.

"It's not guilt. It's the truth. We all want to know you're okay."

"Even you?" she asked before she could stop herself, then wished desperately she could call back the words. Why did she set herself up? Why? Was it a brain injury she couldn't remember? Being just plain stupid?

"Even me."

"Oh."

She didn't know what to do with the information so she ignored it. A part of her thought maybe it wouldn't be such a bad idea to stay with Garth for a while. At least she would have backup. But agreeing felt a little too much like giving up. She'd fought hard to be strong and independent. But at the first sign of trouble, was she going to go running for a big man to solve the problem?

"No," she said. "I can't move in here."

Garth looked more resigned than surprised. "I won't fight you on it, but I want you to promise me that if anything happens, you'll pack your bags and stay here until Jed is in jail."

Would Jed come after her again or had that one stunt been enough? Only time would tell.

"As of right now, if Jed in any way attacks me, I'll come live here with you. You have my word."

"Good. Want to go visit Kathy with me? I usually stop by and see her on Saturdays."

"Sure."

He moved toward her and put his hands on her waist, then lightly kissed her. "What are the odds of you letting me drive?"

She thought of the rental car parked on the street. "Better than you'd expect."

"Going soft on me?"

Keeping secrets, she thought, but instead said, "Making you feel like you're in charge."

"Meaning I'm not?"

She laughed. "Oh, please."

GARTH PARKED BY THE Starbucks in Titanville. When they'd picked up their order, they walked toward the pet store.

"When did you buy the business for Kathy?" Dana asked.

"About ten years ago. She didn't like staying home all the time and there weren't a lot of places that would hire her. She tried volunteering, but she had trouble there, too. She'd always loved animals, even when I was a kid, so this seemed like a good fit."

She sipped her latte, wondering how many other sons would have taken the trouble. "Were you even in high school when she had her surgery?"

"Barely. One of the social workers at the hospital went out of her way to help. She got the word out about the surgery and our bills. The town held a few fund-raisers. A bank set up an account where people could donate. For a while, no one was sure she would even survive the surgery. Once she was conscious, I figured out pretty fast that most of her had been lost."

Talk about terrifying, she thought. All that responsibility, all at once. How had he done it?

"Did you have help?" she asked. "Other family?"

"No family. A few neighbors came in to do what they could. Jed had already thrown me out once. I wasn't going back to him."

"He wouldn't have bothered," she said, aching for the teenager forced to grow up too fast.

"We were lucky in some ways," he said. "Her recovery was easy—she needed a little physical therapy, but nothing too intense. It was her brain that had been damaged. My first plan was to quit school and get a job.

My school counselor talked me into staying in school. She pointed out I would make a lot more money in the long-term, if I went to college."

How had he known how to survive? Just the basics, like buying groceries, paying bills, cooking? Not to mention caring for a suddenly mentally disabled parent.

"What about social services?" she asked. "They didn't try to take you away from her?"

"No. I don't think anyone was willing to report what had happened. They all felt bad. She got disability payments," he continued. "That covered the bills, but not her care. She couldn't stay by herself. I worked after school for a while, but that meant more time I needed to pay someone to be with her, so I got a night job as a janitor. I worked while she slept."

She swore under her breath. "When did *you* sleep?"

"When I got older. I could only pay for someone to be around so many hours a day. We had great neighbors. They would look in on her. College was harder, because I was gone during the week. I could drive home on weekends to check on her and I did, but those years were tough." He hesitated. "She went into a group home for a while. My last two years of college. She seemed to like it, so that was something."

He didn't sound convinced.

"Garth, you can't blame yourself for that. You'd done more than most people. You took care of her when you were still supposed to be a kid. You were totally alone. You can't beat yourself up for that."

"I don't. I blame Jed."

"He deserves it."

She'd known for a while why Garth wanted to destroy Jed, but listening to his story made the reasons more real and immediate. The money to save Kathy Duncan would have meant nothing to Jed. It was pocket change. He'd once cared about her enough to sleep with her and later set up a trust fund that should have taken care of her for the rest of her life. If tragedy hadn't struck. Now all their lives were different, because of one thoughtless act.

"Where does Kathy live now?"

"Around the corner from the pet store. I bought her a little house with a garden. She has someone stay with her when she's not at work. Her caretakers take shifts. They've been with her seven or eight years. It works."

He'd solved the problems he could, she thought. The logistics. But there was nothing he could do to get his mom back. Not to the way she'd been.

They walked into the pet store. The teenager in front greeted them.

"We have new puppies," she said with a grin. "Kathy's taking care of them."

Garth nodded.

Was it always like this? Did he have a coded conversation every time he came in, finding out from people how his mother was doing? What happened on a bad day?

They headed for the rear of the store. Kathy sat beside a large pen watching three black Lab puppies tumble and play. She looked up and beamed when she saw her company.

"Garth!" She scrambled to her feet, then took the latte he offered. "You came to see me."

He kissed her cheek. "It's Saturday."

She nodded, her eyes wide and happy. "You always come on Saturday." She turned to Dana. "You're friends now. I knew you would be."

Dana blinked and tried to smile.

Kathy was casually dressed in jeans and a bright pink polo shirt. A green smock with Titanville Pet Palace on the front covered her from shoulders to knees. She held her coffee in both hands, still smiling, as if her day couldn't get better.

"The puppies are nice," Garth said. "Have you found homes for them yet?"

"Two," Kathy said. "They'll be by later to pick them up." She looked at Dana. "You'll need a dog, but not for a while. You're still not ready."

Dana shifted in place. "I'm, um, not really a pet person."

"You will be."

There was a scary knowingness in Kathy's happy expression, as if she could see dimensions the rest of the world didn't even know existed. Determined not to be totally freaked out, Dana smiled back and shifted so Garth was between her and Kathy.

Kathy put her coffee on a shelf by the pen and took one of his hands in both of hers.

"You're not so sad today." She released him, then returned her attention to Dana. "I've known Garth a long time."

"I know. He loves you very much."

Kathy's smile widened. "I'm lucky."

"Yes, you are," Garth said quietly, then kissed her cheek. "I'll be by to see you later this week," he promised.

"Okay."

Kathy dropped down by the puppies and spoke softly to them. Dana studied her for a moment, wondering if they were forgotten now, until the next time she saw one of them. Did Kathy remember or dream or long for something different? Or was she happy in her own world?

Garth had gone out of his way to give her a good life, but what had he given himself? What were *his* dreams and longings when it came to Kathy? That she could be herself? The parent he'd lost so many years ago?

"God, I hate this," he muttered as they left. He tossed away his half-finished coffee. "Seeing her like that."

"I was just thinking you've made her a lovely life."

"I have money to spend on her, so I'm one of the lucky ones. I know that. But this isn't her. My mother was a vibrant, funny, smart woman who saw the ridiculousness in life. She loved to argue politics and read a book a day. She talked about wanting to travel. We were supposed to go to Europe for the summer when I graduated high school. Every week we put twenty dollars into a special savings account. By the time I graduated, it would have been enough."

His pain was a living creature breathing down the back of her neck. She didn't know what to say—how to help him feel better. Then she realized there would never be the right words. Telling him no one deserved this wouldn't make a difference at all.

Not knowing what else she could offer, she reached for his hand and laced her fingers between his.

He looked at her, his dark eyes clouded with hurt and anger. "You don't strike me as the hand-holding type."

"I'm not. So I'd appreciate it if you didn't mention this to anyone."

"I won't say a word."

DANA GOT HOME A lot earlier than she'd planned. After visiting Kathy, Garth had announced he needed to go into the office. She suspected he mostly needed some time alone to bury himself in work so he could forget…at least for a little while. He'd promised to call her later so they could go to dinner, but she wasn't holding her breath.

Her relationship with Garth was confusing at best and not easily defined. Distance between them wasn't a bad idea.

Dana parked her rental in her space, then walked

toward her apartment. She'd barely pushed the door open when every sense in her body went on alert. Without thinking, she shoved her hand into her purse and pulled out her handgun. The purse dropped to the floor and she kicked it out of the way. Then she stepped into the room.

Everything was exactly as she'd left it, with one very real exception. Jed Titan sat on her sofa, reading a magazine.

He glanced up at her, then showed her the front of the magazine. *"Time,"* he said. "Impressive. I'm glad you're keeping up with current events." He looked from her face to the gun in her hands. "Are you planning on shooting me?"

"That depends on why you're here."

CHAPTER TEN

JED TOSSED THE MAGAZINE onto the coffee table, then pointed to the club chair opposite. "I'm here to talk, Dana," he told her. "Alone. But if it makes you feel like you're in charge, you can continue to hold the gun."

She walked to the chair and pulled it away from him, so she wouldn't be in reach, then sat down. She kept the gun on her lap. "Thanks, but I don't need your permission."

"Still feisty, I see. Not a big surprise. People rarely change. I remember you when you were a little girl. Big eyes and ragged clothes. I never understood why you and Lexi became friends."

Her clothes hadn't been ragged, but she knew he was simply making a point.

She kept her breathing steady, her body relaxed. She wanted to be on alert, but not hyper-vigilant. No need to wear herself out. Jed could be planning a long conversation.

Even as she watched him, she was aware of her surroundings. While she suspected he was alone, as he'd claimed, she didn't want to be caught unawares.

"There's a lot you don't understand," she told him. "Like how to make a point. What was with the car chase? It was practically a cartoon. I would have expected better."

"Don't worry," he said calmly. "You'll get it."

She gave him a faint smile. "Let me guess—you're here to warn me about something. I'm to do exactly what you say or there will be dire consequences. If only there was some movie music to fill out the moment."

"I'm here to tell you to back off or you'll be sorry."

Not a surprise, she thought. "And here I was hoping for more."

"Look at you, Dana. Always the lost puppy, on the fringe of everything. Lexi was good to you, helping you fit in, making you feel like you belonged. Later Skye and Izzy joined her. But you'll never be one of them. You know that, right? They're sisters. You're just someone they know."

He was good, she thought, doing her best not to react. If he'd talked about her lack of money, she would have been able to laugh him off. But talking about belonging was much smarter.

"I'm a big girl now," she said easily. "I can take care of myself."

"Keep telling yourself that. Maybe it will be true. How's Garth?"

She blinked. "I have no idea."

"But you were with him earlier. I saw you in front of Kathy's pet store. Holding hands." He gave her a knowing smile. "So romantic. It's really funny when you think about it. All your life you've been trying to be equal with my girls and now you're dating my son. I should warn you, it didn't work with them and it won't work with him. You'll never be a Titan, Dana. You're not one of us. You know that. You try to pretend it doesn't matter, but we both know differently. After all, your father hit you for a reason."

It took every ounce of control she had, but she was determined not to react. At the same time she sat there, completely still, a voice screamed in her head. What the hell? Had everyone in town known she was being beaten on a regular basis and no one had thought to ask a couple of questions or turn in her old man? Had everyone looked the other way?

Stupid question and she already knew the answer.

"You're trash, Dana," Jed said, almost kindly. "In my day we would call someone like you poor white trash. My girls know that and so does Garth. I'm not saying he doesn't enjoy fucking you. You're athletic. I'm sure you can keep him happy in bed for a couple of months. But it's not going to last. I'm saying that with a full heart."

He actually put his hand on his chest as he spoke, as if to convince her of his sincerity.

"I'm beyond touched," she said dryly. "And officially bored with this conversation. Was there anything else?" She glanced at her watch. "Because otherwise, I need to get going."

Jed rose. She did, as well, keeping distance between them and a firm hold on her gun.

"You'll back off," he said flatly.

"Or I'll find a horse's head in my bed?"

"Nothing that abstract. I prefer to be more direct. If you don't back off, all of you, I'll start hurting the people you love most."

Her mouth went dry. "You already tried that once."

"Next time I won't leave anything to chance. Next time the consequences will be a lot more serious. Lexi or Izzy or Skye might not get out alive."

"YOU OKAY?" Garth asked.

Dana shook her head. She was sure she would never be okay again. "He was so cold," she said, folding her arms over herself and doing her best not to shake. "So casual, the way he talked about hurting his own daughters. Who does that? He's become a monster. When did that happen?"

After Jed had left, Dana had checked the place to make sure no one else was there, then had driven to Garth's office.

He sat next to her on the sofa by the window and slowly rubbed her back. "Do you want me to get you something to calm you down? Tea? Something stronger?"

She glared at him. "I'm not hysterical. I don't need to be sedated."

"I'm just offering."

"Don't. We need to figure out a plan. We need to stop him."

"We have a plan."

"It's not working," she snapped, then shook her head. "Sorry. I'm a little on edge."

"I hadn't noticed."

She managed a slight smile, then took a deep breath. "Okay. What are we going to do?"

"I'll let Mitch, Cruz and Nick know what happened and what Jed said." He hesitated. "If I tell you something, you have to keep it to yourself."

"What are we, in high school?"

"I'm serious."

He looked serious. Determined and a little intimidating. Not that she would tell him that.

"Fine. I won't say anything."

"The guys have hired bodyguards."

He didn't say any more than that, but Dana could fill in the rest. She sprang to her feet, put her hands on her hips and glared at him.

"Are you serious?" she yelled. "My friends are being watched and they don't know it?"

He stood. "Protected. There's a difference and you know it. It's a precaution. Based on what Jed said, do you think it's such a bad idea?"

She opened her mouth then closed it. "No," she grumbled, sinking back onto the sofa.

She bounced back to her feet, then poked him in the chest with her index finger. "You better not have anyone following me or I swear I'll disembowel you."

"There's a visual."

"I mean it, Garth."

He sighed heavily. "I don't have anyone on you. With your professional training I knew you'd be better prepared. I'd like to have you protected…"

"And I'd like to win a megalottery. We all have unfulfilled dreams. You'll have to get over this one."

"That's what I thought you'd say. But with Jed making overt threats, I want you to be really careful."

The man had sent people to run her off the road and then had shown up in her house. She was going to be the poster child for careful.

If only the license plate numbers had helped, but as she'd suspected, they'd been stolen.

"I'm not the only one who has to watch herself," she said. "Jed could just as easily come after you. That's the most direct road to success."

"Are you worried about me?"

Garth put his hands on her waist and drew her against him. She didn't really want to go, but the second he touched her, she didn't seem to have much will to resist. There was something about the heat of his body or the strength of it. It made her want to melt. And she was not the melting kind.

She managed to push his hands off her waist and take a step back. "Worried is too strong a word. I know Izzy would be upset if something happened to you. She's determined to see you as one of the family."

He pulled her close again and kissed her jaw. "What do you see me as?"

"Trouble," she said, trying not to sound breathless. Which was really hard because tingles followed everywhere his mouth touched. Even as he kissed his way down her neck, she felt heat flaring in her breasts and between her legs.

He paused at the edge of her sweatshirt. For a second she thought about just ripping it off, but stopped herself. They were in Garth's office. While it might be Saturday, she'd seen several people around. Anyone could walk in. She wasn't the type who enjoyed being a show.

She managed to push away again, only this time she really, really didn't want to stop.

He cupped her face in his hands. "I'll be careful," he promised.

"Good."

"If you'll go to Skye's fund-raiser with me."

The tingles died.

"What?"

"Skye is having a fund-raiser next weekend. It's an annual event. I promised I'd go and I want you there with me."

"Why?" The question popped out before she could stop it.

"Because you're my girlfriend."

His what?

She stared at him. Girlfriend? As in relationship?

Her mind went completely blank. She wasn't the relationship type. She was difficult and awkward and the most she knew about getting fancy with makeup was to put on a second coat of mascara.

"I don't go to Skye's fund-raisers. It's not my thing."

He dropped his hands to her shoulders and stared into her eyes. "It's not my thing, either, but I promised."

"So you go."

"I will. With you."

She wanted to complain that she had nothing to wear, but he was a guy and he wouldn't get that. She wanted to tell him that events like that made her feel uncomfortable and out of place. Worse, she remembered what Jed had claimed. That she would never fit in. Never be an equal. Did her reaction to the invitation prove he was right?

Garth squeezed her shoulders, then released her. "It wasn't supposed to be that hard a question. If you don't want to go, it's fine."

Pride battled with fear. Was she really going to let Jed get in her head and mess with her? "No. I'll go."

"You could sound a little more enthused."

She forced a smile. "I'll go. Thanks for asking."

He kissed her. "You'll have fun. It's at Glory's Gate."

"Since when? Skye doesn't live there anymore."

Garth grinned. "He's renting out the house. Skye's paying a premium, but it's a good property for this kind of event."

Glory's Gate. At least Dana knew her way around the place. It would be a lot easier than a fancy hotel.

He leaned close, his mouth barely touching her ear. "Just so we're clear—this is a date. I'll be driving."

He expected her to laugh. The punch line was him driving. The "D" word was incidental. To him. To her it was the first step into a terrifying and unfamiliar world from which she might never find her way back.

"F-fine," she whispered, knowing it was anything but.

"WHAT WAS I THINKING?" Dana demanded of Lexi three days later when they met up at an exclusive boutique Dana had never stepped in before. It was easier to focus on her panic about the coming fund-raiser than worry about what Jed might be planning for his daughters. Or try not to see the mysterious male shopper who was obviously—at least to Dana—Lexi's bodyguard. While she didn't like the idea of keeping secrets from her friends, she knew that protecting them came first. None of the Titan sisters would accept the idea of bodyguards. Better pissed at her than dead, she thought grimly, then pushed her conversation with Jed away. If she kept thinking about it, she was at risk of blurting out something she would immediately regret.

"You were thinking it would be fun to see Garth's world," Lexi said soothingly. "Or your brain was momentarily toasted from something he was doing to the rest of you."

"We were only kissing," Dana said absently, staring at all the clothes around her, wishing there was a rack marked Clothes Dana Wouldn't Rather Die Than Wear with a big sale sign on it.

"Interesting. If just his kissing can do that, I wonder what he can do when he puts his mind to it."

"You have no idea," Dana said.

Lexi patted her arm. "You'll be fine. Okay, the outfit. Skye's saying formal but not white tie, so that helps."

Dana was sure it would if she actually knew the difference between white tie and black tie.

"I'm open to suggestions," she said between gritted teeth.

The boutique was well-lit and screamed expensive. There weren't even tons of clothes on display. Just one of everything. Then a salesperson went off and got your size. Shopping in a place like this was the seventh level of hell for her. The only thing that kept her in place was the fear of embarrassing Garth. It should be embarrassing herself, but she didn't care what people thought of her. But Garth would have business associates at the event. Friends, maybe. He would take her, regardless of what she was wearing. He would never ask her to change clothes, but that didn't mean he would be thrilled if she showed up in jeans and a T-shirt.

"Obviously the point isn't just to raise money for Skye's foundation," Lexi said. "It's also a see-and-be-seen kind of party, as well. Dallas society and all that. Senators, congresspeople."

Dana pressed her hand to her suddenly writhing stomach. "You're not making me feel better."

"I'll do that later," Lexi said kindly. "I want you to understand what we're talking about. This is Garth's world."

"And I don't belong there."

Lexi grabbed her arm. "No. That's *not* even close to what I'm saying. You totally belong there. But if you want to fit in, to be comfortable, you're going to have to learn the rules."

She held up her hand before Dana could interrupt. "There's a big difference between fitting in and selling out. I'm not asking you to be someone else. I'm asking you to dress in such a way that you don't insult your hostess, who I would like to remind you, is a close friend."

Dana pressed her lips together. "Fine," she mumbled. "What should I wear?"

"You'll probably be more comfortable in pants and a jacket," Lexi said, moving deeper into the store.

Dana followed her, careful not to brush against anything. She wasn't sure where exclusive boutiques stood on the "you break it, you bought it" policy, but she and her credit card didn't want to get into trouble.

"What about this?"

Lexi held up a tailored jacket. Or maybe it was a blazer. Dana wasn't sure. While she stared at it, her friend was talking. She could see Lexi's lips moving, but there wasn't any sound except for a massive buzzing in her ears.

Had someone blindfolded her and told her that her life depended on her describing the jacket, she wouldn't have been able to do it. Not when all she could see was the small, hanging price tag.

Fifteen *hundred* dollars. You could buy a used car for that.

"What?" Lexi asked. "Are you feeling all right?"

Dana shook her head and pointed. Lexi glanced at the tag, then shrugged.

"It's Donna Karan. Her clothes are beautiful and I think they'd really suit your body."

"Fifteen hundred dollars? It's a jacket."

"It's a designer label." Lexi sighed. "Dana, this is what quality clothes cost."

"Are they sewn by albino virgins born on February 29th?"

"Maybe you'd be happier with something else."

Something that wouldn't make her credit card scream for mercy.

Lexi circled several racks, then glanced back at Dana. "Would you consider a dress?"

Dana would rather consider quality time in a snake exhibit at the zoo. A dress, as in not pants? "I guess."

Instead of circling the racks, Lexi circled Dana. "When was the last time your legs saw sunlight?"

"1943."

"Very funny. Pale is in. Blinding white doesn't look attractive on anyone. I'll get you in at the spa. We'll give you a nice fake tan that glows."

Dana frowned. "What does it matter what color my legs are? I'll be wearing panty hose."

Lexi stared at her. "No. We don't do that anymore. Colored tights are always a possibility with a wool skirt and boots, but…" She seemed to brace herself. "When was the last time you wore a dress?"

"Prom."

"High school prom?"

"It's the only one I went to."

Lexi linked arms with her and rested her forehead on Dana's shoulder. "I have to apologize. I've totally failed you as a friend."

"Why? I'm fine."

"You're many things but fine isn't one of them. We'll go classic," she said. "A little black dress." She straightened and smiled. "The good news for you is you can get one for a lot less than fifteen hundred dollars."

"Lucky me."

Fifteen minutes later, Dana had to admit Lexi might be on to something with the dress thing. She'd tried on three already and each of them looked pretty good.

The first had been made out of a shiny fabric that was a little stiff. The front came up to her collarbone but the back had a cut-out that dipped down to the belt. Lexi had explained something about a specially designed fancy bra that would hold the girls in place, but Dana wasn't so sure about walking around with her back exposed.

The second was silk. She knew because Lexi had gushed about it. It had a wrap-style top and a full skirt.

"Too retro," Lexi said.

"Too girly," Dana added.

The third, which according to legend should have been just right, wasn't. It was cut low enough for most of her breasts to show.

"I'm not flashing the world," Dana said, staring at herself in the mirror and trying not to wince. Then she reached for the zipper and stepped out of the dress. "There will be old people there. I don't want to put anyone off the appetizers."

"Or give them a heart attack." Lexi looked at the remaining dresses. "Maybe. I don't know. Maybe."

"What?"

"I'm thinking."

Dana had to admit there was one advantage to shopping in the exclusive part of town. The dressing rooms were really nice. Large, with a couple of chairs and big mirrors. Now that she thought about it, the space was about the size of her living room.

"Here." Lexi handed over what looked like a latex tube.

"What is that?"

"Your new best friend. It's an indestructible manmade fiber designed to hold every inch of you in place. Otherwise known as shapeware."

Dana turned the black tube over in her hands. "How do I get into it?"

"Wiggling and a lot of prayer."

The task seemed impossible, but Dana stepped into the tube and started pulling up. Lexi got behind her and tugged, as well. It took a few minutes, but finally the tube was in place.

It wasn't just tight—it pressed in from every direction. She wasn't sure she could fully expand her lungs. Eating would be impossible.

"I can't breathe in this thing."

"You'll get used to it," Lexi said, apparently unconcerned about Dana's asphyxiation.

Dana took a few practice breaths and found that by inhaling slowly, she could get more air in her lungs.

"Try this," Lexi said.

The "this" was a simple black dress that looked like it had been created by bands of fabric sewn together. They alternated dull and shiny. The neckline was square and the straps were the same width as the bands.

"It's too small," Dana said, eyeing the dress and hoping it would look good on her.

"It's meant to be fitted. Which is why you're not breathing. Try it on."

Dana slipped the dress over her head. It felt tight, but not too tight. She eased it into place. Lexi fastened the zipper, then sank into one of the chairs.

"My work here is done," Lexi said happily.

Dana faced the mirror. The dress was amazing. It clung to every curve as if she'd been sewn into it. She looked sexy and feminine and not the least bit like herself.

"Shoes," Lexi said, pointing to the boxes they'd brought in along with the dresses. "Try that box on the left. They're satin, too."

They were also armed with a four-inch heel.

"I don't think so," Dana said, staring at them in total fear. "I'll kill myself."

"You'll look good as you go. Try them on."

Dana slipped on the shoes.

Despite being a bit wobbly, she looked good. Better than good. Her legs were endless, with great curves. It was like being in someone else's body but looking into her own eyes. A surreal moment.

Lexi rubbed her lower back. "We'll get you into the spa the day before the fund-raiser. You can get the fake tan and we'll do something about those eyebrows."

Dana peered into the mirror. "What's wrong with my eyebrows? I have two."

"You practically have four. We'll fix it. Then on the day of the fund-raiser, I'll come by and help you get ready."

Dana turned around and looked at her friend. "This isn't me. I'm not into this stuff."

"You don't know that for sure. You've never tried. I'm not saying you have to become a beauty school graduate, but spending a couple of minutes a day on your appearance doesn't make you a bad person. Or a weak one. You can still be as tough as you want and dress nice."

"Maybe," Dana admitted. It wasn't about being bad,

it was about being vulnerable. Which Lexi wouldn't understand.

"He won't know what hit him," her friend added. "More important, you'll feel fabulous."

She was used to feeling competent and in charge. How important could fabulous be?

She glanced back at the mirror. Maybe it was time to try.

DANA DROVE TOWARD HER apartment, doing her best not to think about the packages in the backseat of her rental. She'd never spent that much money on clothes in a year, let alone one afternoon. The good news was the dress and heels together had cost a lot less than the jacket. The bad news was she had to wear them.

Garth had better be appreciative, she thought, both nervous about his reaction and anticipating how he would react. She doubted he expected her to be all glamorous.

She turned left onto her street. It was quiet, as usual. She signaled a few feet before the entrance to her complex. She'd barely started the turn when there was a loud pop and the rear end of her car started to wobble and bump.

Several things happened at once. She checked her mirrors to make sure no one was right behind her, then she jerked the car to the side of the road, braking at the same time. As she quickly came to a stop, she grabbed for her purse and pulled out her gun, then slid down in the seat. Even as she opened the door, she heard a car speeding away. She jumped out to see if she could catch the license plate, but there wasn't one. Then she leaned heavily against the car.

Her gaze dropped to the left rear tire. There was a hole in it, where the bullet had entered. Had they been trying to scare her or had the shooter missed? Either way, another message had been sent. One she couldn't keep to herself.

She reached back into the car and dug out her cell phone. She dialed the number from memory. When the Titanville sheriff's office picked up, she identified herself then said, "I need to report a shooting."

CHAPTER ELEVEN

DANA SIPPED ON THE COFFEE she'd been given, although she figured she wouldn't need caffeine for a month. She was plenty wired from the shooting. She'd already completed her report about the incident, although she wasn't looking forward to talking about it. No one was going to want to hear that Jed Titan was her prime suspect.

As she sipped, she watched the door. She knew Garth would show up. He'd been very quiet when she'd called and told him what had happened, but she hadn't been fooled. He was pissed that Jed had been so blatant.

But the first familiar face she saw wasn't his. Instead Mary Jo Sheffield, his attorney, hurried in.

"Are you all right?" she asked, putting her leather briefcase on a chair.

"I'm fine. But my car was a rental and I don't think they're going to be happy when they see the tire."

"What about the shooter?"

"I never saw the perp. It was a black town car. There

are a thousand in the city. Limo companies use them for airport runs. No license plate."

"Was he a bad shot or trying to scare you?"

"That's my question. If I had to guess, I would say trying to scare me."

Joe Campbell, a guy she'd worked with for two years, walked over. He didn't look happy.

"You sure about your report?" he asked. "You're saying Jed Titan is behind this?"

Mary Jo bristled. "My client," she began.

"You hired a lawyer?" Joe looked hurt. "Dana, you work here."

"I didn't hire a lawyer," Dana told him. "Mary Jo represents Garth Duncan, who's a friend of mine. She can be a little overzealous." She turned to Mary Jo. "Back off for a second, okay?"

Mary Jo nodded, but didn't physically move away.

Dana turned back to Joe. "I realize that this is Titanville and Jed's not only related to the founder, but a model citizen. But I know he's behind this. Did you check with the Dallas PD?"

"Not yet."

"Call them. They'll confirm there's an investigation."

"I also have the names and numbers of people at the FBI and ATF," Mary Jo said. "There are several ongoing investigations. And Jed has threatened Dana."

Joe looked at her. "He threatened you? Did you report it?"

Dana groaned. "Not officially." She glared at Mary Jo. "I never said he threatened me."

"You didn't have to. I'm a good guesser. Based on my instincts, I'm also going to say this isn't the first time he's come after you."

Garth chose that moment to walk in and join the conversation. He'd come from the office, so had on his suit, but for some reason, he looked a little rumpled. And worried.

He walked directly to Dana and pulled her to him. "You okay?" he asked.

She felt awkward being hugged in public, in front of Joe, where she worked. "Um, fine."

"Good." He released her and greeted the others. "What did I miss?"

"Dana was just going to tell us about her previous encounters with Jed," Mary Jo said calmly.

Garth spun toward her. "There have been others?"

"It was nothing," Dana said, wishing Mary Jo had kept her mouth shut. "I was run off the road a couple of days ago."

"Run off the road?" Garth and Joe said at the same time.

"That explains the rental," Mary Jo murmured.

"You have a rental car?" Garth asked. "Since when?"

"It's no big deal." She dug in her purse and pulled out the paper with the license plates on it. "Here, Joe. You won't find anything, but it's all I have."

"What happened?" Garth demanded. "And why the hell didn't you tell me? We had a deal."

She knew he was referring to the fact that she'd promised to move in with him if Jed came after her. "This happened before that," she said.

"You kept it from me. You lied."

Mary Jo slipped her arm through Joe's. "Let's go get some coffee and leave them to work this out."

When they were gone, Garth narrowed his gaze. "Start talking."

Her temper flared. "You're not my boss. You don't get to say what I do."

"You deliberately withheld material information. Dammit, Dana. Jed is coming after you and I'm the reason. Do you think I want anything to happen to you?"

"No. You're worried about everyone. I get that."

He grabbed her arm, his expression intense. "I'm worried about *you*. I wanted you to move in before this ever happened. I let you put it off because I thought you were safe and you let me believe that."

She glanced down then back at him. "You're right. I'm sorry. I didn't think it was that big a deal."

"He hired someone to run you off the road. Then he paid you a private visit. Now this. How big a deal does it have to get before you pay attention?"

She pulled free of his grip. "I'm sorry. Okay? I should have said something."

"Damn straight."

"I don't want to be anyone's responsibility."

"It's too late. Jed knows we're together. You're just as vulnerable as Lexi or Izzy or Skye. You're part of this."

She knew what he meant, but even though he was trying to scare her, she couldn't help feeling a warm little jolt inside her belly. Being part of something was important to her. She hadn't allowed it to happen many times in her life. Just as intriguing was Garth's statement that they were together. Was that how he saw things?

"Dana?"

"I'm listening," she said quickly. "I'm sorry. I should have said something before. I thought he was trying to scare me. I didn't think he would take it any further."

"And now?"

"I'm not so sure."

He seemed to brace himself. "I want you to move in with me. We talked about it before. I know it's not what you want, but things are getting dangerous."

"I know," she said.

"He'll keep coming after you. I swear, Dana, I'll… What?"

"I know," she repeated. "I'll move in with you."

"Just like that?"

"There's nothing like getting shot at to change someone's perspective. He wants to distract us from what's important. I'm not saying living with you will be much protection, but I'll do it. On one condition."

He drew in a slow breath. "Typical," he muttered.

"I don't want Lexi, Skye or Izzy to know about the shooting or him running me off the road. It'll scare them. They're already being protected, so that's not going to change. But if they know, they'll be upset and they'll feel guilty. That won't help."

Garth considered her words. "Fine," he said, after a second. "But I'm telling the guys."

She didn't like that. She didn't want to keep information from her friends, but she hated the thought of them taking the blame. None of this was about them. Jed was the one who'd gone over to the dark side.

She was most worried about Lexi and her baby. If anything happened to either of them, she would never be able to forgive herself. But to let the *guys* know?

"I hate that," she told him. "Just for the record. And when they do find out and they're pissed, I'm so going to blame you."

"Ask me if I care. Do we have a deal?"

She nodded.

"Do you mean it this time?" he asked.

"Ouch. I meant the last one."

"You withheld information."

"That doesn't mean I didn't mean it." She sighed. "I'm moving in with you. Isn't that enough?"

"For now."

DANA FOUND THAT PACKING up everything she owned and leaving her apartment, even temporarily, was harder than she'd expected. She wasn't comfortable with the idea of living with Garth. Despite his statements, she still considered their relationship undefined. What exactly would he expect from her? What were the house rules? While asking would be the most mature way to handle the situation, she wasn't feeling especially grown-up at the moment.

She loaded everything in her nearly restored truck, doing it herself. A concession that Garth had fought. He'd wanted to come with her, as if expecting Jed to be lurking outside her apartment. Or inside—which he'd already done once.

She double-checked her drawers and the closet, trying to make sure she didn't leave anything important behind. Not that she would be very far away. If she needed something, she could stop by and get it.

Still, even with just her clothes and personal things missing, her apartment seemed sad and abandoned. This had been her home for nearly four years. She liked the small, quiet space. She'd bought the prints above the sofa at a garage sale and the coasters, pictures of hunky naked guys under glass, had been a gift from Izzy. There were memories here.

"Get over it," she said aloud. She was moving in with Garth for a few weeks at most. She would be back. Life as she knew it hadn't ended.

But she was feeling uncomfortably emotional as she got into her truck and drove toward his high-rise condo.

When she pulled in front of the building, Garth was waiting.

"I got you a parking spot," he said. "Number one-eighty-two." He handed her a card that would let her into the underground garage. "Use this to get in. I'll meet you by the elevator and help you carry up your suitcases."

She stared at the small, white plastic card. "They have spare parking?"

"I get two spaces with my condo. This is the second one. It's next to my car."

She wasn't sure if she believed him. Did he really have an extra spot or had he rented or bought one for her? Not that she would ask. She didn't trust him to tell the truth. Besides, what difference did it make? He could afford it.

Except telling herself that didn't make her feel any better. She didn't want him buying her things or taking care of her. That implied an obligation she didn't want to have. It made her nervous.

"This is why I keep relationships simple," she muttered as she drove into the parking garage and found the spot in question.

A few minutes later, both Garth and George, the doorman, had joined her at the truck. With all three of them carrying things, they had her truck unloaded in one trip. Once everything was in his condo and George had left, Garth handed her a key on a ring.

"You know the main layout," he said, pointing to the

kitchen. "Help yourself to whatever you want. I don't keep a lot of food around, but if you need girl food, that's fine."

She raised her eyebrows. "Girl food?"

He grinned. "Yogurt. Stuff with soy."

"Because you see me as the soy type?"

"All women keep secrets."

"Maybe, but none of mine involve soy."

She followed him down the hallway. She'd been in his bedroom before and expected him to head in there, but instead he kept walking and pushed open the door at the end.

The room was much smaller than the master, but had a big window and a killer view. There was a queen-size bed, a dresser, a desk and a flat-screen TV on the wall.

He turned to face her. "I thought you'd be more comfortable here. I didn't want to assume…"

It was the first time she'd seen him unsure of himself. He didn't look directly at her as he spoke and after gesturing to the bed, he shoved his hands into his slacks pockets.

A guest room. Who would have thought?

She thought of the big bed in the room down the hall, of sleeping next to him every night, of having him touch her and take her until she was weak with wanting to give all she had. And if she did that, what would be left of her?

"This would be great," she said.

Something flashed through his eyes. Something that

if she'd been brave like Izzy or beautiful like Lexi or emotionally strong like Skye she might have thought was disappointment, but being just her, she ignored it.

He jerked his head to the right. "Bathroom through that door. The closet is big, but if you need more room, I have it in mine." He pulled one hand out of his pocket and looked at his watch. "I have a meeting. Are you going to be okay by yourself?"

"I'm hardly by myself. Our command center, as your sisters call it, is rarely quiet. One of them is forever dropping in. Then there's delivery people, our resident computer geek and the sandwich delivery guy."

"I'll be back around seven. Want me to bring Chinese?"

She nodded.

"If you need anything," he began.

"I'll call," she told him. "I'm good. I'll get settled and be here when you get home."

"Right."

They looked at each other.

Part of her wanted him to kiss her. The girly side she didn't let out much thought a hug would be good. Some kind of physical contact. But she didn't ask and he didn't offer and then he was gone.

Dana heard the front door close, then went to make sure it was locked. She walked through the large living room, crossed to the floor-to-ceiling windows and stared out at the skyline of Dallas.

This wasn't her world. In her tiny apartment, she looked out onto a poorly maintained courtyard. She couldn't see clear to the horizon. An issue she would deal with later. First she had to unpack. But instead of returning to the guest room, she walked into Garth's room.

The bed was made, the dresser tidy. One drawer was partially open. She went to close it, only to realize it was empty. As was the drawer below it and the one below that. She crossed to the bathroom and the big closet beyond.

Garth's clothes still hung in place, but they'd been shifted closer together. While the last time she'd been here, she'd noticed he wasn't using all that much space, the new configuration left more than half the closet empty. As if he had planned to share it.

Is that what he'd been expecting? That she would join him in here? Is that what he'd been hoping? Or were the questions just wishful thinking on her part?

GARTH LEFT THE FINANCE meeting feeling better than when he'd entered. Not only were profits up eighteen percent in the past quarter, the entire company had exceeded benchmarks for the year to date. The news was nearly enough to burn away his disappointment.

He knew he was being a total guy. He'd told Dana he wanted her to move in so she was safe from Jed. At least when she wasn't out on her own. It was the only reason—he'd even discussed it with her best friends.

Or so he'd thought right until she'd taken the offered guest room over sharing a bed with him and he'd been…

What? Hurt? Was he turning into a woman? He wasn't hurt. Of course it was more practical for her to have her own space. Hell, they barely knew each other. They'd slept together exactly one time. Neither of them trusted easily. It wasn't as if she was living with him because they had a relationship.

But he'd wanted her with him and he hadn't known he did until she'd refused.

He pulled out his PDA and checked his schedule. His five o'clock said nothing more than "ST." Who or what was ST? There was only one way to find out.

He took the stairs to the executive floor and rounded the corner, only to see Skye waiting outside his office.

"You're my five o'clock?"

"I made an appointment and everything. You should be so proud."

"That depends on why you're here," he said cautiously. Izzy, he understood. She was straightforward and open. But Lexi and Skye were still a mystery to him.

He motioned for her to enter his office and followed her inside.

"By the way," she said as she took a seat in front of his desk and set her briefcase on the second chair. "Don't worry about dinner. Dana's going out with Izzy."

"You know she moved in."

Skye's green eyes crinkled as she smiled. "Yes, and

I'm not going to ask you how you did it. I'm just happy to know she's protected. My father can be a dangerous man."

More than Skye knew, he thought, remembering his promise not to tell any of the Titan sisters what had happened.

He hovered by his desk. "You wouldn't be more comfortable on the sofa?"

"No. This is a business meeting. Go ahead and sit behind your desk. It will make you feel like you're in charge."

"What makes you think I'm not?"

She gave him an enigmatic smile. "Oh, please."

Wishing he knew why she was here, he did as she requested.

She opened her briefcase and pulled out a folder. "We did a detailed analysis. I have more paperwork to explain the numbers, if you need it."

She passed him the folder. He opened it to find a bill for three million dollars from her foundation. Behind that was another sheet listing various expenses.

"Your pranks, for lack of a better word, cost me money," she said calmly. "Legal fees to fight the rumors, lost donations. I had staff members resign and they had to be replaced. According to my chief financial officer, this should cover all of that, plus give us a little bonus, by way of an apology."

"Because I'm feeling remorse?" he asked, admiring her willingness to simply ask for what she wanted.

"Of course. We're family now."

"So says Izzy." He glanced at the paperwork. "Three million dollars seems high."

"Do you know the number of children right here in this country who go to bed hungry every night? My foundation works every day to feed them. You took money away from that, Garth. Do you really want to complain about an amount you can easily afford and write off as a tax donation?"

She looked determined. Her green eyes snapped with temper. He would bet Mitch did his best to make sure he never pissed her off.

"Three million seems fair," he said quickly. "Will a personal check be acceptable?"

She relaxed in her seat and smiled. "As long as it doesn't bounce."

He reached into his desk drawer and pulled out his checkbook. "Having sisters is a bigger pain in the ass than I thought it would be."

"Part of our charm."

He glanced up and their eyes met. For a second, he felt a connection with her. A sense of shared respect and a certain humor. Then he blinked and it was gone.

He wrote out the check and handed it to her. She reached across the desk and took it.

"Is Lexi going to come after me for money, too?" he asked. "Or Izzy?"

"Only if they think about it."

"Great. Something to look forward to."

She tilted her head. "I'm sorry for what happened all those years ago. With Kathy."

He shrugged. "It had nothing to do with you."

She leaned toward him. "I wish you'd come to us. We could have helped."

"Skye, I was fourteen. You were maybe seven or eight. What would you have done?"

"Oh. Right. I keep thinking it's current because all this is happening now, but your mom got sick a long time ago. I wish…" She drew in a breath. "There's nothing that can be done for her?"

"Nothing. She's been to a dozen experts. The damage is irreversible. It's not like a broken bone."

Her mouth twisted. "I'm sorry my father is such a bastard."

"He's my father, too."

"If only he'd acted like it."

Garth didn't want to think about that. He knew the pain of wishing things could be different. There was no win in that and only a whole road of hurt.

"He'll get his," he said.

Skye didn't look reassured. "Vengeance isn't known for its healing properties. Would Kathy have wanted that?"

"She would have wanted a chance to get better. Jed took that from her. Now he's going to pay for it."

"THIS IS A BAD IDEA," Dana said as she sat in the middle of the dining room while Lexi pulled on her hair. "Do you want to know if that hurts?" she asked as her former friend wielded a very large curling iron.

"No," Lexi said cheerfully. "But yell if your scalp starts to burn. We're talking painful burn here, not mild discomfort."

Izzy strolled back in from her tour of the place. "Very nice," she said. "Love the view. You really do have your own bedroom."

"How do you know that?"

"I opened a few drawers." Dana's expression might have made her nervous because she immediately held up both hands. "I didn't touch anything. Don't wig out on me."

"Wigging out isn't what I had in mind."

Although a good hour of kickboxing sounded really good right about now. Who knew that getting ready for a stupid party could be so time-consuming?

Lexi had shown up nearly two hours ago to work her magic on Dana. Because spending the morning at Lexi's spa hadn't been enough. There Dana had been massaged and endured a pedicure. A cheerful yet vicious woman had practically ripped off seven layers of skin to get, as she had put it, "The perfect eyebrow arch." Individual fake eyelashes had been glued on before Dana had endured the humiliation of standing naked except for a thong in a tanning booth while a complete stranger had sprayed her with fake tan. She'd smelled funny all day.

Now she had on enough makeup to be an extra in

Madam Butterfly and Lexi was determined to curl every hair on her head.

"You should think about growing your hair out a little," Lexi said, moving to another part of her head. "I'm not talking superlong, but maybe to your shoulders. You have a bit of a natural wave."

"Lucky me," Dana muttered.

"Trust me," Izzy said, puffing her own wildly curly hair. "Guys so go for the big hair. It's sexy."

As was Izzy. She wore a halter top and loose black pants, which sounded normal enough. Until Izzy moved. Then the slits that went from the band on her ankles all the way up to mid-thigh were visible. It was the kind of outfit that made a little black dress seem almost plain by comparison.

"Done!" Lexi announced, then sank into a chair. "Just in time, too. My back is killing me."

Dana turned to her. "You should have said something. We didn't have to do this."

Lexi looked at Izzy, who grinned. "Oh, honey, we so had to do this. Go put on your dress."

Dana touched Lexi's arm. "Are you all right?"

"I'm fine. Cruz will be here in twenty minutes to pick me up. Due to my advancing pregnancy, I get to spend the evening at home watching reality TV." She gave Dana a little push. "Go get ready. You still have to squeeze into your shapeware."

"Right. The tube of death."

Dana scrambled to her feet then hurried back to the

bedroom she used. She stripped off her jeans and shirt, then spent five minutes wiggling into something obviously designed by a misogynist. The dress was next. Thanks to the shapeware, it fit her perfectly. She pulled up the zipper, then reached for the diamond dangle earrings Lexi had loaned her. The hideously high shoes were last.

Izzy burst into the room. "He's back. Don't you hate a guy who's prompt. You'd better—"

She skidded to a stop and stared. "Wow! You look fabulous, and I don't say that lightly."

Dana smoothed the front of the dress. "Is it okay? It's not nearly as sexy as what you're wearing. And you have on pants. Maybe this is…"

Izzy grabbed her hand and pulled her into the bathroom. There was a full-length mirror by the tub.

Dana stared at herself, not recognizing the woman staring back. Her dark, short hair had perfect waves with lots of layers that looked amazing. The makeup made her eyes huge, and the long lashes didn't hurt, either. The dress hugged curves she hadn't realized she had. And the tan made her legs look slim and long. She had to admit that while she hated the heels, they looked great with the dress. She was elegant and sophisticated and longed to look this good every day.

"Oh," she whispered. "Okay."

"Yeah," Izzy said, hugging her. "Okay for sure. Let's go dazzle Garth."

"You think he'll like it?"

"He won't be able to talk."

Dana wasn't so sure. She followed Izzy down the hall, into the living room where Garth stood talking to Lexi. He looked like a male model in a perfectly fitted tux and white shirt. Her heart gave a funny little lurch, which she ignored.

"Are you ready?" he asked as he turned toward her.

And then the most amazing thing happened. He stopped talking. His mouth hung open but he didn't say a word. He closed his mouth, then opened it again. But there still wasn't any sound.

Next to him, Lexi sighed. "I love it when a plan comes together."

CHAPTER TWELVE

"The limo was a nice touch," Dana said as they climbed the stairs to Glory's Gate. She'd been in the house a thousand times before. As a kid, she'd spent the night nearly every weekend. There was nothing to be nervous about. So why were her insides quivering?

"You hated the limo," Garth said, putting his hand on the small of her back, as if to guide her.

"I wasn't sure of the purpose. You have a very nice car."

"It was for show. This is all about how things look, not how they are."

"There's a philosophy to embrace."

They reached the top of the stairs and moved toward the open front door.

Dana could see into the main floor of the huge house. Three or four hundred people milled around inside. Light glittered from a dozen crystal chandeliers. Servers in black pants and white shirts circulated with trays of expensive food while the sound of champagne corks competed with the chamber orchestra.

Nothing about this was her, she thought, knowing it was too late to turn back now.

"You okay?" he asked.

She reached for Garth's hand and squeezed it. "I'm fine."

"You're lying."

"Go with it."

They walked into the party. Dana knew she was probably cutting off the circulation in Garth's hand, but she couldn't loosen her grip. Not when there were so many well-dressed strangers everywhere she looked. Senators, oil tycoons, movie stars. Not a crowd designed to make her feel at home.

"Garth, good to see you," an older man said. "You remember my wife?"

His wife was a blue-eyed blonde with a face that didn't move. Dana wasn't sure if she was twenty-five or fifty.

"Of course," Garth said easily. "Amanda, you look lovely. Jason doesn't begin to deserve you."

"So I tell him every day."

Garth chuckled. "This is my friend, Dana. Dana, Jason and Amanda Barkley. Jason is the ambassador to Costa Rica."

Dana smiled and shook hands with the couple. They chatted for a few more minutes, then moved on.

"Want to head to the bar?" Garth asked.

"Do I look like I need a drink?"

"No, but I do. Liquor makes the party easier to tolerate."

"Then I'm glad we came in a limo," she whispered, as he nodded at more people he knew.

When they'd reached the bar, Dana accepted a pale green "drink of the night" with no idea what it was. Garth asked for Scotch.

They moved through the crowd. The downstairs of Glory's Gate had been designed for entertaining. Seemingly solid walls could be moved out of the way, creating an open space that could accommodate nearly a thousand people. There would be less tonight because there was a sit-down dinner. Dana had seen Skye plan for a big event before, but she'd never appreciated the sheer size of the major fund-raisers. Everything she'd ever been dragged to before had been tiny by comparison.

"How does this work?" she asked. "Do people pay to come?"

He nodded. "It's five thousand a plate."

She nearly choked. "Five thousand *dollars?* You paid ten thousand dollars for us to be here?"

"That's nothing. Ask me about the three million she made me pay the other day."

Dana had no idea what he was talking about but she couldn't wrap her mind around the idea of that much money.

"Later there's an auction. She should walk away with a couple of million easily."

It boggled the mind, Dana thought, taking a sip of her drink.

Nick came up and joined them. "Izzy found someone who's actually been cave diving. She's badgering
the poor guy for details. I couldn't listen."

Dana didn't want to think about underwater cave
diving, either. "Do you think she'll really try it?"

Nick shook his head. "We're talking about Izzy. You
want to take bets?"

"No." Izzy had always been wild, although falling
for Nick had calmed her down a lot. She was going
back to college in a couple of months. "Maybe she'll
be too busy with homework."

"We can only hope."

The orchestra started another song.

Nick took her drink and put it on a small table by a
pillar. "Come on, Dana. Distract me with a dance."

The line was smooth enough and Garth gave her an
encouraging push toward his friend, but everything about
the moment felt strange. Rehearsed, almost. She turned
to say something to Garth, only to find him walking
away.

"So this was a plan," she said, following Nick a
few steps, then coming to a stop. "Want to tell me
what's going on?"

"No."

"What is he up to?"

Nick sighed. "It's not what you think."

"I don't know what to think."

"It's not another woman."

"I never thought it was." Which was true. So why

would Garth want to go off on his own? A business deal?

She dismissed that. Not here. Not at Skye's party.

"Is it Jed? Is he here?" she asked.

"Apparently he bought a ticket."

She didn't like the sound of that. "Garth shouldn't be alone with him. Something could happen."

"Don't worry. Garth can take care of himself."

"That's what I'm worried about. Jed will do anything to win, including trap Garth." She turned to walk away.

Nick grabbed her arm. "Dana, leave him be."

She shrugged free. "Are you really going to stop me?"

Nick stared into her eyes. "No. But tell him I tried, okay?"

"Sure."

She went in the same direction as Garth, hoping she could find him before something bad happened. Unfortunately the tiny evening bag Lexi had loaned her hadn't been big enough to conceal any of her handguns, so she wasn't armed. Fashion was a big pain in the ass.

She reached the edge of the main room and hesitated. Glory's Gate was a really big house. There were a dozen places the men could be. But only one Jed would consider his own, Dana thought, and opened a door leading to a long hallway.

She walked the familiar route to Jed's study. The door was partially closed. Dana debated simply pushing her way inside, but then what? Better to find out what was going on.

She shifted so she could see into the room, but there wasn't anything in her view. Slowly, carefully, she pushed the door open a little more, then nearly gave herself away by gasping. Garth stood behind Jed, his arm around the older man's throat. He held a lethal-looking knife at Jed's chin.

"She bleeds, you bleed," Garth said, his voice low and threatening.

"All this for a woman," Jed said, obviously trying to sound relaxed, but the fear in his eyes and the lack of color in his face gave him away. "I didn't think you'd have that much trouble getting laid."

Garth tightened his grip. "Is there any part of you that doubts me, old man? You *will* leave her alone."

Dana hesitated. While she wanted to bargain and stop the man games, she was more curious about Garth's plan. Still, she didn't want him putting Jed in the hospital and himself in jail. Just when she was about to step inside, Jed nodded once.

"I'll leave her alone."

Garth released him.

Dana stepped back, then turned and walked toward the party. Her mind jumped from image to image. She could still hear the anger in Garth's voice.

No one had ever tried to protect her before, she thought, confused by what he'd done. No one had ever flirted with an assault charge to make a point on her behalf. She knew Garth was more than capable of making good on his threat. He had the physical scars on his body as proof of his strength. Strength he could use against anyone at any time. But to risk it all to protect her?

She slipped back into the party, then headed away from where she'd left Nick. She walked around the perimeter of the crowd, not ready to talk to anyone. She felt uncomfortable, but couldn't say why.

A few minutes later, she walked by one of the many bars and ordered the drink of the night. She'd barely taken a sip when the hairs on the back of her neck stood up.

"No one is fooled," Jed said, standing right behind her. "No one thinks you belong here."

She turned to face him. He was still a little white around his mouth, although she doubted anyone else would notice. Were words all he had left?

"Do you hear that ticking?" she asked coolly. "There's a big clock counting down to your destruction. Your own family wants you in jail. That says something. What I can't figure out is why you did it. All those years ago when Garth showed up, you could have easily paid for the surgery. That's all he wanted. Then none of this would have happened."

Jed's lip curled. "You're going to lecture me?"

"No. I'm just curious. You should never have gone after Izzy. Lexi and Skye could have forgiven nearly anything else."

"Collateral damage. The price of war. I didn't plan on her getting hurt."

"You arranged for a bomb to blow up an oil rig. What did you think would happen?"

He shrugged. "That she'd be scared. The purpose of the explosion had nothing to do with Izzy. The Duncans needed to learn a lesson."

Oh, God. Because he'd been setting up Garth, she thought. Then she replayed his words in her head. "The Duncans? Not just Garth? Kathy has a part in this?"

How could he have anything against Kathy? "Is this about the past?" she asked. "About what happened between you and Kathy all those years ago?" She tried to read his expression and couldn't.

"This is about making sure Garth doesn't win."

"He's already got you beat."

"Don't be so sure, Dana. Garth has a lot to lose."

WHEN GARTH FINISHED with Jed, he had trouble locating Dana. She wasn't with Nick, or with Skye. Eventually he found her with Lexi who was seated on a chair by the wall while Cruz hovered nearby.

"I thought you weren't coming," he said to Lexi as he approached.

She smiled. "I wanted to see Dana dazzle. We're only here for a few minutes." She put her hand on her belly. "Someone else wants to party."

He frowned, not sure what she meant. She grabbed his wrist and pulled him closer.

"The baby's kicking. You can feel it."

There were a whole lot of things he would rather be

doing than touching her stomach, but he couldn't figure out a polite way to refuse. Then his palm was against the surprisingly hard curve of her belly and he felt a jab right under his thumb.

He looked at Dana. "Have you felt this?"

She nodded, then looked away.

He grinned at Lexi. "It's really a baby."

"The alternative was that I was developing an unnatural affection for fast food."

An older couple joined them and started talking to Lexi and Cruz. Garth stepped back, then put his arm around Dana's waist and led her away.

He'd thought she might resist, but she went with him. When they were relatively secluded beside a large leafy tree in a massive pot, he released her.

"What's wrong?" he asked.

"Nothing."

The right word, but she wouldn't look at him. He stared at her.

"You followed me."

She drew in a breath and finally looked him in the eye. "He could press charges."

"He won't and that's not the problem."

"No, it's not."

He couldn't figure out what bothered her. "You were shot at. I couldn't let that go."

"If the person with the gun had wanted me dead, I'd be dead now. It was a warning."

"Just being a warning doesn't make it okay."

"But it's perfectly fine to hold a knife to someone's throat?"

"Is that what's bothering you?"

"It doesn't make me happy."

"Jed isn't someone who responds to quiet conversation. Dana, he can't be allowed to think there aren't consequences. Jed has never had to answer to anyone before. Now he has to answer to me."

"Vigilante justice is still illegal."

"I'm not interested in breaking the law."

"No. You just want to win at any cost. You're more like him than you think." She drew in a breath. "Has he had any contact with Kathy since the surgery?"

"No, why?"

"He said something."

"You spoke to him?"

"Mostly he wanted to tell me I didn't belong here, with you. Which isn't important. He implied there was something he owed the Duncans. Not just you."

Garth swore. "As far as I know, he hasn't spoken to her since I was born. Certainly not since the surgery. Her caretakers would have told me."

"You have someone watching her?"

"Yes."

"Good." She looked around. "I can't be here right now. I'll see you back at the condo."

She was leaving? Just like that?

He wanted to tell her she couldn't. Or that he would take her home. But something about the set of her body, the way she held her purse so tight that her knuckles were white, made him stay silent.

"I won't be late," he said quietly.

She nodded and then left.

Garth watched her go, wondering how everything had gotten so screwed up and how, if he didn't understand the problem, he couldn't possibly fix it. First Jed threatened Dana, now his mother. In addition to adding security, he would talk to Kathy's caretakers. Explain a little of what was going on. He could have a guard move into her house until this was wrapped up.

DANA SAT CURLED UP on the sofa in Garth's condo. The lights of Dallas seemed to twinkle in the light rain, but she wasn't enjoying the view. Her stomach hurt and she had a strong sense of dread. Telling herself that she was safe, that nothing bad was going to happen, didn't make her feel any better.

Cruz and Lexi had driven her home, and because they were good friends, they hadn't asked what was wrong. She'd changed into sweats and a T-shirt, washed off the makeup and slipped on thick socks. Now all she had to do was wait.

Garth was going to want an explanation. The real question was did she tell him what was wrong, or did she come up with some half truth to put him off? Could she even talk about what she was feeling?

If he'd been one of the guys she usually dated, none of this would have been an issue. No one she knew would be willing to take on Jed Titan that way. In all her other relationships, she was the one in charge. Now she wasn't so sure.

She heard a key in the lock and straightened, braced for Garth's temper.

He walked into the condo and tossed his keys on the small table in the entryway. He closed the door, then locked it, shrugged out of his jacket and pulled off his already undone tie. Then he crossed to the living room and sat on the coffee table in front of her.

"I'd never hit you."

She did her best not to wince. Talk about getting it right in a single guess.

She drew in a breath. "When I was fourteen, Jed wanted to put Lexi into these after-school classes. They pretended they were something different, but it was basically a charm school for rich kids. She didn't want to go, but Jed insisted. Finally she agreed, but only if I went with her." Dana shook her head. "It wasn't much of a win for me."

Garth watched her without speaking.

"Some of the guys there were from our school, but a lot were from a prep school I'd never heard of. They wore blazers with patches on the chest pocket and gray flannel slacks. They were our age, but they seemed older and a lot more sophisticated."

She drew her legs to her chest and wrapped her arms around her knees. "There was this one guy. He was really good-looking and funny and I liked him a lot. I guess he was my first crush. He would always dance with me. One day we snuck out of class and were hanging out behind the building. He kissed me, which was fine, but then he tried to take things further."

"What did you do?"

"Kicked him in the balls. It was just a reaction. Apparently I nailed him really good because they ended up taking him to the hospital. I got thrown out, Lexi refused to go back without me and Jed…"

She looked out the window, but instead of the view, she saw the familiar book-lined study and a younger Jed looking both stern and amused.

"Jed told me that it was a man's world and the sooner I figured that out, the easier things would be for me. I knew he was probably right, but I didn't want easy. I wanted safe."

"Because of your dad."

She nodded, still not looking at him. "I never knew when," she whispered. "I'd be sitting at the kitchen table, doing my homework and he would walk by. Sometimes nothing happened. Sometimes he jerked me to my feet and started hitting me. He hit hard. There's a sound a fist makes. I'll never forget it."

"I'd never hit you," he repeated.

She did finally look at him, at the familiar dark eyes, the full sensual mouth that knew secrets about her body even she hadn't discovered.

"I know, but sometimes knowing isn't enough."

"You're not that scared little girl anymore."

"I haven't been for a long time," she agreed. "But that doesn't mean she can't influence me. We can talk and talk, and you'll never get it. You don't understand the fear. I control it through training and my job. I'm in better shape than you, but if it was a fight to the death, you have sheer size and strength on your side."

He stood up suddenly. The coffee table went skidding back a few feet. "I'm not that guy," he yelled. "There's no fight to the death. Are you going to spend the rest of your life hiding because the alternative is to take a risk?"

"I'm dealing with the aftermath of having my father beat the crap out of me for years. It will probably always be something I wrestle with. What you did tonight, with Jed… I get it. I know why you did it. I understand the motivation, the fury you feel. I totally get the desire to protect those around you." She'd almost said "protect what's yours," but that was yet another place she wasn't willing to go.

"You did what you thought was right," she continued, standing. "But there are consequences to every action."

"Meaning now you don't trust me?"

"Meaning I never saw you as physically dangerous before," she admitted. "I have to figure out what I'm going to do with that information."

He walked to the end of the kitchen, then turned back. "Dammit, Dana. Don't do this. Don't go there. I'm not a violent man. I've seen violence. I've lived it."

He ripped open the front of his dress shirt, exposing the scars. "I still have nightmares. Not that often, but they come. And I wake up soaked in sweat, trying not to give in to the terror." He hesitated. "I know what it's like to live with fear and how hard it is to let it go."

He crossed to her and cupped her face in his hands. "I'd never do that to you. I'd never do it to anyone."

She saw the pain in his eyes and behind it, a truth. That ugliness changed a man forever. It couldn't be helped. But *how* the change happened was determined by the man's character. Garth hadn't given in to the darkness that could have claimed him. If anyone had reason, it was him. Even his revenge against Jed had been civilized and thought out. He didn't need to hurt someone physically to feel like a man.

"There's a part of me that wants to fly to Florida and have it out with your old man," he admitted, still staring into her eyes. "I want him to feel what it was like."

"Would you do that for me?"

He didn't hesitate. "No. He's old and it serves no purpose. It wouldn't change the past. If he were still a threat to you, I'd take him on in a heartbeat, but he's not. Empty violence teaches nothing."

"You used violence on Jed."

"I used fear. There's a difference." He dropped his hands to her shoulders. "How much have I screwed up things?"

She touched his chest, traced a scar. "Not as much as you'd think."

"Yeah?"

She looked up at him and smiled, then raised herself up on tiptoe and kissed him.

She'd been avoiding physical contact with Garth as much as possible, telling herself that she'd imagined the passion between them.

But now she was unable to resist the feel of his mouth on hers. She needed to be close to him, to touch all of him and be touched by him. Their connection had been broken and she wanted it restored.

He didn't disappoint. The second her lips met his, he kissed her with a hunger that burned. His arms tightened, then they were straining together, as if trying to climb inside each other.

She parted for him, then groaned as he plunged his tongue inside of her mouth. She met him stroke for stroke, wanting to excite him as much as he excited her. Wanting turned liquid and flooded her. Even as they kissed, she tugged at his shirt. His hands swept under her T-shirt and found her breasts.

His fingers were warm and knowing. He cupped her curves, then brushed across her already tight nipples. Even through the fabric of her bra, the gentle touches aroused her.

She touched his back, then rubbed her hands up and down his chest. It wasn't enough. They had to touch more.

"Wait," she gasped, pulling back.

She jerked her T-shirt over her head, then unfastened her bra. Before she'd even tossed it away, he'd already bent his head and took one of her nipples in his mouth. He sucked deeply, using his tongue to caress sensitive flesh. She clung to him, feeling the tugs all the way between her legs. Her blood pulsed, causing her to swell.

Without thinking, she pushed down her sweats. Her panties went with them. Even as he shifted to her other breast, he slipped a hand between her thighs and found her wet, swollen center. Two fingers pressed against that one spot, then began to circle it.

He straightened enough to kiss her mouth. Their tongues tangled, she held on to his shoulders, all the while his fingers created magic. She couldn't think, couldn't do anything but feel the pressure. He moved steadily, rubbing over and around. Her body tensed. She wanted to part her legs but her stupid sweatpants were in the way. If she could just open a little more and he kept doing that, she would come in a heartbeat.

She tried to kick them away. He broke the kiss then pushed her back a couple of steps.

"Table," he said, his voice thick with passion.

She stepped out of her sweatpants and panties. He grabbed his shirt and put it on the wood table, then helped her jump up onto the cool surface. She parted her legs and went to grab his hand to show him exactly where she wanted him, but he was busy unfastening his belt and shoving down the zipper.

He pushed into her, filling every inch of her. She

stared into his eyes, seeing the fire there, knowing it was matched by the need on her own face. He pulled out and thrust in again, but this time he used his fingers to rub her at the same time.

It only took a few seconds for her to lose herself in her release. Every muscle in her body convulsed as she cried out, clinging to him.

He waited until the shudders had stopped before grabbing her hips and hanging on as he pumped in and out of her. Soon he stiffened and groaned.

They held on to each other. The sound of their rapid breathing filled the quiet kitchen.

"Are you all right?" he asked, stroking her head and kissing her bare shoulder.

"Yes."

And for that moment she was. She wouldn't think about tomorrow right now. Or the day after. Or the niggling sense that she was afraid of the wrong thing. It wasn't that Garth would hurt her physically that should have her on edge. It was that the more she knew him, the more she liked him. And that liking made her vulnerable.

For the first time she realized the true danger wasn't to her body, but was instead to her heart.

CHAPTER THIRTEEN

IZZY SHOWED UP the next morning with Danish, coffee and a copy of the paper. Dana had spent the night in Garth's bed and there hadn't been a lot of sleep on the agenda, so she was still groggy and not feeling like she wanted company.

"I should take the food and run," she said, then yawned. "But that would require too much energy."

Izzy followed her into the kitchen. "Someone got to bed late last night," her friend teased. "Want to share details?"

Dana got out plates and napkins, then led the way to the dining room. The small table in the kitchen should probably be wiped down before anyone ate at it.

"He's your brother," she said as she took a seat and reached for one of the containers of coffee. "Are you sure you want details?"

"Never mind." Izzy had already gone through the paper. She pushed a folded page toward Dana. "Brace yourself. You made the society page."

The hot coffee seemed to get stuck halfway down

Dana's throat. For a second she couldn't seem to swallow. She finally managed to get it down only to cough until she gagged.

"W-what?" she managed, then cleared her throat. "There's a society page in the paper?"

"Uh-huh, and you're the star. That's what happens when you go out with one of the city's most eligible bachelors. Being one of Garth's women comes at a price. By the way, you look great."

She turned the page so Dana could see the picture of herself standing next to Garth in front of Glory's Gate.

Dana felt the beginnings of a headache right behind her eyes. "Seriously? I didn't see anyone with a camera." She'd been too freaked about the whole party to notice details. That didn't bode well for her returning to a career in law enforcement. "I'm losing my edge."

"You were probably trying not to trip in high heels."

"True, but not an excuse."

Dana studied the picture. She had to admit, she looked good. The dress fit perfectly and Lexi had worked magic with hair and makeup. But seeing herself with a caption under the picture was beyond surreal.

There were several other pictures, including one of Skye with Mitch, and an article about the fund-raiser. She scanned it.

"They print the menu?"

"The little people are curious," Izzy teased. "Now that you're no longer one of them, you'll have to learn to be kind."

"Bite me."

"That would be Garth's job."

Dana drank more coffee. The society page. "How do I keep this from happening again?" she asked.

"Avoid society events."

Dana didn't think it would be too hard. Then she remembered something else her friend had said. "What do you mean 'one of his women'? He has others?"

Izzy shifted in her seat. "Not that I know of. It was just an expression. I'm sure he's not dating anyone else."

Dana winced and reached for a Danish. "You're the wrong person to be asking. That's a conversation I need to have with him."

She told herself not to worry. He was home early every night. All the time she'd been following him, he'd never gone out with anyone.

Izzy sipped her coffee. "Is it getting to the point where you need to know that kind of thing?" she asked.

"I don't know. I'm sleeping with him. I'm a big fan of serial monogamy. But I didn't bother asking about *his* preferences."

"He's a good guy," Izzy reassured her. "I wouldn't worry."

"You don't have to. It's fine. We'll have a rational, adult conversation."

"Because you like him."

Dana raised her eyebrows. "I don't care how athletic you are, I could so take you."

"You'd have to catch me first."

Dana nodded. Izzy was skinny, but she was also fast. She sighed. "I guess I do like him. A little."

Izzy grinned. "Casual like or serious like?"

"I'm not sure."

"That means serious like, or you'd be willing to say."

Dana glared at her. "Because it's impossible to believe I'm actually not sure?"

"Oh, please. You're very decisive. You wouldn't be sleeping with Garth if you didn't already like him."

"Maybe."

Izzy stared at her. "How serious?"

"I don't know." Dana took a bite of Danish. Maybe the sugar rush would help her think more clearly.

"He's not like the guys you usually date."

She swallowed. "Tell me about it. I don't know. There are things I really admire about him, but sometimes…" she looked at Izzy "…he scares the crap out of me."

"That's how all good relationships start. You can't be scared if you have nothing to lose."

"Meaning?"

"You're putting your heart on the line. That's good."

"Not for me or my heart." Dana licked her fingers. "Want to go work out?"

"Ick. No. But I'll go rock climbing with you."

"Anything that works up a sweat and keeps me from thinking is fine."

Izzy grinned. "Have you ever been rock climbing before?"

"No."

"You are so going to love it."

GARTH WALKED INTO ONE of the smaller conference rooms after lunch to find his three sisters waiting for him.

"Thanks for coming," he said.

"We were summoned," Izzy said. "I, for one, keep a very busy schedule, so this had better be important."

"What she said," Lexi told him.

"Ditto," Skye said.

Garth winced. "I shouldn't have my assistant call and ask you to stop by?"

"Probably not," Izzy told him. "Although if you had snacks, that would help."

"I'll remember that." He took a seat.

Women were complicated at the best of times. The Titan sisters were more complicated than most. But they were also smart and funny and he liked spending time with them. Guilt flashed through him. Guilt for what he'd done, how he'd upset their lives. But there was more. A sense of loss. How different his life would have been if he'd gotten to know them earlier. If he'd grown up with them as his family.

Enough with the emotion, he told himself. They had a bully to ruin.

"I want to talk about Jed," he said.

"We figured that," Izzy told him. "It's not like you want to ask about our plans for the holidays."

"Which are quickly approaching," Lexi said. "I'm

guessing we won't be at Glory's Gate this year. So where are we celebrating?"

"Your place," Izzy told her.

"Why me?" Lexi sounded faintly panicked. "I'm seriously pregnant. I can't be expected to cook."

"Skye's talking about a Christmas Eve wedding at Mitch's house. Nick and I live too far away. That leaves you. But don't worry. I'll help with the cooking."

Lexi winced. "You know less than me."

"That's true, but I have a secret weapon. Nick's cook, Norma, has said she'll help, too. So we're fine."

Lexi didn't look convinced. "Are you coming?" she asked Skye. "Or will you be off on your honeymoon?"

"We'll be there. We're not leaving Erin on Christmas. We'll head out a few days later. So expect a crowd."

"You were in on this!" Lexi sounded annoyed. "Ganging up on me. That is just so typical." She rubbed her belly. "You have very mean aunts. You'll have to watch them carefully."

Garth held up his hands in the shape of a *T*. "If we could get back to the subject at hand."

"Which is?" Izzy frowned, then relaxed. "Right. Jed. How did we get on Christmas?"

"That would be your doing," Lexi told her.

He ignored that and reached for the stack of folders in the center of the table, then passed one to each of the women. "I need you to look these papers over and sign them. I'll be buying shares in Titan World in each of your names. The amounts of the shares will require disclosure. Jed will see your names. He already knows we're working together but he may consider this a different level of betrayal."

They all stared at him with identical expressions of outrage.

"Excuse me?" Lexi asked.

Garth felt trapped. Had he misunderstood? Didn't they want to take down Jed?

"We, ah, talked about this," he reminded her, then glanced at Izzy and Skye. Neither of them looked especially friendly, either. "Working together. Letting Jed know we're a united front."

"You're giving us money," Skye said mildly. "That's why we're upset. No one is upset about taking on Jed."

"Okay." Relief swept through him. They *were* on the same page. "Then what's the problem?"

"You're giving us money," Izzy repeated. "We don't want your money."

Once again the female mind baffled him. "Why not? I have more than all of you."

"That warm, delicate nature," Lexi said, shaking her head. "He gets it from Jed." She leaned toward him. "We can buy our own shares."

"No, you can't. I'm talking hundreds of thousands of dollars here. Several million in total. None of you have it. You'll be filing forms with the SEC showing ownership."

"Isn't that technically illegal?" Skye asked. "You giving us money to buy shares?"

"I have a very expensive lawyer making sure we're doing everything the right way."

"Which isn't the point," Lexi told him. "We don't want your money. This isn't about getting anything from you."

Izzy shook her head at Lexi, then turned to him. "We love that you're including us, but we can't do this. It feels funny."

"I don't care how it feels," he told her. "It's about getting Jed."

"It's too much," Skye told him. "Garth, you mean well, but there has to be another way."

They were hung up on the amount? "If it was twenty bucks you wouldn't care. Is that it?"

"Sort of," Izzy said, giving him a sympathetic smile.

"This is part of the plan." He did his best not to give in to frustration. The last thing he needed was them digging in their heels. "We talked about this."

"You didn't say anything about giving us nearly a million dollars' worth of shares."

"I'm not doing it to give you anything," he said, trying not to clench his teeth. "I'm doing it to get Jed."

"No," Skye said, pushing the folder toward him. The other two did the same.

Women, he thought, leaning back in his chair.

He could tell them that they could sell the shares when all this was over and give the money to charity, but he wasn't sure that would actually help. Which left him with a pounding sensation over his left eye.

Buying the shares was important. But how to convince them?

He straightened. There was one card left to play.

"Jed went after Dana."

Three pairs of eyes locked on him. Lexi and Skye both went pale while Izzy looked ready to take on her father and beat him into submission.

"How?" Lexi asked.

"First he had someone run her off the road, then he had a guy shoot at her. That's when she moved in with me."

Skye's green eyes filled with tears. "She's all right, isn't she? We just saw her and she's fine."

Lexi nodded. "She didn't say anything. She didn't want us to know. She didn't want us to worry."

Garth held in a groan. He just remembered he'd promised Dana he wouldn't say anything to her friends. "Look, you can't tell her I told you."

Lexi and Skye glanced at each other. Izzy gave him a pitying look. "You poor, poor man."

"Seriously, she doesn't want you to worry."

"Too late," Skye whispered.

She was so going to kill him, he thought grimly. But before that happened, he might as well get it all out. "I spoke with Jed at the fund-raiser. Told him to lay off." He'd done more than talk, but he was in enough trouble already.

"You think that's going to work?" Lexi asked.

"I don't know. But the quicker we get Jed in jail, the safer everyone will be. We all want to take him down." He pointed at the folders. "It's the best way."

His sisters looked at each other, exchanging information in that silent way women did.

"We'll sign," Skye said. "But we're not keeping the money."

"I don't have a problem with that." They could cash out and light it in a bonfire for all he cared. "Just don't…" He stopped. Maybe he should have asked the other guys to come to the meeting, as well. They would have understood the next step.

Izzy looked at him, her eyebrows raised. "Don't what?"

"Stay safe," he said instead. "Once Jed finds out, he's going to be pissed."

The three of them exchanged another look. "We will," Lexi told him. "Don't worry—we're not interested in annoying Jed for sport. We want to get him out of our lives as quickly as possible." But she sounded sad as she spoke.

"You don't have to do this," he said. "I can find another way."

"After you went to all this trouble?" Izzy pointed to the folders. "They have our name on them and everything."

Skye smiled at him. "This isn't about you, Garth. We're sad because it's come down to trying to ruin our father. It's not a decision we've made lightly. But he nearly killed Izzy and we can't forgive that."

He nodded cautiously, not sure if he was being let off the hook or lulled into a false sense of security.

"You'll take care of Dana?" Lexi asked as she signed the paperwork.

"Yes."

Izzy looked up at him. "Does she know that?"

"It's an ongoing negotiation."

DANA SPENT MOST OF her afternoon poring over computer printouts. She was doing her best to find traces of Jed's foreign deposits, which sounded easier and more interesting than it was. Fortunately, a distraction arrived in the form of all three Titan sisters walking into the command center.

"Look at you, all businesslike," Izzy teased as they hugged. "I never thought I'd see the day."

"Me, either." Dana hugged Skye and Lexi. "I'm learning how to hack into computers. It's not as fun as it looks on TV."

The sisters pulled up chairs.

"Not that I'm not thrilled to see you," Dana said. "But what are you doing here?"

"We came to give you a stern talking-to," Lexi said grimly. "Dammit, Dana, what the hell is wrong with you?"

Skye frowned. "Lexi, don't make her defensive. It doesn't help anyone."

"I'm pissed," Lexi said. "In my condition, that's not a good thing."

Dana stared at them. "What are we talking about?" These women were her friends. They were never upset with her.

Izzy started to speak, but Skye shook her head. "I'll do it," she said. "Dana, we know what happened with Jed and we're very upset and hurt that you didn't tell us yourself."

Dana sprang to her feet and circled behind the desk. "I told Garth not to say anything. I asked for one thing, but could he do it? Of course not. Typical man."

"Garth is many things, but typical isn't one of them," Lexi said. "And it's not his fault. We were being difficult about signing some papers. He needed to point out how serious the situation is with Jed."

"By using me." She was furious. He could have told them something else. Anything else. She looked at her friends. "I'm sorry. I didn't want you to worry."

"It comes with the relationship," Izzy said. "Worry are us. Or something like that."

Lexi still looked upset. "Dana, Jed is our father. You've been a part of our lives since we were kids. We have the right to know if he's threatening you."

"Why? It has nothing to do with you."

"It has everything to do with us," Skye said, standing and facing her. "We love you and don't want anything to happen to you. If it does, we have a share of the responsibility."

Dana held up both hands, as if to push them away. "That's crazy. You can't control what Jed does and you're not responsible. I don't accept that."

"You must," Lexi said quietly. "Otherwise you would have told us. You knew how we'd feel."

Talk about a tidy trap, Dana thought, feeling both small and guilty. "I didn't want any of you to be upset."

"If he divides us, he wins," Skye said. "We have to remember that. The only way we're strong is if we're together." She stared at Dana. "We want you to promise that you won't keep any more secrets about Jed."

"I can take care of myself," she reminded them.

"This is about more than you," Skye told her.

"Did you get the *we love you* part?" Izzy asked. "You're one of us. You know—family."

Because that's what they had always believed. Family. Was it possible?

Lexi struggled to her feet, then waddled over to hug her. "You're stuck with us. You need to stop resisting. It's exhausting."

Skye and Izzy joined in the hug. The women holding her tight should have made her feel trapped. She should have been wanting to escape. Instead she felt warm and safe and loved. The emotion filled up a space that had been empty for so long, she'd nearly forgotten it was there.

"No more secrets," she whispered, telling herself the burning in her eyes came from a lack of sleep and nothing else.

"This is so cool," Izzy said. "Now let's all go get matching tattoos."

Skye sighed. "Someone hit her."

GARTH WALKED INTO THE condo that night, took one look at Dana and knew his time of being confronted by the women in his life was far from over.

"You're pissed," he said by way of greeting.

She sat in the living room, dressed in jeans and a sweater, a glass of wine in her hand.

"Hardly a greeting to treasure," she said. "Especially after I slaved all afternoon, cooking you dinner."

The words sounded right, but there was something flashing in her eyes. Something that, had he been less secure in his masculinity, would have scared the crap out of him.

"You cooked?"

"I'm full of surprises." She pointed to the chair opposite the sofa, next to a small table where a second glass of wine waited. "Have a seat."

He shrugged out of his suit jacket, then did as she suggested. He reached for the wine.

"Are you going to poison me?" he asked.

"You mean go behind your back and do something you've specifically asked me not to do?" she asked, coming to her feet and glaring at him. "You mean upset people you've cared about all your life and then not even warn you?"

He winced. "They came by."

"You bet your ass they came by. What the hell is wrong with you? First, you told them what happened with Jed, then you didn't even have the grace to warn me."

"I, ah, didn't think they'd say anything. At least not that fast."

"Because you've never met a woman before? Dammit, Garth, I had my reasons. I trusted you and you betrayed me."

He stood and faced her. "Look, I'll accept that I screwed up, but betrayal is going too far. I didn't have a plan. I needed them to sign some papers and they were resisting."

"So you sold me down the river."

"That's dramatic."

"It's the truth!" she yelled.

"It's what had to be done. I thought we all had a goal here—to take down Jed Titan. At least that's what everyone is saying they want. But when it comes to action, no one is showing up. I asked them to sign some paperwork to buy shares of his stocks. They resisted."

She watched him warily. "Why would they do that?"

"For the same reason you will." He reached for his briefcase and pulled out a folder. "I have the same thing for you. I'll be buying nearly a million dollars' worth of Titan World shares in your name."

She jumped back as if he'd burned her. "What?"

"That's what they said, too."

"I'm not taking your money."

"I've already had this argument today," he said, rubbing his forehead. "Look, Dana—"

"No, *you* look. This is bullshit. It's bad enough I have to live here, but I'm not taking your money."

He told himself she was upset—that her complaint about living with him wasn't personal. But he felt the sting, all the same.

"Then go back to your own place," he said, his voice low and angry. "I'll get you a full-time bodyguard."

She stood very still. "That's not what I meant."

"It's what you said."

"I'm sorry."

Two words he'd never expected her to say.

She drew in a breath. "I can't take your money. I sleep with you. If you give me money, then I'm your whore."

"Dana, we have a plan here," he said, doing his best to stay calm. "We're trying to back Jed into a corner. Having him know everyone is buying into his precious company is going to seriously piss him off."

She tucked her hands behind her back. "No. And while we're negotiating—"

"Saying no and changing the subject isn't a negotiation."

She ignored that. "I want to go back to work."

He tossed the folder onto the coffee table and swore. "Sure. Why not? Spend your day totally in the open with no protection. That's smart. When the bullets come, what are the odds you won't be the only victim? What happens when they take out your partner or some innocent citizen?"

She looked uncomfortable, as if she hadn't thought that part through. Not that he was prepared to accept victory. He wasn't that clueless.

"I'm supposed to be a deputy," she snapped. "I want my career back and my life, as well. You don't understand. You have a life, a place to go, people to see. Probably women. By the way, who else are you dating?"

If he lived to be five hundred and eight he would *never* understand women. "Who else would I be dating? Are you serious? When would this happen? If I'm not at the office, I'm with you. We're sleeping together. Are *you* seeing anyone else?"

"Oh, please."

That pissed him off. "So it's fine for you to accuse me, but not the other way around? That's fair."

"We're not talking fair," she yelled. "You're this rich, successful guy. We were in the society pages after Skye's fund-raiser. My picture was in there with you. That doesn't happen to me."

He still didn't understand the problem but was thinking wine wasn't going to be close to enough. It seemed more like a Scotch night.

"I don't control the press. I didn't even know there were society pages."

"Me, either," she snapped. "So you'd better fix this."

"Fix what?"

"Everything."

They stared at each other. Tension filled the room. There was anger and frustration and something else he couldn't figure out.

He had no idea what to say, so he settled on the truth. "I'm not seeing anyone but you. I wasn't seeing anyone before I met you. I want you to sign the papers because it's the next logical step in bringing down Jed. Signing them doesn't say anything bad about you and when all this is over, you can sell the shares and give the money to the charity of your choice."

He watched her watching him, trying to read her expression, but he couldn't. For all he knew, she was going to pull out her gun and shoot him.

"I get that it's frustrating for you to be stuck here. Going back to work is dangerous, not just for you but for everyone around you. Nick needs some help out at the ranch. You'd be fairly isolated there and probably safe. If you're interested, I'll ask him. But I'd want you to have a driver or a car tailing you on the trip there and back. It's a long drive that would leave you exposed. Or you could stay there. Which wouldn't be my choice, but as you've said, this isn't about me."

"Damn straight."

He held up both hands. "I'm not trying to run your life. I just want to keep you safe. I don't want anything bad to happen to you." He lowered his hands. "That's it. You can yell at me now."

One corner of her mouth twitched. "I'm not a yeller."

"Right. You're calm and diplomatic. An iceberg of emotion."

The twitch turned into a smile. "You can call me Ice if you want."

"Can I?"

The tension eased from the room, leaving them alone. Dana walked toward him. He wrapped his arms around her and kissed the top of her head.

"I just want you safe," he repeated.

"And Jed in jail."

"I've always been a high achiever. Is this okay now? Are you going to turn on me again?"

She looked into his eyes. "I won't turn on you. At least not for this."

"At the risk of making you froth at the mouth, are you going to sign the papers?"

She glanced at the folder, then back at him. "Yes, but I won't like it."

"Duly noted."

She stepped back, then slugged him in the upper arm. "Next time, keep my secrets."

The place she'd hit stung like a sonofabitch, but he was a guy. He couldn't rub it. "You have my word."

"Like I believe that." She sighed then went into his arms again. "Want to get Chinese?"

"I thought you cooked."

"Like I know how."

"That's my girl."

CHAPTER FOURTEEN

THE DOWNSIDE of not being annoyed with Garth meant having to go with him to events like this one, Dana thought a few nights later as they circulated through a business cocktail party held at a large, fancy hotel. She wasn't sure of the purpose of the party. Her best guess was someone had opened a new law firm, but she hadn't seen the invitation. Garth had tried to explain but she'd glazed over.

Dating a captain of industry was time-consuming and expensive. She didn't have anything close to the right wardrobe. Not that she cared about being fashion forward, but she didn't want to embarrass him. Fortunately she and Skye were nearly the same size and her friend had opened her impressive closet for Dana's borrowing pleasure.

"What are you thinking?" Garth asked as he passed her a glass of wine. "That you'd like to be anywhere but here?"

She looked around at the well-dressed crowd. At least it was an after-office-hours event that wouldn't go too late and she'd been spared having to wear shapeware.

"That tomorrow I'm going to stand in front of the mirror practicing telling you no."

He leaned in until his mouth brushed against her ear. "But I like it when you say yes."

A shiver tiptoed down her spine and her skin broke out in goose bumps. He was good, she thought, resigned to being weak where he was concerned. Better than good.

She distracted herself by looking at the jewelry the other women were wearing and trying to calculate an approximate cost. The flaw in the plan was that she had no idea what your average diamond was worth, let alone twenty set in a fancy necklace. Or bracelet. Or in earrings.

She frowned. Talk about people with money, she thought, turning in a slow circle and taking in the sparkle. Jewels glittered from every direction.

"What are you doing?" Garth asked.

She stopped and discreetly pointed to an older woman in a black suit. "Look at that leopard pin on her lapel. Do you think it's real? Are the blue eyes sapphires?" She frowned. "Is that the blue stone? I know emeralds are green, but isn't there another blue stone?"

"You're checking out the jewelry?" He raised his eyebrows. "Socialites everywhere would be so proud."

She rolled her eyes. "I'm not checking it out as in I want it. I'm amazed at how much there is."

"An entire industry survives because we like pretty things. Wars have been fought over diamonds."

"You're making that up."

"You ever hear of blood diamonds?"

"No, and I don't want to talk about them now." She touched her simple gold hoops. "Skye offered to lend me a couple of things along with the clothes. I should have said yes."

Garth got the strangest look on his face.

"What?" she asked.

"You're borrowing clothes from Skye?"

"Do I look like the type to have a wardrobe suitable for this kind of stuff? I bought the dress for the foundation party, but I'm not spending a bunch of money on clothes I'm never going to wear again."

"Would you let me take you shopping?"

"No."

"It's my fault you're here," he said, sounding almost reasonable. "It could be fun."

"No and no. Not every shopping experience is like what happened in *Pretty Woman*. I don't like shopping. Skye's closet is great. Lexi's would be better but she's so damn skinny. Well, not now, but I'm not ready to settle into the maternity look."

He glanced at her neck. "Maybe some pearls."

"Don't make me shriek in public. No pearls. No anything. I took that stupid stock because I had to, but that's it."

"I'd like to buy you something."

"I could use a new handgun."

"I don't want you armed."

She smiled and sipped her wine. "Too late. I already am."

He dropped his gaze to her small handbag. "Seriously?"

The man knew nothing about women's accessories, which wasn't a bad thing. The handbag was way too small to conceal a regular handgun, but there was no need to tell him.

"You'll have to wait and find out."

He looked like he wanted to say something more, but wisely didn't. Dana returned her attention to the mammoth ring on a woman walking by and wondered if the money wouldn't have been better spent on the national debt or saving a third world country.

Not that she objected to pretty things, as Garth had called them. She wouldn't mind a few little pieces that sparkled…one day. But they would have to be subtle and something she bought for herself. No gifts of obligation, although she wasn't sure if she meant the giver would feel obligated or she would.

Husbands bought their wives presents, so that would be okay. Or an engagement ring. If she were ever going to get married, which she couldn't imagine. Marriage was another form of surrender. Although plenty of people seemed happy doing it. She would have to be sure—more sure than she'd ever been in her life.

"Senator Davis is here," Garth said, pointing. "I want to say hello. Do you mind?"

She took a step forward, only to have one of the

servers passing by her trip and bump her arm. White wine splashed down, sprinkling Skye's black pants with tiny drops.

"I'm so sorry," the waiter said quickly, looking terrified. He reached for the glass. "Are you all right?"

"Fine." She shrugged. "It happens. Don't worry." When he'd left, she turned to Garth. "I want to go wipe off the pants so they don't get stained."

"Should I wait?" he asked.

"No. Go have your bondy moment with the senator. I'll clean up, then join you in a few minutes."

He leaned in and kissed her on her neck, just under her ear. "Don't be long."

The stupid shivers returned, but she ignored them. Maybe she could find some kind of Garth vaccine. Something that would keep her from reacting every time he was close by.

She made her way to the restroom. It was huge and contained everything from hairspray to spot-removing cloths. She wiped off the few drops of wine, decided nothing was ruined, then washed her hands and returned to the party.

It took her a few minutes to spot Garth, then wished she hadn't. He was in the same crowd as the senator, but instead of talking to a portly older man, he seemed to be having an intense conversation with a petite, beautiful blonde.

The woman was maybe thirty, with features so perfect they didn't look real. She was almost a doll come to life. A doll with large breasts that moved under the low-cut fitted top she wore over a slim, dark skirt.

It wasn't so much the conversation that got her attention, or the woman's exquisite features. It was the way she looked up at Garth, all wide-eyed and hopeful. As if he could make her world exactly right just by smiling at her.

Dana shook off the thoughts, reminding herself that unless she'd had a recent brain injury, being fanciful wasn't her style, then walked up to join them. Just before she got there, the woman excused herself.

By the time Dana joined Garth, he was talking to the senator and there was no chance to ask about the blonde.

Garth introduced her to everyone in the group. She nodded and smiled and did her best to remember names, but couldn't seem to keep her attention on the conversation. Instead she found herself watching the other woman, who circulated through the party. She seemed to know nearly everyone. When she stopped by an older woman, dripping in jewels, they embraced.

The blonde laughed, then put her hand on the older woman's arm.

If Dana hadn't been watching so intently, she wouldn't have seen what happened next. There was a quick shift with the blonde's hand, then the diamond bracelet that had been winking from the older woman's wrist disappeared. Seconds later Dana watched the blonde slip it into her small handbag.

"Excuse me," Dana said then walked toward the blonde. Even as she crossed the space between them, she argued with herself.

She had to be wrong, she thought. But she knew what she'd seen and every instinct, not to mention her police training, insisted she find out what had happened.

Dana walked up to the blonde, who had started to move on, and stepped in front of her. The other woman smiled up at her.

"Hi."

"Hi," Dana said, staring into eyes the color of the Caribbean. True aqua-blue fringed by long, dark lashes. "Tell me she's your grandmother. A relative? Not that it would necessarily help your story."

"What?"

"That woman you were just talking to. Grandma? An aunt?"

"No."

"Then you probably want to give her back the bracelet." Dana grabbed the blonde's purse and opened it. The bracelet glittered against the black lining, as did a watch and a ring. "You've been busy."

The other woman's eyes widened. "Who are you?"

"Someone who is going to be calling the police."

A large, masculine hand covered hers, closing the small handbag. Garth stepped between them and put his arms around their waists.

"We should take this somewhere else," he said. "It's a party."

"Tell that to the jewel thief."

"Fawn already knows."

"FAWN?" DANA REPEATED as she paced the length of the meeting room on the same floor as the party. "Her name is Fawn? Who does that to a child?"

"It's a family name."

"Great. So her mother is Doe and her father is Buck?" Dana swung around to face Garth. "Wait a minute. How do you know her name?"

He didn't even bother to look uncomfortable, she thought bitterly as he leaned against the wall and put his hands in his pants pockets. "I've known Fawn and her family for several years now. And no, her father isn't named Buck."

Dana wanted to spit. "Tell me we're calling the police. If we're not…" She didn't know what she would do but it would be really, really painful. She wasn't sure who she was going to hurt, but someone was going down tonight. There would be blood. Or at least serious bruising. "Where is *Fawn,* by the way?"

"Her name isn't her fault."

"How nice for her. And the stealing?"

Garth had led both women out of the ballroom, then a tall, older man had collected Fawn. While Dana seethed in frustration, Garth had whispered to him and then led Dana into this empty room.

"Don't think you can distract me into forgetting," she said. "I'm pissed."

"I can tell."

"She stole. Not just the bracelet, but a watch and a ring. I don't know what they were worth, but there were a lot of diamonds. What is she? A professional jewel thief?"

"Not exactly."

The door opened and to Dana's amazement, Fawn rushed in. She ran directly to Garth. Worse, he didn't back away or sidestep. Instead he let her wrap her arms around him and hold on as if she would never let go. Things went to hell very quickly as he returned her embrace.

Dana knew she was the wronged party in this trio, but righteous indignation didn't make her feel any less awkward. Fawn was tiny and perfect. Next to her Dana felt half mutant. Fawn belonged—Dana never would.

Garth looked at her over Fawn's head.

"It's not what you think," he said.

"You don't know what I'm thinking."

Fawn turned in his arms, but grabbed his hand. "I'm making a mess of everything, aren't I?"

"Yes," Dana snapped, not caring when the other woman winced.

The older man from before stood at the open door. "Fawn, we have to go."

Fawn raised herself on tiptoes and pressed her mouth to Garth's. "I'm sorry," she said as she backed away. "You know that, don't you?"

He nodded.

Then they were gone.

Dana folded her arms across her chest. "If she'd been the gardener instead of a pretty socialite, you would so be throwing her ass in jail," she said bitterly. "It's all about power and social position. And looking like an angel doesn't hurt, either." She turned to him. "Tell me I'm wrong."

Garth hesitated.

"Figures," she muttered and started past him.

He grabbed her arm. "Wait. Fawn has a problem. She takes things. She has plenty of money and could afford to buy anything she wants, but sometimes…"

"Ask me if I care," Dana said, pulling free of his grasp.

"She's trying."

"Not very hard. Give me a break. Poor little rich girl has a problem. So what happens now? None of you will press charges, so it never happened. Let me guess, Daddy takes her home and we go on with our lives."

"Everyone likes her," he said.

"So that makes it okay." But Fawn wasn't the entire problem, she admitted to herself. There was a bigger one she couldn't ignore anymore. "How do you know her?"

He hesitated.

She waited. The information was only a few computer clicks away. Skye would know her last name and then a quick Internet search would give her more than she wanted to know.

"It was a long time ago," he began.

Dana felt beyond stupid. They'd gone out. Of course. Why hadn't she figured that out the first second she'd seen them together?

But Fawn was the opposite of her. How could he have been interested in Fawn and then want to be with her? Which brought up a whole lot of other questions she didn't want to answer.

"We were engaged."

"YOU DON'T WANT TO do this," Lexi said, standing beside Dana's chair.

Dana ignored her and typed in Garth's name along with the phrase "and women." The Internet responded instantly, producing over ten thousand listings. She picked one at random.

There was a picture of Garth with a tall skinny woman who had to be a model of some kind. No one normal had such bony knees and elbows. She clicked on other articles and saw Garth with plenty of heiresses, successful businesswomen and even an actress. There was a theme to his women—they were all beautiful and accomplished. They had style, possibly grace and moved effortlessly in his social circle.

She was a small-town deputy who, until a few weeks ago, hadn't worn a dress in nearly ten years.

"What was I thinking?" she whispered.

"I can't answer that until you tell me what's going on," Lexi said, then pulled up another chair and sat heavily. "My back hurts."

Dana turned to her, the search forgotten. "Are you all right? Do we need to go to the hospital?"

"No. My back hurts. I'm seven and a half months pregnant and getting bigger by the second. Of course my back hurts."

Dana drew in a breath. "Don't scare me like that. I have enough stress in my life."

"If you tell me what happened, I can help."

It was a reasonable statement, especially considering Dana had shown up that morning with a suitcase, asking if she could stay.

To her credit, Lexi hadn't asked a lot of questions, but instead had shown her to a guest room. Dana had gotten out her laptop and gone online to find out the truth about Garth. Something she should have done weeks ago.

Everything was right there, in the pictures. Woman after woman, smiling at the camera. Leaning against him or holding hands or linking arms.

She'd been a fool. Worse, for him, she'd been convenient. He didn't even have to make a booty call. The booty was right there in his condo.

"I don't need help," she said. "I'm fine."

"You are so going to tell me what's going on," Lexi said. "Dana, I mean it. What happened?"

Dana turned to her friend. "I'm sorry. Everything is totally screwed up and it's all my fault. Well, his, too. Mostly his."

Lexi covered her face with her hands and shrieked. "What are we talking about?"

"Garth was engaged."

Lexi dropped her hands to her lap. "I knew that. It was a few years ago. Three or four. Rich girl. Then she sort of disappeared. What does that have to do with... Oh. You met the ex."

"I more than met her."

Dana told her what had happened, ending with Fawn's father taking her away.

"She was stealing?" Lexi asked, sounding outraged. "And nothing happened. Why am I even surprised?"

"That's what I said."

Dana thought about Fawn in Garth's arms. Jed had been right. She would never fit in.

"I don't belong with him," she said.

Lexi frowned. "What does Fawn have to do with you and Garth?" She held up a hand. "I know finding out about someone's past is never easy. But I'd like to point out all you have to deal with is an ex-fiancée. Cruz didn't tell me he had a teenaged daughter. We all keep secrets, Dana."

"I don't." There wasn't anything secret-worthy in her past. She wasn't excited to talk about how her father had treated her, but Garth already knew the basic story.

"He's not with her now."

Dana logged off the Internet. "Lord, I know. Garth didn't know she was going to be there, blah, blah, blah. But when it came down to it, he protected her. She was stealing. And he let her get away with it."

He'd chosen Fawn over her.

Dana would never say that. She wasn't sure she would admit to even thinking it, but that was the bottom line.

"Fawn obviously needs help," Lexi said. "She needs to learn to take responsibility."

"That's not going to happen while everyone steps in to protect her."

"I agree." Lexi frowned. "I'm surprised Garth did that."

"Why?"

"He's pragmatic," Lexi said. "Why would he get involved with someone like that then or now?"

"He probably didn't know when they started dating. Besides, you haven't seen her. She's so beautiful, she doesn't look real. Talk about a trophy wife."

"Garth doesn't need a trophy. He's young and successful. He can have anyone he wants."

Dana sighed. "This would be you making me feel better?"

Lexi smiled. "Do you need me to? Is there something you want to tell me?"

"No."

"Are you falling for him?"

"No one says 'falling for him' anymore."

"I do, and stop avoiding the question."

Dana leaned back in her chair. Falling for Garth? Not possible. They weren't anything alike. He was from another planet, while she lived on this one. He was…

"I don't know," she admitted. "I want to tell you no. I want to tell you he's just someone I know, but I can't. It's too confusing. We aren't following any rules I know."

"Then maybe it's time to start breaking the rules."

"Have you met me? I don't break the rules, I enforce them."

"How's that working for you?"

Dana shrugged. "Good point. I just wish she hadn't been there." Or that she could forget seeing Fawn melt into Garth's arms.

"You can stay here as long as you'd like," Lexi said.

"Thanks."

"Are you sure you don't want to talk to Garth about this?"

"And be rational? No, thanks. I like wallowing in uncertainty. It's a new experience for me."

"Welcome to the real world."

"When do I get to go back to the old one?"

Lexi smiled. "I have no idea."

Later, Lexi went to her office, while Dana wandered through Cruz's large house, feeling more uncomfortable than she did at Garth's place. The only bright spot in her otherwise boring afternoon was a wild game of chase the string with C.C. the cat.

At three-fifteen, the doorbell rang. Dana opened it to find Garth standing there.

As always, the sight of him made her whole body go on alert. If only she could look into his dark eyes without imagining them bright with passion. She wanted to be able to look at his arms without seeing them around Fawn.

"You left me," he said.

Why did he have to say it like that? "I needed to think. Wait a minute. It was just this morning, after you'd gone to work. How did you know?"

He shrugged. "I had a feeling. I went home and you weren't there."

"So you called Lexi?"

"No. I knew you'd be here."

How? When she'd left his condo, she hadn't known where she would go. She'd driven here without thinking.

She waited for him to ask her why. Or to get angry with her for walking out. Or to blame her for everything that had happened. Instead he stared into her eyes and said, "I'm sorry. Please come home."

CHAPTER FIFTEEN

DANA WANTED TO TELL HIM it wasn't home, that she had a home. A lovely little apartment where she was never confused. But she knew what he meant and what he was asking. As she had no answer, she held the door open a little wider, to let him in, then closed it behind him.

Emotion complicated everything, she thought grimly as she followed him into the large living room. If she wasn't confused about her feelings, she could make a decision easily. Stay with Garth because right now it wasn't safe to be on her own. Or move in with Lexi. Or hire a bodyguard and stay at her place. There were multiple solutions…until she started thinking with something other than her brain.

Garth stood in the center of the room, watching her.

She motioned to the sofa, but he shook his head. She shrugged. "This is your party. You should do the talking."

"Fair enough." He cleared his throat. "I met Fawn about five years ago. She was dating some European duke or prince or something back then. I can't remember."

"I have that problem all the time," Dana murmured.

He ignored the comment. "I didn't think that much about her until she called me the next day and invited me to lunch."

Dana found it difficult to believe any man could be in the same room as Fawn and think about anything else, but stranger things had happened.

"We went out a few times," he continued. "I liked her well enough. She was a fun date. A violinist, so we went to the symphony a lot. I wasn't thinking about anything serious until her father came to see me." He looked at her. "You met him last night."

The tall, older man who had collected Fawn? Guessing was enough—she didn't need Garth to confirm the information. "Go on."

"He wanted Fawn married and I seemed like a good choice. He let me know there would be many advantages to being his son-in-law."

"Did he mention her problem with other people's possessions?"

Garth's expression didn't change. "No. He didn't say anything. I thought about what he'd said, then I talked to Fawn about it."

"How did she feel about Daddy trying to sell her off?"

"She wasn't surprised. I sensed there was a catch, but I couldn't put my finger on it. We went away together for a couple of weeks to see if we could consider marriage. When things went well, I proposed."

"So it was a business arrangement," she said, wishing she could believe him. It was all just a little too convenient.

"At first," he said cautiously. "The more I was around Fawn, the more I liked her."

Why didn't he just say he was in love with her? That was the significant information. She didn't want to hear the words, but once she did maybe the ache in her chest would go away.

"A few months later, I found out about her problem. She liked to take things."

"You mean steal jewelry that didn't belong to her."

"Yes."

"Does it help to make the words pretty?"

His gaze narrowed. "Does it make you feel better to make them ugly?"

She stiffened. "I'm not the one who did anything wrong here. I'm not the one who protected a potential felon."

"You're being dramatic," he said.

"Do you really think the world is a better place because Fawn is free to steal at will?"

"Would it be better with her in jail?"

"Maybe it wouldn't but it would be really nice if every now and then people were reminded there are consequences for their actions. Maybe the world can't be improved, but maybe Fawn would take her problem a lot more seriously if she suffered a little instead of heading off to another five-star luxury rehab facility."

He flushed slightly.

"So that's it," she said, telling herself not to be surprised. "Fawn will be readmitted to whatever program has already failed to help her."

He nodded.

"Is that why you ended the engagement?" she asked.

"What makes you think I ended it?"

Because Fawn had walked into his arms with the certainty of a woman who knows she was going to be welcomed. And if she'd dumped him, she wouldn't have been sure. Garth wasn't the type to forgive and forget.

"Am I wrong?" she asked.

"No," he said, looking away. "I found out about her stealing and I finally knew why her father was so anxious to marry her off. While I believe Fawn cared about me, I think she cared a lot more about finding someone to take care of her. She wasn't big on taking responsibility."

Dana wanted to say that she still wasn't but that seemed like a cheap shot.

"I broke the engagement and she went away. I haven't seen her since."

Dana had so many other questions. Like did he still love Fawn? If she'd been cured would he want to be with her now? Did he have any regrets? Did he want another chance with her?

"So she's the one who got away," she said, hoping her voice sounded light and casual.

"That's making it more than it was."

"You weren't sorry to see her."

"No, but I wasn't happy, either. I'm sorry she's still having problems. She probably will all her life. It's why she had to give up playing professionally. She couldn't go on tour and not steal. Apparently the compulsion hasn't gone away." He stared at her. "If I'd known we would run into her, I would have said something. Warned you."

"Why? Don't you have ex-girlfriends at most of the parties you go to? There are dozens and dozens of them out there."

He frowned. "What are you talking about?"

She tried to smile and wasn't sure she succeeded. "Come on, Garth. I looked you up on the Internet. You've done more than your share of dating in the past dozen or so years. Models, actresses, women who come from money. I will say you don't have a physical type. I guess that keeps things interesting."

He looked more wary than annoyed. "I'm a single guy. Dating is allowed."

"You're right." She moved around so the sofa was between them. "I really appreciate you coming here and explaining all this. Now I know who Fawn is and what she means to you—"

"She doesn't mean anything."

"Whatever."

"You're pissed."

Actually, she wasn't, which was too bad. Pissed would feel really good right about now. Pissed would give her energy and maybe stop the ache she felt inside. The pain was general, rather than specific, and as she didn't know what had caused it, she didn't know how to make it stop. She just knew the longer she talked to Garth, the worse she felt. It was as if... As if...

As if she was devastated that he'd wanted to marry Fawn because she was so different from her. A man who had been in love with Fawn could never love Dana. Never marry her.

The thought slammed into her. If she hadn't already been leaning against the back of the sofa, she might have fallen over in shock. What a ridiculous idea. She didn't want to marry Garth and she certainly didn't care what he thought about her. She was with him because of her personal safety and maybe because the sex was good. But she wasn't interested in him as anything other than a guy in her bed. He didn't *matter* to her. He wasn't...

"Dana? Are you all right?"

"I'm fine. Just fine. What were we talking about?"

"You being pissed."

"I'm not. Everything is great. Thanks for telling me about Fawn. I appreciate knowing the story. She's, um, very pretty. Don't you think she's pretty?"

He stared at her as if she'd grown another head. "Do you feel okay?"

"Uh-huh." She bobbed her head as she spoke. "Anything else or do you have to go?"

Please let him have to leave, she thought. The faster he was out of here, the quicker she could bang her head against a wall and knock some sense into herself. There was no way on this planet or any other that she was so damn stupid that she had fallen for a man like Garth Duncan. Not like him, she reminded herself. Him exactly.

"You haven't said if you're coming back with me."

His place. That's what this was all about. Keeping her safe from Jed because he felt responsible for what was happening. She'd agreed because it made sense and she didn't want her friends to worry. And maybe because she'd wanted to.

So now what? Go back and stay with him, knowing that she could never be…never be Fawn. That she was trapped being herself and even if she could change that, she probably wouldn't.

"If you'd rather stay with Lexi and Cruz, I'll understand," he said quietly.

But his dark eyes said he wouldn't understand at all. Or maybe that was just wishful thinking on her part.

It would be safer for her emotional self to put distance between herself and Garth. But there was more at stake here. Did she really want to impose on her friend and Cruz? Getting a bodyguard was also an option, but how would she pay for that? Garth would insist on covering the expense and that would freak her out.

Or she could go back with him.

It was what she wanted. She was self-aware enough to know that. She wanted to be with him because… well, better not to go there. But to risk everything she had on a man who would never be interested in her for more than something temporary?

"I'll come back," she said slowly. "To the condo. Not to your bed."

Nothing about his expression changed. She had no idea what he was thinking, nor did she ask.

"When?"

She drew in a breath. "It will only take me a minute to pack."

JED READ THE SINGLE-PAGE report a second time, then looked over the sheet at his chief financial officer.

"You're sure about this?" he asked.

"They've already filed with the SEC," Brock told him, looking worried. "They're following the law to the letter and they're not being quiet about their intentions. They're buying up shares with the idea of forcing you out. I'm getting calls from some of the institutional stockholders. Jed, this isn't good."

Not something he wanted to hear, Jed thought furiously. His own daughters turning against him. How could they, after all he'd done for them? He was their father, for God's sake. What happened to family loyalty?

"Do you know why the girls are doing this?" Brock asked tentatively.

Jed thought about the explosion that had injured Izzy. "Women," he muttered. "Who knows why they do anything?"

"A couple of financial reporters have been trying to get me to comment," Brock admitted. "They're wondering if the federal charges are the reasons. If your daughters think you're going to jail and you aren't willing to hand the reins over to them directly. So they're being forced to take control on their own." He shifted uncomfortably. "The problem is they're family, Jed. This doesn't look good."

"I know they're family," Jed roared. "Goddamn insufferable bitches, all of them. They're making everything worse." He glared at his friend. "Can we stop them?"

"They're allowed to buy anything they want."

"But how are they getting the money? They don't have enough. Skye's put all her inheritance into that asinine foundation of hers. Izzy's money is tied up in trust and Lexi never had much of her own. Cruz could be funding this, I suppose."

But a future husband giving his fiancée money to buy family stock was hardly illegal.

He didn't like this—any of it. He hated the questions, the looks he was getting. How people were starting to whisper. The federal investigation continued as the probe went deeper. He wanted to tell them they weren't going to find anything, but he wasn't sure. Had he buried the trail deep enough or was he in danger of being caught?

"They should be after Garth," he snapped. Enough clues had been planted. "He's the problem in all this. Bastard."

The irony of the word didn't escape him but he was too furious to see the humor.

"We'll have to start buying up stock ourselves," he told Brock. "Beat 'em at their own game."

"An excellent plan, but the company doesn't have the money. If we take out a loan now, while this is going on, everyone's going to know we're nervous."

"Not through the company," Jed said. "I'll do it personally. That will give us a little time before we have to report the transaction."

Brock shook his head. "You don't have the money, either, Jed," he said quietly. "You're cash poor."

Jed didn't want to hear that, even though it was true. His legal expenses had been chewing up money for months now. He was hemorrhaging cash. Selling his horses had raised millions, but they weren't enough to buy back the number of shares he needed.

"Land rich and cash poor," he said with a heavy sigh. "A rancher's lot for generations. What about borrowing on Glory's Gate?"

"Don't do it," Brock told him. "I've been your friend for over forty years, Jed, and I'm telling you not to do it."

"You saying I couldn't raise the cash?"

"You could get plenty, but it would be too risky. You really want to put the last of the Titan land on the block?"

"It's a loan, Brock. I'm not selling."

"And if you have to default?"

"I'm winning this fight." He always won. This time was taking a little longer than he was used to, but the outcome would be the same. "Find me some fool with money."

Something flashed across Brock's face.

Jed raised his eyebrows. "You have someone already?"

His friend hesitated. "I've been approached. There's an offer on the table."

"Why didn't you tell me?"

"Because it's a bad deal. The interest rate is reasonable, as is the price, but the note…it's callable."

Jed nearly laughed. "It's Garth," he said gleefully. "He thinks he can trap me the way he nearly trapped Lexi. A callable note. What are the terms? No, wait. Let me guess. Minimal payments for as long as I want, but the note is callable with sixty days' notice."

Brock swallowed. "Seventy-two hours."

Jed's humor faded. "Sonofabitch. That's armed robbery."

"That's the offer. And there aren't any payments. He's just giving you the money. But when he calls it, the principle and interest are due at the same time."

It was like a giant game of poker, Jed thought, hating Garth Duncan with every fiber of his being. If it were up to him, he'd take the man out back and horsewhip him to death.

"He said you'd never do it," Brock said. "He's challenging you. It's a taunt."

A damn good one. But if he could take the money and trick Garth into thinking he was more desperate than he was… Yes, Jed thought slowly. Turn the game around.

"Do it," he growled.

Brock stared at him. "No, Jed."

"Do it," he repeated. "Take the offer. Let him think he's got me where he wants me. Let him get cocky. We'll only buy what we need to push up the stock. Let word leak out there's in-fighting in the family for control. That will get people thinking there's a reason we all want control. The price will go up, we'll sell and I'll pay him back."

Brock looked unhappy. "I don't think this is a good idea."

"There isn't another choice. Don't worry, I have a good idea of what to do next. I plan to win it all back in one big hand of poker. Then I'll crush Garth and my daughters along with him. I'll teach them all not to screw with Jed Titan."

DANA HAD THOUGHT shopping hell would be defined as the fancy boutique Lexi had taken her to a few weeks before. She'd been wrong. True pain and suffering came in the form of a well-lit, beautifully furnished wedding salon. Not even a store or a boutique…no, this was definitely a salon.

Here, tasteful music played quietly in the background. The carpet was plush, the mirrors carefully polished, the chairs well-padded and covered in some kind of tapestry. Those buying were clients, not customers, and gowns had names instead of inventory numbers. First names. You didn't ask for Vera Wang. Just Vera was enough.

"It helps if you keep breathing," Izzy whispered, grinning over her fancy teacup. "And remind yourself to bring a flask next time."

"I would have brought a flask this time if I'd been thinking," Dana muttered, shifting on her too-soft chair and wishing she could fast-forward through the next hour.

She loved Skye. She would even take a bullet for her, but sitting quietly while her friend tried on wedding dresses was a new and uncomfortable form of torture. Still, when Skye had asked, she'd been unable to say no.

Until Skye had e-mailed her the address, she hadn't known this place existed and she could have died happy without the knowledge. She didn't know what dresses here cost and she wasn't going to ask. Still, the sisters seemed happy. Lexi had been ushered to a plush chaise where she half reclined, sipping herbal tea and having her feet massaged by the in-house masseuse. At least she was having a good time if the groans were anything to go by.

Skye walked out of one of the big dressing rooms and stepped onto the round platform in front of the half circle of mirrors. She smoothed the narrow cream-colored skirt.

"What do you think?" she asked, looking hopeful, but not sure.

Dana studied the tasteful, tailored suit. It was silk, a fact she knew only because she'd overheard the sales-woman describing the fabric as she'd picked it out. There was lace on the lapels and a pretty scalloped hem, if one was into that sort of thing.

"You look great," Lexi said, through half-closed eyes. "It fits you great."

"One of the advantages of being a size ten," Skye said with a sigh. "Getting married in a month means buying a sample. So at least they fit. It's pretty." She sounded more doubtful than sure.

"Very elegant," Izzy said. "It's great."

Dana studied the suit. It was beautifully made and probably cost a whole lot of money. It even suited Skye's curves and coloring, but it wasn't the dress of her friend's dreams.

"You hate it," Dana said. "Why are you trying on suits? You wear suits to the office, not to a wedding."

Skye bit her lower lip. "It's a second wedding," she said. "At home. The dress shouldn't be anything, you know, too much."

"Why not?" Dana asked. "It's your wedding. Wear what you want. Who's going to complain? Plus, what is Mitch going to think when he sees you in a suit? Skye, you're into princess dresses. Not this."

"But I shouldn't…"

"Yes, you should," Lexi said. "Dana's right. This is your wedding to Mitch. Go try on something that will make you happy."

Skye's mouth turned up at the corners. "Really?"

"Don't make us have Dana get violent," Izzy said. "As long as we're not bridesmaids, I totally support you covering yourself in tulle and fluff. Go for it."

Skye grinned, then hurried back to the dressing room. Seconds later two salespeople went scurrying into the back, no doubt to drag out a dozen or so dresses for her to try on.

Dana set down her herbal tea and stood. While she wanted her friend to be happy, the afternoon already seemed endless. She wasn't sure she could sit through more of the fashion show.

She headed outside, then stood on the sidewalk, under the awning, as a light misting rain chilled her. Izzy came out after her.

"You all right?" she asked.

"Yeah. I just needed some air."

Izzy's eyes darkened with concern. "Want to talk about it?"

The fact that it had been a week since Dana had gone back with Garth? A week of sleeping in a separate room, which he apparently didn't notice because he hadn't said a word. Hadn't tried to change her mind. Not that he was ever home, she thought grimly. She'd barely seen him. She knew he was avoiding her, what she didn't know was why.

Was he missing Fawn? Did he regret breaking up with her? Was he angry with himself? With Dana? Or was he just busy at the office? She couldn't bring herself to ask him. Mostly because she was afraid of the answer.

"Dana?"

She looked at her friend. "Sorry. I'm not feeling well."

"Flu sick or man sick?"

Dana shook her head. "Tell me the difference."

"That bad?"

"It's not bad, it's just…confusing."

Izzy touched her arm. "Lexi told me about what happened at that party. With Fawn and all."

Dana wasn't surprised. Lexi had been worried about her. She didn't mind Izzy knowing, even if she disliked being the object of concern. Or worse, pity.

"He has a past," she said firmly. "We all have pasts, right? His happens to be a little more complicated than most. It happens to have a problem with stealing, but what does that matter?"

"Are you afraid he's still in love with her?"

Trust Izzy to cut to the heart of the matter, Dana thought. "Maybe," she admitted.

"Because he's important to you."

"I don't want him to be. I tell myself he's just a guy. No better or worse than the others."

"Garth is many things, but he's not just a guy."

That's what terrified Dana the most. That he was different. So different that she couldn't protect herself from him. What if he hurt her and she couldn't ever recover?

Dana drew in a breath. "She was so beautiful. Seriously, alien beautiful. As if she wasn't completely human. I'll never be that. I'll never be anything like her."

"Do you want to be?" Izzy asked.

"No. But then I think I should wear makeup or dress better or cook. It's horrible. I'm turning into someone weak."

"Wanting to please someone isn't a sign of weakness—it's a sign of caring."

"I'm not changing my life for a man," Dana snapped.

"No one's asking you to."

"I know." She sighed. "It's me. The voices in my head saying I should nest and bond. What if I want to buy an apron? It'll be the death of hope."

Izzy grinned. "You'll never want to buy an apron."

"I want to buy eye shadow."

"You want to be pretty. You want Garth to think you're pretty."

All true, but still hard for her to hear. "I can't be who I am with him."

"Sure you can. Maybe you'll even figure out who you were supposed to be, if you hadn't spent so much time trying to make sure no one hurts you."

"Ouch."

Izzy's humor faded. "You know I love you."

"So that's your excuse for playing hardball?"

"It's okay to care about Garth."

"No, it's not. Caring means being vulnerable." It meant opening herself up and risking everything. She glanced back at the etched glass door. "Tell Skye I had to go, okay?"

She didn't wait for an answer. Instead she stepped into the rain and hurried toward her truck.

CHAPTER SIXTEEN

DANA RODE THE ELEVATOR UP to the penthouse, then unlocked the door. Before she'd put her purse on the table in the entryway, she knew she wasn't alone. Someone else was in the condo.

Silently, she pulled out her handgun, then eased the door closed behind her. She moved toward the hall, using the wall as cover. Deep breaths kept any apprehension at bay, while adrenaline sharpened her senses. Was it Jed? Or had he sent someone else?

"Dana?"

Garth's voice surprised her. She frowned at her watch. It was barely two in the afternoon. She shoved her gun into her purse and walked toward the living room. He stood by the window, facing the room.

"You're home early," she said. "Is everything all right?"

"No."

With the light behind him, it was difficult to see his face or read his expression. She couldn't tell what he was thinking. Not that she usually could.

"What happened?" she asked. "Is it Jed?"

"It's not Jed."

There was something strange about his voice. The tone was off, or maybe it was more the clipped way he formed the words. Uneasiness swept through her, making her stomach hurt.

She took a step toward him, then stopped. If she'd been someone else, she would have admitted he was scaring her. Not in a dangerous way but in an "I don't want to hear this" way.

"How long are you going to be mad at me?" he asked. "It's been a week and you're still pissed. Tell me how to fix that."

She blinked at him. He thought *she* was pissed? "You've been going to work early and staying late. You're barely talking to me."

"I was giving you space."

"For what?"

"To work out your feelings. You were mad."

She'd never been mad—not in the way he meant. She'd been hurt. Not that she would tell him that.

"I was upset," she admitted. A nice, neutral word. Not much risk there. "You asked me to come back, then you disappeared. I didn't know what to think."

He swore and moved toward her. When he stepped away from the window, she saw the concern in his eyes and maybe a little worry.

"I know this is complicated," he growled as he approached. "We're dealing with Jed and all he's doing. You're here against your will. There are—"

She put her hand on his arm. "I'm not here against my will."

"You didn't like the idea of moving in."

"Maybe, but that's very different than saying it's against my will."

His dark gaze locked with hers. "So you want to be here?"

Oh, God. Why did he have to ask that?

"I don't *not* want to be here."

"What the hell does that mean?" he demanded. "Dammit, Dana, do you think this is easy for me? I started this. If someone gets hurt, it's my fault. I didn't care before. It was easy. Bring down the Titans. But now it's different. Complicated. I have to worry about my sisters and you. Jed's come after you. What if he hurts you? What if something happens?"

He sounded almost panicked, which was oddly comforting.

"We'll deal," she told him.

"That's not good enough. And you've been mad."

"I'm not mad. I was giving *you* space." She sucked in a breath and risked a piece of the truth. "I thought you were upset about seeing Fawn again. That you had regrets about letting her go."

He grabbed both her arms and stared into her eyes. "I was never in love with Fawn."

"But she's so beautiful."

"Sure. If you don't mind waiting a couple of hours for her to get ready, it's a great show. But she also has a lot of problems and while I feel sorry for her, I'm not interested in spending the rest of my life worrying with her. I'm not that sensitive a guy. I'd screw it up. I need someone tough and strong and smart and determined. I need someone who can take me on and give as good as she gets."

Hope filled Dana. Dangerous, growing hope that made her want to believe he was talking about her.

"Good luck with that," she whispered.

"I don't need luck. I have you."

Maybe it was real or maybe it was just a line. She couldn't be sure, but for now, hearing was enough. She reached up to hug him. He wrapped his arms around her, pulling her hard against him.

They'd made love before, had kissed and touched and played in bed, but nothing they'd done had ever been this intimate. They hung on to each other for a very long time, as if neither wanted to be the first to let go. Finally she shifted back enough to be able to look into his eyes.

"I missed you," she whispered, exposing her heart one word at a time.

"I missed you more," he murmured, and then he kissed her.

"Maybe next time you could surprise me with something good," Dana muttered as she followed Lexi back into the bridal boutique.

"Like an afternoon on the shooting range?" Lexi asked.

"That would work."

Izzy was waiting for them inside, already sipping tea and looking both happy and beautiful. "Maybe I should have a big wedding," she said. "Get all fancy. Invite people I barely know, get presents."

Lexi patted her shoulder. "You're not really a wedding kind of person."

"I know, but every now and then I like to talk about a big ceremony. Just to watch Nick sweat."

"You have a mean streak," Dana murmured. "That makes me like you more."

"Then you shouldn't mind being here," Izzy said. "Because you like Skye, too."

"The things I do for my friends," Dana grumbled.

The manager of the salon rushed over and greeted them. She smiled vaguely at Dana before fawning over Lexi and Izzy. Lexi was immediately shown to a plush chaise and urged to relax.

"Does she get another foot massage?" Izzy asked. "I'd love a foot massage."

"You're not pregnant," Lexi said, relaxing into the soft cushions and sighing. "This is how I want to live my life."

"It *is* how you are living your life," Dana said.

"Lucky me." Lexi turned to Izzy. "Why don't you show her what we picked out? Then she can choose the least offensive one."

"Don't you want a say?" Dana asked, almost meaning it. She would actually prefer getting the final choice, but it seemed polite to offer the choice to Lexi.

Lexi put her hand on her belly. "All the ones she picked will do a great job covering this, so I'm good." She smiled at the petite dark-haired woman who approached. "Eva, I've missed you. And my swollen ankles have missed you more."

Izzy grabbed Dana's arm. "Come look. You should be happy. I went with black rather than red or green. I know it's a Christmas Eve wedding, but seriously, that color of green doesn't flatter anyone over the age of eight."

Although Skye had said no one had to dress up as her bridesmaid for her second wedding, all of them knew that she would love to have her sisters and Dana as part of the ceremony. Izzy had come up with the idea of surprising her at the wedding in matching dresses. Dana thought that idea was right up there with a root canal, but they were talking about Skye, whom she loved very much. Sacrifices would have to be made.

"Erin's dress is adorable," Izzy continued, leading Dana into a large dressing room and pointing at the dresses hanging along the wall. "I saw it earlier and chose elements for our dresses that would complement the style. I also picked what would look good with Skye's gown."

Dana pushed down a flash of guilt. The gown she hadn't stayed to see. So she wasn't really in a position to know which dress worked best.

Fortunately all the dresses Izzy had chosen looked pretty nice, considering they were bridesmaid dresses. They were long and simple. One had more ruffles than the other, one had lace, but none of them would make Dana gag.

Izzy pointed to the one on the left. "That one has the best shot at a second life," she said. "Chop it off at the knees, shorten the sleeves and you have a fancy cocktail dress."

Dana studied the dress in question. The black lace sleeves looked three-quarter. The top was beaded, but there wasn't any lace and the skirt hung fairly straight. No ruffles, no flounces.

"Can Lexi get into that one? Where would her stomach go?"

Izzy crossed to the dress and held out the sides. "There's a lot of material here and the empire waist means it's more flattering than most."

Dana would have agreed, had she known what an empire waist was. "Let's try it on," she said.

Five minutes later she stood in front of the big mirror in the main room. Lexi raised her herbal tea in salute. Eva had apparently worked her magic and left.

"You look nice. I like it. Can they get them here in time?"

Izzy nodded. "They're not custom. It's just a matter of calling other stores and getting them here. So what do you think?"

Dana stared at her reflection. Apparently an empire waist was one that sat up higher, just below her breasts. The dress was pretty and not so girly that it made her want to run screaming from the room.

"I like it. Are you sure Skye won't mind us wearing black?"

"She'll love it. Then we're agreed?" Izzy asked. "We'll get this and surprise Skye right before the wedding."

"Uh-huh." Lexi sipped her tea, her gaze intent. "Dana, are you all right?"

"Fine."

"You don't look fine. You look…tired. But not in a happy, I've-been-having-sex kind of way."

"Maybe I need a new moisturizer," Dana said. "Or highlights."

Lexi wrinkled her nose. "Don't toy with me. You'd never get highlights. But I think they'd look nice. Is something wrong?"

Dana glanced at Izzy, who shrugged. Dana didn't know if that meant Izzy hadn't told Lexi about their conversation the last time they'd been in the salon or if Izzy didn't know how to distract Lexi.

"Not wrong, exactly," Dana mumbled. "Just…confusing."

"How?" Lexi asked, lowering her voice. "This is about Garth, right?"

Dana shrugged. "Mostly."

"Because you're not running this time?" Lexi asked.

"I don't run."

"You don't stay," Izzy said. "It's practically the same thing. You pick guys who aren't interesting to you, then leave when you get bored. You go safe. Garth is anything but safe. Of course it's uncomfortable. You're stepping into the unknown."

"This is a good thing," Izzy said, coming up next to her. "The other guys were never what you wanted."

Dana really didn't like being the center of attention. "How do I know Garth is?"

"He's a step closer," Lexi said.

"And you know that how?"

Lexi smiled. "Because your eyes light up when you talk about him. Because he makes you crazy and you can't wait until you see him again. Because when the phone rings, there's only one person you want it to be."

Dana swallowed. She would never have thought to explain her relationship that way, but when Lexi said it, everything made perfect sense.

She leaned against the gilded chair by the chaise. "I'm confused," she admitted. "Some things are clear. I know he'll do whatever it takes to get the revenge he wants. But at the same time, I don't think he'd hurt any of you, anymore. So that's good, right? But it means he changed and I don't believe people change."

"Maybe you've been wrong," Izzy told her. "Stranger things have happened."

Dana nodded. "Maybe. I just…" She cleared her throat. "How much of what's going on is about me and him and how much of it is just about keeping me safe? Are we together or is it convenient?"

"Have you tried talking about this?"

Dana stared at her.

"Right," Lexi said. "Why would you do the rational thing?"

"Oh, please." Izzy rolled her eyes. "Because you discussed everything with Cruz while you were pretending to be engaged. There were no surprises, no misunderstandings."

Lexi sniffed. "I have no idea what you're talking about and that isn't the point. Dana, you should talk to Garth. Ask some of these questions."

"What if I don't like the answers?"

"What if you do?"

That almost scared her more, she thought, not wanting to admit it even to herself. "I'll wait until this is over," she said. "Right now he's too distracted. I wouldn't want to get in the way."

Izzy made a clucking sound.

Dana turned and glared at her. "You *so* want to take that back."

"Why?" Izzy put her hands on her hips. "I call 'em like I see 'em. You're scared. Taking down Jed could take weeks or months. Are you really going to wait that long to figure out what's going on?"

The only problem Dana had with that plan was admitting it to her friends. "There are other considerations."

Izzy rolled her eyes. "Name one."

"Izzy, stop," Lexi said.

They both looked at her.

Lexi smiled at Dana. "The problem isn't Garth's

busy, the problem is you don't want to know the answer to the question. If he's interested, you have to deal with an adult relationship with a man you can't control. You have to risk your heart and that's terrifying. If he's not interested, you're in trouble because you've passed the point where you can protect yourself. You're emotionally engaged and there's no win in that. At least from your perspective."

Dana stared at her friend. She heard a faint buzzing in her ears. She had a feeling that it was her protective wall crashing around her, leaving her fully exposed.

Izzy moved close and wrapped her arms around her. "Wow," she whispered. "Don't you hate it when Lexi gets it right?"

"More than you know." Dana hugged Izzy back. Lexi grabbed her hand.

Izzy drew back first. "Don't get mad, but are you in love with him?"

"I don't know."

"That's honest," Lexi said. "Could you be?"

"Maybe. I want to be sure."

"That doesn't happen," Izzy said. "I wish it did, but love requires a step of faith. Make that a leap."

"It's worth the risk," Lexi told her.

"It was for you." Dana squeezed her hand, then released it. "You don't know that it will be for me." Put it all out there for a man who may or may not be interested in her. "I want to believe," she said slowly. "But his world is too different. I don't know if I belong there."

Izzy shook her head. "Sorry, but it's not that complicated. You can belong if you want to. If he's worth it."

Is that what it came down to? Was Garth worth it? Or was she really afraid that the question on the table was more along the lines of her being worth it to him?

GARTH KNEW THAT DANA would get home after him. Something about Skye's wedding or dresses. He wasn't sure exactly, but he knew it wasn't a subject he wanted to talk about. Girl stuff.

He'd decided to surprise her with dinner from their favorite Italian restaurant. Mario, the head waiter, had given him easy instructions for heating the entrées. The salads would stay in the refrigerator until they were ready for them. He'd chosen a great bottle of wine and there was tiramisu for dessert.

She was back. Physically she'd been back for a while, but she wasn't…distant anymore, and he wanted to celebrate that.

There was something about her, he admitted to himself. Something challenging. She was unique. Not just because she never met a hair product she didn't hate, but also because she was stubborn and determined. She expected more of people and didn't mind letting them know. She was loyal and honest. He could trust her. There weren't a lot of people he trusted.

The phone rang. He reached for it, checking caller ID as he picked up the receiver. It was the front desk downstairs.

"You have a visitor, Mr. Duncan," George said. There was a pause, then when his voice came again, it was slightly muffled. As if he'd turned away. "It's Miss Applegate. Shall I send her up?"

Fawn? He glanced at his watch and calculated how much time he would reasonably have before Dana came back. "She can come up, George. Thank you."

He hung up the phone.

His first feeling was guilt—as if by inviting Fawn into his condo, he was doing something wrong. He reminded himself that Fawn was an ex-fiancée, that before the party he hadn't seen her in years and talking to her now meant nothing. Which was all true, but truth wasn't always a defense where women were concerned.

Fawn knocked on his door. He crossed to it and let her in.

She smiled as she entered, all big blue eyes and a slightly lost expression. "I wasn't sure you'd see me," she admitted as she set her designer bag on the table by the door.

"There's no reason not to," he told her. "Come on in."

She followed him into the living room, then crossed to the window before turning to face the room. "I like what you've done to the place."

He looked around. "Is it different?"

"Very. When you and I were together, you'd just bought it. Remember? It was all cold grays and blacks.

That guy who'd owned it before, he was a lawyer. He sure thought he had something to prove. Like everything had to be modern for anyone to think he was sophisticated."

Garth shrugged. "Maybe he had a point."

"This is better," she said. "Warmer. It has a homey feel."

"Thanks."

"You're welcome." She smiled. "You look good."

Not words he wanted to hear. "Fawn," he began.

She shook her head. "I know, I know. You don't have to freak out or anything."

"I don't make a habit of freaking out."

"So that hasn't changed, either?"

She stared at him with an intensity that could have left him shaken, if he hadn't known that lost-waif look was her trademark. That, her beauty, and a pedigree for the taking. There weren't any problems, unless you minded the stealing.

Looking at her, Garth wondered if they could have ever made each other happy. The marriage would have been more business deal than relationship, but that didn't mean it couldn't have worked. He'd never expected anything beyond what she'd offered. Had never thought about falling in love. His mother had, and look what had happened to her.

"You want to know why I'm here," she said into the silence.

"That would be nice."

"I wanted to say I'm sorry about what happened the other night. I came to apologize."

"You didn't do anything to me."

"Then to thank you. That woman who was with you—"

"Dana."

She nodded. "Dana. She was…intimidating."

"She has a way about her."

"Is she a cop?"

"Deputy."

She tilted her head. "And you're together?"

"Yes."

"I wouldn't have thought she was your type."

He thought about how Dana made him laugh and frequently threatened him. How she thought she was so damn tough, but she had a heart easily bruised. He thought about all she'd been through as a kid and how it had made her who and what she was today.

"My type has changed," he said.

"Oh. So there's no chance you'd want to go out to dinner, for old time's sake?"

An unexpected question. "I thought you were going back into treatment."

"I suppose. I'd rather not. I'd rather be with you." Fawn moved toward him. "It used to be good, Garth. Didn't it? Don't you remember?"

He stood his ground. "Not as much as you'd think."

She licked her lower lip. "I don't tempt you at all? I used to tempt you."

There were a lot of things he could say. That her father had offered him a massive sum of money, not to mention a company, to take her off his hands. That she would always look good on his arm and that she was the kind of woman who distracted other men and made doing business easier. But those would only hurt her.

"This isn't about you, Fawn. I'm with Dana. I want to be with Dana. You should go."

"But Garth, if you just gave me a chance…"

"Not tonight, honey, but it was really sweet of you to stop by."

The words came from behind him. Garth held in a groan. Did she always have to be so damned prompt? He turned and saw Dana standing by the door.

He ran the conversation over in his head. He knew he hadn't said anything wrong, but he was a man so there was every reason to think he was in a boatload of trouble.

"Hi," he said awkwardly. "Fawn stopped by."

"I see that." Dana smiled at the other woman. "Are you staying long?"

Fawn's expression turned wounded. She looked like a just-kicked puppy. Her wide eyes filled with tears. "I won't stay where I'm not wanted," she whispered, her voice thick with suffering. "I guess he's yours. You won."

"And here I didn't know there was a competition," Dana said, opening the door. "Have fun in rehab."

Fawn gave a little choked sob, then hurried out of the condo. The door closed, followed by the sound of a lock turning.

Garth wanted nothing more than to duck and cover. He told himself he'd absolutely, positively done nothing wrong. And still there was a sinking sensation in his gut.

Dana shook her head. "That woman needs to get a job at Walmart and learn what it's like to pay the bills in the real world. Only then will she have the slightest chance of becoming an actual person."

"She just stopped by."

"I heard."

"I didn't ask her to."

"I never thought you did."

He stared at her, not sure it was really going this well. "You can ask George."

"I don't have to. I believe you."

"Yeah?"

"You look hopeful," she said.

"I'm feeling hopeful. I didn't think… You're not mad?"

"No." She crossed to him. "What, exactly, did you see in her? Aside from the pretty? Okay, and the cultured. Tell me her father offered at least fifty million."

"It was more."

"You're an idiot."

He could live with the insult. "It seemed like a good idea at the time."

"And now?"

He touched her face, then kissed her. "I'm much smarter now."

"I thought so."

CHAPTER SEVENTEEN

DANA PERCHED ON THE EDGE of the guest-room bed and told herself she would be amazed. Enchanted, even. Delighted. Skye hung the long dress on a hook on the inside of the closet door, then pulled away the protective plastic covering.

"What do you think?" Skye asked anxiously.

The dress, actually it was a gown, glimmered in the afternoon light. It was ivory, silk—a fact Izzy had shared—and lightly beaded. The style was simple, an empire waist, with long sleeves and a full skirt. Dana could see Skye in it. The gown was totally her.

"You'll be beautiful," she said honestly. "I'm sorry I didn't stay to see you try it on."

"Don't worry. You can suffer through the fittings I'll have later this month," Skye teased. "And I appreciate you were willing to be there for part of the shopping experience. I know it's not your thing."

"I still feel bad," Dana said. "I was distracted and I shouldn't have been. It was your time."

Skye finished putting the cover back on the dress. "You can make it up to me."

"How?" Dana was cautious. More than cautious. She was worried. Wedding details were not her thing.

"I need help addressing the invitations."

Dana winced. "Why do I know this means more than putting on return address labels or stamps?"

"Calligraphy."

"That fancy writing?" Dana's stomach began to hurt. "You know I can't do that, right?"

Skye grinned, her green eyes dancing with laughter. "Don't panic. I'm not going to ask you."

"Good, because I don't want to learn how."

"It's pretty easy." Skye led the way out of the guest room. "There are special pens that help."

"I'll take your word for it."

They walked down the stairs and into the kitchen. Dana sniffed the air. Something delicious and spicy simmered on the stove.

"Do I want to know?" she asked.

"Carnitas."

"Am I invited to stay for dinner?"

"If you want. It would mean being away from Garth for a few hours."

Dana sighed. "For carnitas, I would suffer through the pain."

"I'm not sure Garth wants to hear that." Skye poured them each a cup of coffee.

Dana sat across from her at the kitchen table. "What's wrong?" she asked. "You're not glowing with happiness. Shouldn't you be?"

"I'm glowing on the inside," Skye said, then sighed. "I'm happy about Mitch. I love him more than I can say. Marrying him and being with him is everything I've ever wanted. But…"

"But?" Dana prompted. There was more. She could see it in the shadows behind the smile.

"I hate what's happening with Jed. He's our father. He should be here with us. We should be working together. Instead we're trying to bring him down because he nearly killed his own daughter. Why does it have to be like this?"

"Because Jed wants to win at any cost, although if it helps, I don't think he was trying to kill Izzy." She told Skye what Jed had said at the party a few weeks ago.

Skye listened, then sighed. "So he might not have been trying to kill her, but it was okay if she or anyone else got hurt? What a guy."

She frowned. "And what he did to Garth and Kathy? I still can't wrap my mind around it."

"I know." Dana hesitated. "But maybe there's more to it than what Garth told us."

"I'm not sure we'll ever find out," Skye said. "Jed confirmed the facts, but won't give us any details and Kathy can't."

"I'm sorry this is all such a mess."

"Don't be. You're one of the few things keeping me sane—knowing I can count on you means a lot.

"I'm getting married," Skye whispered. "I want to

tell my father. I want him to be happy for me. But that's never going to happen. He doesn't care." Tears filled her green eyes. "I thought my dad would walk me down the aisle. I was wrong."

Dana wanted to writhe in her seat. She hated seeing anyone she cared about suffering, especially when she couldn't fix the problem. While she would never want to see her father again, she understood Skye's ambivalence. Knowing Jed was the bad guy was one thing—putting that thought into practice was another.

She remembered Skye's first marriage. It had been a huge society event, with half a dozen bridesmaids and a horse-drawn carriage. The ceremony had been held in a big church in town, followed by a reception at Glory's Gate. Over half a dozen senators had attended, along with a former president. People had talked about the party for weeks.

This time was different. This time Skye was marrying out of love rather than duty. This time everything was the way *she* wanted it and not because of how it would play in the papers. But not having Jed walk her down the aisle would still leave a hole in the day.

"Ask Garth," she said without thinking.

Skye blinked at her. "What?"

Second thoughts crowded in, but Dana ignored them. "Ask Garth to walk you down the aisle. He's your older brother. Doesn't that count?"

"I hadn't thought of that. Do you think he'd do it?"

What Dana thought was that he was so going to

want to kill her. She refused to feel the least bit of apprehension. He owed her for being so understanding about Fawn's visit. "I think he'd have a hard time telling you no," she said honestly.

"Not exactly a rousing endorsement," Skye said with a laugh. "But good enough. I'll call and ask him."

"You should."

Skye's humor faded. "How did we get here?" she asked, tears returning to her eyes. "He's our father. He's supposed to love us."

"A lot of people don't like following the rules," Dana said, thinking of her own father. "Jed's one of them."

"We have to do this. We have to put him in jail. He can't be trusted. Who knows who he'll come after next. Erin, maybe. Or Lexi's baby." She held on to the coffee mug with both hands, but didn't drink. "I never wanted it to be like this. What happens when Mitch and I have a baby? He or she will never know who Jed is. He'll just be a name, not a grandfather."

"Do you think he cares about that?" Dana asked gently.

"No. He doesn't. But knowing that doesn't make me hurt any less."

"I'm sorry."

"It's not your rock, as Fidelia would say. It's mine." She shrugged. "So much that has happened over the past few months has been unexpected. Lexi meeting Cruz, Izzy meeting Nick. Me falling in love with Mitch all over again. And Garth."

"He's a stunner," Dana said dryly.

"Now you're being sarcastic."

"I don't mean to be."

"Then tell me what you really think about him."

Trapped, Dana thought grimly. Trapped with no-where to go. "I think he's complicated."

"And?"

"And he looks good in a suit."

Skye wrinkled her nose. "That's not an answer. Are you in love with him?"

Dana wanted to throw herself out of the nearest window. "Do you have to ask it like that? Don't you want to at least lead up to the question?"

Skye smiled. "Are you?"

"I don't know," she yelled, pushing back her chair and coming to her feet. "I don't know what I think about him. Being with him is hard—maybe the hardest thing I've ever done. Not because I question him, although I do that plenty, but mostly because I question myself. Am I good enough? Am I different enough? Am I too different? I hate feeling like I have to be worthy."

"You're plenty worthy. Garth is lucky to have you."

Loyal words spoken by a loyal friend.

"Is he?" Dana asked, sitting down again. "What do I bring to the table?"

"You're wonderful. Funny and smart and caring. You're brave and feisty."

"Feisty isn't always a good thing."

"Why not?"

"Because it requires effort and from what I've seen, most people don't bother with anything that's too hard."

Skye sipped her coffee. "Loving Mitch is easy," she admitted. "Although being with him can be a challenge. Is loving Garth easy?"

"Do you think you're being subtle?" Dana asked. "Because you're not."

"Yeah, yeah. You don't impress me. Answer the question."

Was loving Garth easy? The implication being she did love him.

"Loving him would take me places I don't want to go," she admitted.

"Meaning?"

"I would have to let him in."

"But haven't you already? You live with him, Dana."

Dana held her breath. Was Garth already inside of her, making a place for himself in her heart?

She'd always been so careful not to get involved with someone who could really touch her, really hurt her. She didn't want that. Not the pain or the risk. She wanted to be safe, even if that meant always being alone.

But while she wasn't looking, something else had happened. Something significant. Something that made her want to take a chance and try flying—as if love really had given her wings.

"Maybe," she whispered. "Maybe I do love him."

Skye didn't say anything.

Dana turned the words over in her mind. She wasn't running screaming from the room. That was something. Did she love Garth? Was it possible? A few days ago, with Izzy and Lexi, she hadn't known, but now, everything was different. Clearer, somehow.

"I love him," she said slowly. "I love Garth."

Skye grinned. "Wow. I never thought I'd hear you say those words."

"Then we're even, because I never thought I'd say them."

"When are you going to tell him?" Skye asked.

"When hell freezes over."

"Why? You should tell him."

"No, thanks. I like my disappointment in small doses."

"Because you think he doesn't love you back?"

"Well, duh."

"He does. Dana, you're amazing."

"You *have* to say that. You love me."

"And it's very possible Garth does, too. Someone has to be the one to risk it all. Someone has to be the first one to put it on the line."

"That someone can be him."

Skye shook her head. "I thought you were strong."

"There's a big difference between strong and foolish. I like to keep on the right side of that line."

"You're really not going to say anything?"

"Isn't it enough that I'm willing to tell you?"

"That is something," Skye admitted. "But it would be better if you'd tell him."

"Better for everyone but me."

"At least think about it."

Dana groaned. "For about sixteen seconds. Then I'll be done."

"It's a start." Skye grinned again. "Soon we'll have you caring about your shoes."

"Did I mention the hell freezing over part?"

"Yes, but I wasn't listening."

GARTH PACED THE LENGTH of Lexi's office, but walking didn't make him any more comfortable. Part of the reason was the space itself. Her office was in her day spa. It was done in rich colors and textured fabric. While it was a functional space, it was way too fussy for him. And there were bowls of stuff that smelled everywhere.

But it wasn't just being in a totally female space that had him feeling ready to jump out of his skin. It was the material Lexi was reading. Or rather her reaction to it.

"This is everything?" she asked, looking up from the list he'd detailed.

He'd barely spent an hour putting the list together, but it had taken him the better part of a week to decide if he was going to give it to her. Talk about handing over the last weapon to the enemy. Except Lexi wasn't his enemy and she wouldn't use the information as a weapon. Something he kept telling himself but wasn't sure he believed.

"Impressive," she said, leaning back in her chair. "Are you going to keep pacing or do you plan to sit somewhere?"

"I'll be pacing for a while."

She smiled. "Because you're nervous."

"You could hang me with that."

She touched the paper. On it he'd listed everything he'd done to the Titan family. From the callable note he'd offered to her, to the false tip about Skye's foundation being a front for money laundering. Some of the things on the list had come from facts he'd dug up—like Jed being involved in illegal arms shipments. But for every fact, there were dozens of rumors. Acts designed to hurt.

"I won't take this to the police," she said.

"I know."

"Then why won't you sit down?"

He shrugged. "Trust doesn't come easy to me."

She pulled out her own list of what had happened, then handed both to him. "You look them over," she said. "By comparing them, we can figure out what Jed has done. I'm going to guess it's a lot more than we think."

"But you asked me to prepare the list," he said, not sure what she was doing. "Don't you want to keep it?"

"No. I wanted you to put it together, but it doesn't

matter who does the comparison. Obviously you'd be more comfortable if it was you." She smiled. "I'm not out to get you, Garth. Not anymore."

He moved toward her desk, then took a seat opposite. "Okay."

Her smile widened. "You don't sound convinced."

"That'll take a minute."

"You're such a guy."

"That's the rumor." He leaned back in his seat. "We're getting close. It's just a matter of time until Jed is forced into a corner. There's no going back."

"What makes you think I want to?"

"I'm checking. I talked to Skye."

Lexi's smile faded. "She's upset about what we're doing."

"So she said." His conversation with his sister had been long and rambling, but a few key points had been painfully clear.

"Her relationship with Jed is different," Lexi told him. "She lived at Glory's Gate longer. She acted as his hostess for years. I think she believed that would protect her. Not that it was why she did it. Skye loves Jed. We all do. But for a long time, it seemed she had more to lose."

Until Jed had turned on Skye, threatening to have her declared an unfit mother and thrown into a mental hospital. All because she wasn't willing to do what he said.

"She wants Jed taken down," Lexi continued. "But

the idea of having to be a part of destroying him doesn't make her happy."

"She can back out."

"She won't. He nearly killed Izzy. Skye protects those she loves. She's tougher than she looks."

All the Titan sisters were, he thought. Tough and beautiful and strong. Not to mention stubborn. "Did she, ah, mention anything about the wedding?" he asked, trying to sound casual and not sure he succeeded.

"What do you mean?" Lexi's blue eyes widened slightly.

"The ceremony."

"It's on Christmas Eve, at Mitch's house. You're coming, aren't you?"

Garth narrowed his gaze. "You already know."

The grin returned. "That Skye asked you to walk her down the aisle? She might have mentioned something."

He swore softly, then pushed to his feet. "What was she thinking? I can't do that. I'm not the right guy. There has to be someone else. A friend of the family. Someone."

He'd been sure that nothing could ever surprise him again. He planned nearly every part of his life, worked hard, understood the risks and outcomes. Then Skye had called and asked him to walk her down the aisle. Like he was…was…like he was family.

"She wants you," Lexi told him. "You're her brother."

Technically. "It can't be me," he said and started pacing again. When he got to the far end of the room, he noticed a damn bamboo plant in the corner. Was everything in this stupid place renewable?

"Did you hear what Izzy said?" Lexi asked. "She wants you in the family, Garth. Apparently you're not objecting too much, since you're here."

"This is different."

"It's what the bride wants. Are you going to tell her no?"

He turned and glared at Lexi, but didn't speak. Tell Skye no? Hardly. The last thing he wanted was to make her cry or something. But why did she have to ask? Walk her down the aisle. He'd never done anything like that.

"Do I have to say anything?" he asked.

Lexi's mouth twitched, but this time she didn't smile. "I believe the minister asks who gives the bride in marriage and you say 'I do.' It's not a speech."

"She's old enough to walk herself," he muttered.

"Maybe, but that's not the point."

"Fine. I'll do it."

"Ever gracious."

"You think this is funny."

"Yes, and I'm enjoying every minute of it. Oh, and consider this your invitation to Christmas at my house. Cruz and I are hosting. We start early with breakfast." She hesitated. "Kathy would be welcome, too."

Kathy at a Titan Christmas? There was irony.

"I'm not pushing," Lexi added. "I don't know if the crowd would frighten her or not. She's met most of us."

Now it was his turn to hesitate. "She usually goes to a special program Christmas morning. It's through one of the churches."

"Then maybe dinner? We're one of those families who has a big meal around two."

"That she could make."

"Good. We'd love to have you both." The smile returned. "And I'll give you a sisterly warning. There are lots of presents under our tree. They're not always fancy, but they are plentiful. Everything from socks to sticky notes to chocolates. Usually one or two special gifts. I've seen the wrapped pile in Cruz's closet, so I happen to know I'm in for a spoiling. Both Nick and Mitch have called me for suggestions, so I know they'll be overdoing it. I'm not saying you have to participate, but if you don't want Dana to feel left out, you might want to get her something."

Because he would be spending Christmas with Dana. She would be part of the Titan celebration. And they were together. Involved. Whatever the hell that meant.

Was it him, or was it getting hot in here? He resisted the urge to loosen his tie. Damn.

"There's the face of a man looking to bolt," Lexi said. "Want to tell me why?"

"I don't make a big deal about Christmas," he said. "I see Kathy and then I go away."

"That sounds lonely."

"I go to five-star resorts and stay in the best room in the hotel. There are plenty of parties and women." It was his world—a world he liked very much.

"Still sounds lonely."

It had been, not that he would admit that to her. But he'd accepted the feelings. Or rather he'd ignored them. Because being by himself meant being in control.

"I didn't spend Christmas with Fawn when we were engaged."

"Hmm, that's pretty telling, but not relevant here. Don't think you can escape us, Garth. We're your sisters. We'll hunt you down and make you beg for mercy."

It wasn't just them, he thought. It was Dana. It was the image of them waking up together on Christmas morning. Of coffee in front of a tree and opening presents. He could get her something lacy and sexy in red velvet and lace. She would hate it and mock him, but then she would put it on.

He imagined her in that and then he thought about her in diamonds and nothing else. He could see them together and that scared him more than his months of being tortured in the jungle.

"No," he said, taking a step back.

"Men," Lexi said with a sigh. "Take a deep breath. Everything will be fine. You're worried because you're falling in love with her and you're not the kind of man who does that easily. It's okay. She's prickly, too. You can take it slow. It's probably better if you do."

She kept talking, but he wasn't hearing anything else. He was stuck back on "you're falling in love with her."

The panic was as ready and immediate as the passion had been. Love? No way in hell. Not him, not ever.

"I don't love her," he said flatly.

Lexi looked more pitying than surprised. "It's okay, Garth."

"It's not. If that's what you all think, you're wrong. I don't love Dana. I don't do love. Ever."

He spoke with a certainty that left no room for doubt, Dana thought as she paused just outside Lexi's office. She'd been in the area and had stopped by to have lunch with her friend. She'd been happy enough to risk sticks and twigs passing for bread and something vaguely slimy made into a sandwich. She'd wanted to talk about her newly discovered feelings for Garth and maybe, just maybe, have someone show her how to wear eye makeup. She'd been floating with hope and promise because she was in love for the first time in her life.

In love with a man who obviously wasn't going to love her back.

GARTH WALKED INTO THE Titan World building. It was one of those great, old high-rises, with old-fashioned elevators and murals in the lobby.

His mother had brought him here when he'd been

ten or eleven. She'd never said why. As they often drove to interesting buildings in the city, he hadn't thought anything of it. Not until he'd found out that Jed Titan was his father.

He looked around at the grand old structure. Ever since Jed had kicked him out on his ass nearly twenty years before, he'd promised himself one day he would own every inch of this place. Now that the day was nearly here, he waited for the feeling of accomplishment and elation. Surprisingly, there was only a faint sense of disappointment—he'd thought Jed Titan would be a more worthy opponent.

He crossed to the guards and got a visitor pass, then made his way to the executive floor. Jed's office was in the back. It would be the grandest, with the best view. The building was worth saving, Garth thought as he approached Jed's assistant. It would survive even as the Titan empire crumpled around it.

He gave the woman his name, then added, "I don't have an appointment, but he'll see me."

She looked doubtful, but picked up her phone. "There's a Mr. Garth Duncan here to see you, sir." She paused, then nodded. "Of course." When she hung up, she pointed to the closed door. "Mr. Titan will see you now."

The last time Garth had been in Jed's office, Garth had been all of fourteen. He'd come to beg for his mother's life. He hadn't wanted to go to the old man, but there hadn't been anyone else with enough money to save Kathy. He'd been young enough to assume that when someone asked for help, he got it. He'd never thought that Jed would tell him no.

Now, as he crossed the thick carpet to the man who was his father, he remembered being stunned when Jed had refused him. He'd tried explaining again, thinking that the other man simply hadn't understood. He hadn't made his case well enough. Then Jed had interrupted him, saying Kathy's brain tumor wasn't his problem and that if Garth didn't leave, he would have security throw him out on the street. Jed made it clear he would have Garth arrested if he ever showed up again.

Time bent and blurred. For a second Garth wasn't sure if this was the past or present, then decided it didn't matter. The journey had been long and hard, but he had finally won.

"I'm glad you stopped by," Jed said from his place behind his big desk. "I'm celebrating." He pulled out a box of cigars and offered one.

Garth shook his head. "Why?"

"Did you see the closing price of the stock? Titan World is up nearly fifteen percent."

"You're buying shares, I'm buying shares," Garth said. "The stock market likes it when shares are in demand."

Jed picked up a cigar and sniffed it appreciatively. "You gave me a good run, son. I'll give you that. You're a slick player and a worthy opponent. With a little more seasoning, you might have had a chance."

"You think you're winning?" Garth asked, amused.

"Sure. Even with the recent jump in prices, the rumors have caused the price to drop enough that I'm buying up double and triple the amount of shares I could have picked up three weeks ago. In a couple of days I'll own enough to drive you out. You shouldn't have offered me the loan. But I suppose you couldn't help yourself. It took you full circle. You started by offering Lexi money and you end it by offering it to me."

Garth took a seat. "But here's the part that confuses me," he said. "You've spent more than I've loaned you."

"You're not the only one interested in helping me, Garth. I still have friends. With a loan from a few of them, I have the cash I need to buy back Glory's Gate. So call the note any time you want. I'm covered."

Garth pulled a piece of paper out of his jacket pocket and passed it over to Jed. "Would these be the friends and the amounts? I'm asking because I know they've all promised you money, but they haven't given it to you yet. And I'm thinking they're not going to. I do business with every one of them. Once they got word of your illegal dealings, they weren't so anxious to be associated with you. Still, they were willing to do me a favor by pretending they were. Those loans you're depending on? They're not coming, Jed. And tomorrow, when the Securities and Exchange Commission expects you to make good on your stock purchases, you're going to have a problem."

Jed's face went white. He sprang to his feet, knocking over the box of cigars. "You goddamn sonofabitch," he yelled. "What the hell have you done?"

"Won," Garth said simply. He put another piece of paper on the table. "I'm calling the note on Glory's Gate. You have seventy-two hours to come up with the cash or the entire property is mine."

"Fucking bastard." Jed's face twisted with rage. "I'll kill you. I swear, I'll kill you."

"Hard to do from prison," Garth said as he stood. "You should have paid for her surgery, Jed. The money wouldn't have mattered that much to you, but it would have saved her. I would have watched your back for the rest of my life."

"You think I care about that? You were some kid. You didn't matter to me."

"I do now," he said and then he left.

CHAPTER EIGHTEEN

DANA DROVE FROM LEXI'S office to her own empty apartment. It was the only place she could think to go where no one would bother to look for her. It was a place to be alone. A thousand thoughts swirled through her brain, but the only one that mattered was that the pain wasn't as bad as she thought it would be.

She'd thought she wouldn't be able to breathe, that her entire body would ache, that she would want to cry but couldn't. There was almost nothing. As if every part of her was numb. Maybe it was.

She walked into her apartment and checked each of the rooms. Everything was as it should be, if a little colder. She'd turned down the heat before moving in with Garth. Now she checked the small bathroom and the kitchen, all the windows, then ran out of things to do. Standing alone in the middle of her kitchen, she accepted the truth. Life was nothing, if not consistent. Lead with your heart and you'll get hit over and over again.

Later, she would go back to the condo and see Garth. She would pretend that nothing was wrong and he

would let her. Or maybe he wouldn't know the difference. He didn't know what she'd heard. He didn't
know that she loved him. She'd spent her whole life
protecting herself only to fall for someone who would
never love her back. Talk about irony. Jed would be delighted.

Dana leaned against the counter and kept her breathing steady. If she focused on her breathing, she wouldn't
feel the growing emptiness in her heart. She wouldn't
notice the hollow place in her chest or the ache in her
soul. If she worried about standing and not collapsing
or screaming, she would be too busy to admit how
much she'd lost.

It wasn't like with her father, she told herself. That
was something. Garth would never hurt her on purpose.
He didn't know she'd been standing there to hear his
damning words. He'd been good to her, someone she
could trust with just about everything but her heart.
What made it so hard was how long it would take to
heal.

She told herself that eventually she would appreciate that at least she'd put herself out there. She'd
given it her all. That hadn't been enough, but at least
she hadn't held back. She'd gone kicking and screaming into the relationship, but eventually she'd made it.
She'd fallen in love with Garth and lived to talk about
it.

She'd also learned a lot. She'd learned that love
wasn't easy or fair. That she didn't get to pick who

would be the one. Garth was an amazing man. She was grateful for the time they'd spent together and would enjoy whatever was left. And then she would leave.

She wasn't the type to make a scene, or worse, beg. He didn't know what she'd heard and she wouldn't tell him. As far as he was concerned, nothing had changed. They'd established the rules together—she'd been the one to break them.

Oh, but it hurt. The sense of loss devastated her. Hopes and dreams she hadn't known she had crowded around her, making her ache for what could have been. For Garth and the life they could have had together.

Her eyes burned and it took a second for her to figure out what that meant. Tears. Foolish tears.

"I'll save them for later," she said aloud. For when it was really over. Then she would cry and eventually tell her friends what had happened. She would figure out a way to move on with her life. She would heal and be better for the experience.

All words that sounded so great. If only she had a clue as to how to make it happen.

But whatever the outcome, she'd learned a lot in the past few months and she had changed. Eventually, when she healed, she would start over. No more safe guys. No more boring men who didn't challenge her. She would find someone who could be important to her, not just someone who was convenient. Assuming she ever wanted to risk her heart again. Right now, that didn't seem possible.

She left her apartment and drove back to the condo. It was nearly dark. The ride up in the elevator seemed to go by too fast. As if time had started to speed up. She wanted to slow everything down, to make the minutes she had left crawl. She wanted to savor every second with Garth.

He was already home. She knew it the minute she put the key in the lock and pushed open the door. Lights were on. Soft music played. Garth stood in the center of the room, looking both pleased and a little uncomfortable. For a second she thought he knew she'd been outside the room when he'd told Lexi he would never love her, but then he held open his arms.

She walked into his embrace and hugged him. As she held on to him, she breathed in the scent of him. She needed to remember as much as she could so that when this was over, she would have the memories forever. Maybe that was a sign of weakness, but she didn't care. She loved Garth—she didn't want to forget anything about being with him. She might not get him forever, but at least she had him for now. There was still time.

He stepped back and touched her cheek. "You all right?" he asked.

"Sure. Why?"

He studied her. "I'm not sure. There's something."

She forced a smile. "I'm fine. What about you?"

"I just had a meeting with Jed."

"Did I know about that?"

"No. I've been working on a few things." His dark eyes crinkled slightly. "Some I haven't mentioned because you wouldn't approve."

So typical, she thought fondly. "We discussed you not breaking the law."

"I'm not, but there's gray area and you don't need to know the details."

Because he would look out for her. Because despite not loving her, he cared about her.

"It's a long story, but the bottom line is he has seventy-two hours to come up with a lot of money. If he doesn't, and he won't, I'll own it all. The company and Glory's Gate."

So fast? But she'd thought they would have more time. Seventy-two hours? And then what? If he was already confronting Jed, then it was nearly over.

"He can't have been happy," she murmured, hoping he couldn't read the shock in her eyes.

"He wasn't. Things are going to get ugly. Everyone has to be careful, especially you. He came after you before."

"I'll be fine."

"No crazy stunts."

She managed a genuine smile. "Not my style."

"I don't know. You can be pretty wild." He touched her cheek again. "I've spoken with everyone. Skye's taking Erin to school and back rather than letting her ride the bus. Cruz won't let Lexi out of his sight. Izzy and Nick will cover each other. It's seventy-two hours and then we're done."

Three days and then it was over. She would return to her life. Go back on duty. Pick up the pieces and try to forget what it had been like to be in Garth's world. To love him and have him with her, wanting her.

"I hope everything goes well," she said.

"Me, too. Jed is cornered and he's going to lash out."

"What about your mom? Kathy's protected, right?"

"Yes. There's a guard watching round the clock, and I've spoken to her caretakers. They're being extra careful. By this time next week, everything will go back to the way it was."

"Lucky us," Dana said softly, reminding herself to ignore the impending doom. She would cry later, when she was alone. When Garth had moved on and their relationship was in the past.

GARTH OPENED DANA'S car door, then closed it behind her. As they walked up to Cruz's house, he took her hand. While he knew in his head that everything was fine, he kept having a nagging sensation that something was wrong. It wasn't doom exactly—more like a low-grade worry. He was a man who always took care of details. After years of planning, he was finally going to take down Jed. It made sense that he would want everything to go well.

"Do you know what this is about?" he asked as he rang the bell.

"No. Izzy said we were all getting together for

dinner and that saying no wasn't an option." She grinned. "That's Izzy. Always a gracious hostess."

Nick opened the door. "You made it," he said with a laugh. "Come on in."

They walked into the house. Nick gave Dana a quick kiss on the cheek, then pulled Garth into a bear hug.

"It's good to see you," Nick told him.

Garth returned the embrace. "You, too," he said, appreciating that their friendship had been nearly restored. "You're in a good mood."

"I know."

Nick led the way into the kitchen where Cruz and Lexi and Mitch and Skye already waited. Izzy poked around in the refrigerator. She straightened as they approached.

"You made it," she said happily. "We're all together. It's practically a greeting-card moment. I'm just digging out some cheese. Skye informed me appetizers are expected. I was excited that I remembered to get food for dinner, but apparently she has higher standards."

He and Dana greeted everyone else. While Izzy put out cheese and crackers, the women gathered around to help. Nick and Garth joined Mitch and Cruz.

"It's been pretty quiet," Cruz was saying. "I'm surprised. I thought Jed would come after all of us."

"He's scrambling for money," Garth told him. "I've heard that he's going everywhere, but no one is willing to take a risk on him. Everyone knows I'm buying up large blocks of shares. With his own daughters also buying a piece of the pie, people know he's about to lose control. No one bets on a sinking ship."

"As long as we stay safe," Mitch said.

"Tell me about it." Cruz grimaced. "At least Lexi isn't interested in taking any risks. As slow as she moves these days, she would be a prime target."

Garth knew the conversation was important, but he found himself distracted by watching Dana from across the room. She laughed at something Izzy said. The sound carried to him, making him want to pull her close to him. Not to protect her but because being near her made him feel good.

She turned her head and the light caught the different colors of brown in her hair. She was so beautiful. He'd thought she was pretty and sexy as hell, but now, as he stared at the shape of her mouth and the curve of her cheekbones, he saw how stunning she was. Maybe because one was lit by what was inside of her and that took a while to be visible.

His gaze drifted to Lexi and Skye, then to Izzy. His family. How curious. He'd begun this journey with every intention of destruction. Instead he'd found a place to belong. They'd dragged him into their world. Or as Izzy had promised, they'd loved him into being a part of them. The irony was if he hadn't set out to ruin them all, they never would have found their way to each other.

Izzy and Nick exchanged a look, then Nick walked to the refrigerator and pulled out a bottle of champagne.

"We want to thank you all for coming," Izzy said. "We would have had you out to the ranch, but it's a long drive and someone should be using Lexi's kitchen."

"Hey," her older sister said from her seat by the round table. "I cook. Sometimes. I think it's a personal choice. It's not like you know your way around anything more complicated than a toaster oven."

"True," Izzy said. She pointed at the champagne bottle. "Where are the glasses?"

"I'll get them," Cruz said, walking to a cupboard and opening it. "What are we celebrating?"

Izzy looked at Nick, who said, "They're your family. You tell them."

Izzy reached into her jeans front pocket and pulled out a diamond band, then slid it on her left ring finger. "Nick and I got married yesterday."

The news was followed by silence, then a shriek from Skye and Lexi. Both descended on Izzy, as did Dana. There was a girl hug, while the guys all slapped Nick on the back and shook his hand.

Garth went last. Nick looked at him. "You always said you owed me for pulling you out of that damn jungle. Because of you, I met Izzy. We're even now."

Garth nodded, mostly because his throat was a little tight. He must have allergies or be getting a cold, he thought, hugging his friend again. "Bringing you two together was my plan all along," he joked.

"Right." Nick grinned. "Who knew?"

Champagne was poured. There was a bottle of

sparkling cider for Lexi, who grumbled about missing out on the fun.

"We're not really big wedding people," Izzy told them. "We'd talked about waiting, mostly so everyone would be focused on Skye and Mitch's wedding. But then we were talking and…"

"It's my fault," Nick said. "I insisted."

Izzy snuggled close to him. "He didn't have to insist. I love him and want to be with him. We're very happy. We saw a judge yesterday and now it's official."

Nick kissed the top of her head.

Garth watched them. Their happiness was visible. He was delighted everything had worked out, not only because Nick was his friend but because he'd come to care for Izzy. She was wild and exactly what Nick needed. At the same time, she would be there for him. They were a good match.

His gaze drifted to Dana, who looked excited by the news. She glanced up and saw him. Their eyes met. He felt the connection run between them. For a second he wanted to go to her and hold her, or at least be near her.

"There's more," Izzy said with a shrug. She set down her champagne glass and picked up a second one filled with sparkling cider. "I'm pregnant." She looked at Lexi. "I didn't want you getting all the attention."

Lexi stood and hugged her. "That is just so typical."

Izzy hugged her back. "You know I'm kidding, right? The baby wasn't planned."

"In this family, they rarely are," Lexi told her.

"Now I want a baby," Skye said, joining them.

Garth looked at Mitch, who looked both pleased and terrified.

Dana clutched her glass and took a step back. "Just in case it's contagious," she murmured.

Cruz laughed. "You'll get there."

"Maybe," she said.

Garth noticed she was careful not to look at him. Why? Because she would never want a child with him? Because she didn't want children at all? He didn't know her feelings on the subject, mostly because they'd never talked about it. They'd never talked about anything beyond the moment.

Why was that? Most of the women he knew were anxious to label everything. To discuss their feelings and plan for the future. Why didn't Dana?

"How far along are you?" Lexi asked, sitting back down.

"About two months."

"This is so cool. Our kids will be less than a year apart."

"I know." Izzy eyed Skye and Dana. "You two had better get busy if you want to keep up."

"Apparently." Skye looked meaningfully at Mitch. "Talk about pressure."

He put his arm around her waist and kissed her. "I'm completely up to anything you want."

"Good."

Dana took another step back. "So what about those Cowboys? Aren't they having a great season?"

"You're not hearing any ticking sound?" Izzy asked. "No 'tick tock' in the background?"

"I don't hear a thing," Dana said.

"There's no need to pressure anyone," Lexi said briskly. "Izzy, this is about you and Nick. We're all happy for you. Now knowing you as I do, I'm sure even though you eloped, you'll want to register for wedding gifts."

Izzy grinned. "I hadn't thought of that, but sure." She grabbed Nick's arm. "We can get some fancy china."

Conversation continued to flow. Garth was fairly sure he was the only one who had noticed the subtle conversation shift. Lexi hadn't wanted to let Izzy pursue the subject of Dana having a baby and he knew why. The obvious assumption would be that they were a couple and he the most likely candidate for the father. But after what he'd told Lexi in her office the other day, she knew that wasn't going to happen.

He wanted to take her aside and tell her it wasn't as bad as he'd made it out to be. Dana was special. More than that. He liked being with her. He liked her. And that didn't happen often enough in his world. But love and babies? It wasn't a place he'd ever planned to go. He'd always assumed he would have a marriage of convenience. One that was more business deal than romantic match. Lexi's claim that he was falling for Dana had thrown him. More than that, it had terrified him and he wasn't a man who easily admitted to fear.

Love. No. He knew what love did. He'd seen what it did to his mother. The only reason she'd stopped loving Jed Titan was because a surgeon had physically cut out that part of her brain. Otherwise, she would still be missing him. Not that she'd ever talked about it or admitted her feelings. When he'd encouraged her to go out and find someone, she'd always said she'd fallen in love once and that was plenty. Her heart could only belong to one man. The same man who hadn't bothered to help when she'd needed him most.

He wasn't willing to go there. Wasn't willing to risk that much. The price of love was too high.

He watched Dana laughing with Izzy. He wanted her and needed her, but love? It was impossible.

JED SAT IN THE FRONT seat of his car, drinking whiskey. The noon sun was bright in the big Texas sky. It was a perfect late-fall day—crisp and clear. Around him the storefronts in Titanville had been dressed for Christmas. Lights and garland circled every window and door. Bells rang and carols played in the town square. It was a little piece of paradise.

Normally he enjoyed strolling through Titanville. Everyone knew him and respected him. He'd worked hard for that respect. There were those who thought he'd had it easy, but they were wrong. Sure, he'd been born a Titan and that was saying something, but he hadn't simply accepted what God had given him. Jed had taken a good-sized fortune and grown it into something impressive. He'd expanded the company, made a name for himself. He could walk into any restaurant in Dallas and get the best table. Senators and heads of state wanted to be seen with him. He'd lived the kind of life that made most men envious. He'd had it all…until Garth Duncan had decided to take it from him.

Jed took another sip from the bottle. He was a little drunk, but not so drunk that he couldn't imagine how good it would feel to destroy Garth. To hurt him in ways he hadn't known were possible. Jed had never hated anyone as much as he hated his own bastard son. Garth was going down. The little shit might think he'd won, but he was wrong. Dead wrong.

Jed screwed the top back on the bottle, then stuck it in the paper bag on the passenger seat. He got out of the car and walked up the street, joining a group of kids walking together. He trailed behind, looking like a parent making sure everyone stayed safe.

They passed the Titanville Pet Palace. The windows had been painted in bright colors. Santa drove a train and all the open cars had pets in them. Puppies and kittens and birds and lizards. There was a man standing next to the door. He was tall and maybe fifty. Ex-cop, Jed thought grimly.

Jed had dressed carefully, in a cowboy hat, sunglasses, a biker jacket and worn boots. He could have been anyone.

He glanced toward the kids still walking, then back

at the pet store. He sighed loud enough for the guard to hear. "See my daughter over there?" he asked. "There's this kitten." He faked a smile. "She wants it for Christmas and I made the mistake of hinting Santa might bring it."

The guard nodded sympathetically. "My youngest wants a puppy. It's a slick road."

"Tell me about it." Jed glanced back at the kids. "Would you make sure they get across the street okay? I just want to run in to see if they'll hold on to that kitten for me."

"Sure. Go on in."

"Thanks, man."

Jed ducked into the pet store. Once inside, he nodded at the teenager at the front counter, then made his way to the back.

He'd been in here once, years ago. Had watched Kathy from a distance. She'd never noticed him, or maybe she had and hadn't wanted to talk to him. Either way, he'd left. Not so this time. He walked up to her and stared into her face.

"Morning," he said.

She turned and frowned when she saw him.

Her eyes were the same and despite the thirty-plus years, she didn't look all that different from the last time he'd seen her. She'd been pregnant then, and defiant.

When she'd first told him she was having his baby, he'd assumed she was trying to trick him into marriage. He'd broken things off with her, telling her if she ever came after him for a penny, he would throw her ass in jail.

She hadn't cried, but her look of sadness had ripped him apart. With tears in her eyes, but her head held high, she'd walked away.

Three months later, he realized he was wrong about everything. That he wanted Kathy, wanted their baby. So he'd proposed.

And she'd refused him.

"I won't marry you, Jed Titan," she said, looking him in the eye. "I'll love you forever, but I've seen a dark side to you."

He'd tried everything. Begging, swearing he would change. He'd even managed to seduce her back into his bed. Nothing had worked. In the end, she hadn't changed her mind. When the baby had been born, a boy, he'd offered her money. At first she hadn't wanted to take it, but an early fever had landed her son in the hospital. With minimal insurance and no income because she wasn't back to work yet, she'd seen the value of his offer. The transfer had been made. It was more than she'd expected, enough for her to live on for the rest of her life, if she was careful.

He hadn't seen her after that. He'd married—twice—had daughters, but no other son. He'd told himself it didn't matter, that Kathy was in the past. And there she'd stayed until that day Garth had shown up, begging for money to save her.

And it had given him great pleasure to refuse the boy. To finally punish Kathy for rejecting him.

Now, staring at her, feeling something stir inside he'd thought dead for a long time, he wondered if maybe he'd been wrong.

"Do I know you?" she asked.

There was something about her speech. Not the words, but the way she said them. Something off.

"I'm Jed."

She frowned slightly. "Did I know you? Before?"

"Yes." He moved toward her. "I thought we could go somewhere and talk."

Her expression cleared. "We were friends."

"Yes, we were."

She smiled. "We can go get coffee."

"I'd like that." Jed smiled.

CHAPTER NINETEEN

GARTH STOOD IN FRONT of his office window, staring down at the street below. Even driving over the speed limit, it would take Nick at least two hours to get into town. Two hours Garth didn't want to waste. But he knew better than to go after Jed on his own. Not that he was worried about what the old man might do to him, but because he needed a witness to say it had all been in self-defense.

He kept his mind on the plan, on tactics, because the alternative was to worry about his mother. While no one ever wanted to be kidnapped, Kathy was the least prepared to handle the situation. And Jed would hardly be considerate as he grabbed her.

Anger bubbled. White-hot anger. He'd known his father would come after someone, which was why he'd made sure everyone was protected. But he'd underestimated Jed's willingness to risk it all. The fault was his.

Because of him, his mother was being terrorized by an asshole out for revenge. He'd started this and he would finish it. He vowed that one way or the other, Jed Titan would cease to be a threat. Today.

The door to his office burst open. Dana rushed in. She had a small, black duffel in her hand.

"I don't have a lot of new information," she told him. "The police are keeping the kidnapping quiet as long as possible. Once the press finds out, they'll be all over us. Later, that will be to our advantage, but not right now. The last thing anyone needs is Jed bolting. The cops think he's still in the city somewhere. They told you that, right?"

He nodded.

She dropped the duffel on the floor and crossed to him. "I'm sorry about Kathy. I know she must be scared, but she has an inner strength. She'll be okay."

Garth stared into her brown eyes. "We don't know that."

"He won't hurt her. It wouldn't benefit him in any way."

"That's some comfort." He pulled her close, then kissed her. "You don't have to be here."

"Hey, I'm a professional and I can be very useful. You're lucky to have me at your beck and call."

"That part I know."

The door opened again. This time Skye and Izzy hurried toward them.

"We just heard," Izzy said. "Lexi wanted to come but Cruz made her stay home and relax. This totally sucks. You're going to get him, aren't you? I can't believe it. I should, but I don't."

"I'm sorry," Skye said quietly.

Both women embraced him, hugging him close.

"Oh, Garth," Skye whispered. "You must be so scared."

"She'll be fine," he said automatically, because now that was what he had to believe.

"The police will find Jed," Izzy said.

"They won't have to."

Izzy and Skye stared at him. Dana didn't look surprised.

"You're going after him?" Skye asked.

"Not a question you want to ask," Dana told her.

"You're in on this?"

"No, but I will be." She stepped back and pointed to her duffel. "I came prepared."

Dana wasn't coming along, but he would deal with that problem later.

"I don't like this," Skye said, folding her arms across her chest.

Izzy wrinkled her nose. "Imagine how I feel. You're waiting for Nick, aren't you?"

Garth didn't want to say anything, but he didn't have to. Izzy knew Nick better than Garth.

"He's driving in from the ranch," she said, then nodded slowly. "Okay, but we just got married and I'm pregnant. I don't want anything to happen to him."

"Nothing will," he said, meaning it. This was his fight.

"No offense, but…" Izzy turned to Dana. "You'll keep him safe?"

"Yes."

"My stomach hurts," Skye murmured. "You probably want to talk about your plan. We'll go and leave you to it, but you have to promise to tell us the second you know anything."

Garth nodded. "I will."

They left.

Dana picked up her duffel. "You can yell at me while I get changed."

"Why do you think I'm going to yell?"

"I saw your face when I said I was going with you." She paused at the doorway to his private bathroom. "Someone has to make sure you don't go to jail over this. Jed is the only one I want behind bars. Nick has to stay safe—I promised Izzy. So that leaves me to watch your back."

She looked determined, but he wasn't intimidated. "I'm capable of getting Kathy out and staying on the right side of the law."

"It's not about being capable. It's about being pissed, which you are."

"I won't sacrifice you."

She smiled. "Nice sentiment, but I'm the only professional in the room. I'm coming with you, Garth. That or I'm calling the police and telling them your plan. Then you'll have to get by them as well as by me."

Frustration tightened his chest. "You're damned annoying."

"You're not the first man to tell me that."

He clenched his teeth. "Fine."

"Good."

He looked pissed enough to throw something, Dana thought, but she wasn't backing down. This was too important. They hadn't come all this way to lose Jed now. She knew Garth believed he was in total control of his emotions, but she wasn't so sure. Jed had kidnapped Garth's mother. No one could think rationally through that.

She walked into the bathroom and shut the door behind her. Three minutes later she'd changed into black jeans and a black T-shirt. She walked out with a bulletproof vest and handed it to Garth.

"Are you wearing one?" he asked.

She picked up the second one she'd brought. "Jed's a wild card. We're not starting out stupid."

"But we may end up that way?"

"Maybe. Do you know how we're going to find him?"

Even as she asked the question, she had a feeling she already knew the answer. Garth wasn't the type to leave anything to chance. She respected his need to protect what was his. It might not be her, but that wasn't his fault.

"Do you really want to know?" he asked.

"Sure. I'm on a leave of absence."

"I have a GPS tracking device on his car. I had it put there after he shot at you."

"Impressive."

"You don't sound surprised."

"I'm not."

"It's against the law."

She smiled grimly. "Not today."

LESS THAN AN HOUR LATER, they were parked by a ratty hotel near the highway, their car concealed from the room windows by a van. Dana looked at the run-down cars in the parking lot. Only one stood out. A late-model Suburban belonging to one Jed Titan.

"I'll go ask the desk clerk which room he's in," she said, reaching for the door handle.

Garth grabbed her arm. "Wait a minute. You think he's going to tell you? Just like that?"

"I can be very charming."

He didn't look convinced.

"Someone has to ask and I would rather it was me," she said. She reached into her jeans pocket and pulled out her ID. "Does it sound better if I say I'm the only one with an official badge? Let me talk to him. You can explain to Nick why he's staying in the car."

"What?" Nick yelped. "I'm here for backup."

"Not anymore," Dana said as she got out and walked to the front of the motel.

It was the kind of place made famous in the movies and not in a good way. Places like this catered to the desperate and those on the run. The guy behind the counter wore a short-sleeved shirt stained with sweat and had stringy hair tied back in a ponytail.

"Hey, darlin'," he said around his cigarette. "You need a room for an hour?"

"No, thanks," she said and showed him her badge. "I need information."

He held up both hands. "We run a real clean business here."

"Uh-huh. That's why you rent rooms by the hour."

"The customer's always right."

"Then I'm your best customer. The guy in the Suburban. What room is he in?"

The clerk looked at her badge, then shook his head. "That's private information."

Dana put her badge back in her pocket. "Don't make me show you my gun."

The clerk sighed. "Seventeen, but I don't want no trouble."

"Stay out of my way and you won't get any." She started for the door, then paused. "How much did he pay you to call if anyone came asking for him?"

"Two hundred."

She stared at the guy.

He shifted in his chair. "Seventy-five."

She dug out two twenties. "Here's another forty. Give me a two-minute head start, then you can call." She narrowed her gaze. "I want the two minutes. Don't try cheating me. I'm mean to the bone."

The guy nodded. "I'll spot you three."

She returned to the car. "Got it," she said. "It's downstairs, on the end. The doors are solid enough but the locks look flimsy. You feeling macho enough to kick them in?"

"I could kick in a door," Nick grumbled.

"I'm sure Izzy will reward you later," Dana said.

Garth nodded and they moved toward the building, careful to keep concealed behind cars. They headed for the left side of the motel, then walked around the back, coming out on the other side, next to number seventeen. Dana pulled out her gun and got ready. She looked at Garth.

He held up three fingers, then two, then planted his foot right by the lock. It gave instantly, the door swung open and Dana circled inside.

She crouched low to avoid any flying bullets. It took less than a second for her to train her gun on the people inside. Not that there was any need. Kathy sat on the bed, her legs pulled up to her chest, her arms around her knees. Jed sat in a corner chair, his head in his hands. He looked up when they burst in.

There was a stark pain in Jed's eyes that surprised Dana. A shock and disbelief, as if everything he'd ever known was gone.

"She's not there," Jed said dully. "Kathy's gone."

Garth was silent for a minute. When he spoke, it was with a quiet anger. "What did you think she would be like? I told you what she needed. I told you what would happen if she didn't have the surgery."

"I didn't believe you. I thought she was going to be all right."

Kathy glanced between them. "He's very sad. He keeps crying. He thinks I'm someone else, but I keep telling him I'm me." She scrambled to her feet. "Can I go home now?"

IT TOOK NEARLY TWO HOURS for everything to get explained and Jed to be led away. By then the press had arrived. They swarmed around like ants at a picnic and, try as she might, Dana couldn't seem to avoid them.

"Deputy Birch," one of them called as she walked by. "We'd like to talk to you."

"And I'd like an all-expenses paid trip to Tahiti," she muttered without slowing. "Neither is going to happen."

Just then a familiar Mustang pulled up. Izzy got out and smiled at the reporters. "I have something for you," she called, waving a stack of folders. "A little light reading."

Dana moved toward her, but the reporters got there first and grabbed every copy.

"What do you think you're doing?" Dana asked.

"Giving them background information. Don't get your panties in a bunch. I ran it all by Mary Jo. Now there's a lawyer with attitude. She said it was fine. We were very careful not to give out privileged information or anything the police might want to keep for themselves. But I wanted to move things along. The sooner Jed gets shoved into jail, the better for everyone."

She glanced over Dana's shoulder toward the motel room. Garth was still inside with Kathy. "How are they doing?"

"Garth still wants Jed's head, but Kathy's doing okay. Apparently she remembered Jed enough to simply go with him and he doesn't seem to have hurt her. The medics gave her something to help her relax. Once it kicks in, Garth will take her home. She's given a preliminary statement to the police, but they'll want more. That won't be fun."

"Did Jed fight back or try to escape?"

"He seems broken," she said and explained what had happened. "He'd already lost to Garth and apparently realizing what had happened to Kathy pushed him over the edge." She still couldn't believe he'd thought her condition was a trick to get more money. Talk about an ugly twist of fate. If only he'd been willing to take some responsibility, everything could have been different.

Izzy stared at the motel building. "It's going to be a hell of a story. The rich and powerful Jed Titan brought to this."

"By his own family. They'll be writing about it for months."

"That'll be a pain in the ass, but at least it's over. He won't be able to hurt us anymore." Izzy sounded more resigned than sad.

"You okay?" Dana asked.

"No, but I will be."

"When Garth's done with Kathy, can you give me a ride back to his place?"

"Sure."

"Great. I'll just need a second to talk to him."

Izzy nodded, then pointed to the motel. "You should take your second now. He has Kathy."

Dana turned around and saw him leading Kathy to his car. She was wrapped in a blanket and seemed to be half asleep. When he got her in the car, he carefully closed the door, then crossed to them.

"I'm going to take her home," he said. "Hey, Izzy."

"Hey, yourself. I'm sorry he hurt her."

"Me, too."

She looked around. "I should head back to Lexi's. Nick will be pissed when he finds out I left by myself." She pulled a folder from the front seat of her car. "A copy of what Mary Jo and I put together for the reporters. Just so you know what they'll be writing about."

"Thanks."

Izzy got in her car and pulled off to the side. Dana turned to Garth. There were shadows under his eyes and lines by the corner of his mouth.

"You look tired," she said.

"It's been a hell of a ride. At least it's over now."

Almost, she thought. There was just one more thing to take care of. "How's Kathy?"

"Pretty out of it. Whatever the doctor gave her is strong. She'll sleep through the night. I've already got a psychologist coming in to talk to her about what happened."

Right. Because Kathy would have more trouble processing what had happened. "Is there anything I can do to help?" she asked.

"Not tonight. I won't be back until morning. Are you going to be all right on your own?"

She'd told herself she was staying until it was over. This was pretty much the final moment. Oh, sure, she could make excuses and string things along for a few more days but to what end? Postponing the inevitable wouldn't make it go away.

"I won't be there in the morning," she told him. "I'm going to pack my things and head home."

He frowned. "Why?"

She stepped toward him, then cupped his face. "Because Jed is no longer a problem."

He grabbed her wrist. "You don't have to move out. Dana, I want you there when I get home."

He probably did, she thought sadly. This worked for him…for now. But what happened when this wasn't enough? When her love for him caused her to make demands? Then he would be forced to tell her the truth. And she knew deep down, he wouldn't want to hurt her.

"I want that, too," she said. "Too much and that's the problem." She drew in a breath. "I love you." She shifted her fingers so they covered his mouth. "I don't want you to say anything. I've never let myself be with anyone I could seriously care about. I've never risked falling in love. Despite my past and being terrified, I'm putting it out there. But I don't expect anything in return."

Something flashed through his dark eyes, something she could read. Relief? His own brand of fear? Did it matter?

"You won against a formidable opponent," she continued. "You took down Jed Titan. Now you need to let go of the past and move on with your life. Start over. You have a family. You need to be in the moment and then go find your future." She dropped her arm to her side.

"Dana," he began, then paused.

She knew why. What else was there to say?

"We'll run into each other," she told him. "At various Titan events. Skye's wedding will be hard, but after that, it will get easier. I don't regret loving you, Garth. All that crap about love transforming us and making us better? Damn if it isn't true. I love you. I'll do my best to get over you, but you're going to be a tough act to follow."

She raised herself on tiptoes and kissed him. "I want the best for you. Always."

She turned and walked toward Izzy's waiting car. As she moved through the darkness, she listened for footsteps, foolishly hoping he would come after her, maybe beg her to stay. She wanted him to tell her that of course he'd fallen in love with her, too. That they would be together forever.

There was only silence.

She reached the Mustang, then opened the passenger door. As she turned to get in, she looked across the car to where Garth stood in the parking lot. Their eyes met, but he didn't say anything. Didn't try to stop her.

"Everything okay?" Izzy asked.

"Everything's going to be fine," Dana said, and nearly meant it.

GARTH UNLOCKED THE FRONT door to Glory's Gate and walked inside. The house was silent and cold, as if it had been abandoned a whole lot longer than a few weeks.

The first time he'd been in the house had been eight or nine months before, when he'd come to one of Skye's fund-raisers. He'd wanted to see the Titan family home. Now he'd taken it from Jed. There was no more Titan World, no Titan empire. Just pieces of the whole, his to do with as he pleased.

He crossed through the big entryway, past the grand piano. He took the stairs two at a time, then walked along the long second-floor hallway until he found the master bedroom.

The huge closet was empty, as were the drawers. It didn't look as if anyone had lived here for a long time. It was the same with the other bedrooms. He returned to the main floor and discovered Jed had cleared out the study.

He must have a place in town, Garth thought, walking through the large kitchen and out onto the back porch. From here he could see acres of land. Titan land. *His* land.

He won, just like Dana said. He'd beat Jed at his own game, had taken everything the old man valued. As a bonus, Jed's illegal activities were going to land him in jail for a very long time. Things had turned out better than he'd hoped.

He should celebrate. There was only one problem— the person he wanted to share this with wasn't with him anymore. True to her word, Dana had been gone when he'd returned to his place. She'd moved out, leaving behind empty closets and drawers. The fate of Glory's Gate on a smaller scale.

He told himself it didn't matter. That he'd enjoyed her company but nothing more. That their time together had been great, but she was right. It wouldn't have lasted. Surprisingly, she turned out to be like every other woman, speaking of love as if it were the ultimate gift.

He turned back to the house, but didn't go inside.

Except she *hadn't* been like everyone else. She hadn't begged or pleaded or threatened. She'd told him she'd loved him and then she'd left him. As if saying the words was enough. As if that was all she wanted to do.

He didn't understand that. She had to want something from him. Everyone did. She couldn't just be giving her love to him. Who did that?

He tried to convince himself it was nothing but a mind game, only he knew Dana. She was the most straightforward person he'd ever met. She was tough and vulnerable, powerful and giving. She loved fiercely—he'd seen her love in action.

Given her past, what her father had done to her, it was kind of a miracle she was willing to love at all. Especially someone like him. He knew he wasn't exactly easy or even safe. She'd exposed herself. He could have hurt her. Not that he would, but why would she risk it? Why did she want him to know?

Too many questions, he thought as he walked into the house and locked the back door. He crossed through the kitchen, then went down the long hallway to the living room.

This would pass, he told himself. The ache inside that he couldn't explain. The empty silence in his condo. He believed in traveling light. Dana would only slow him down. Better to be ready at a moment's notice. Now if only he had somewhere to go.

CHAPTER TWENTY

DANA DIDN'T WANT TO answer her front door, but the person knocking didn't seem to be in the mood to walk away. She crossed the small living room and undid the lock.

"Finally," Lexi said, walking inside. "Do you have any idea how swollen my ankles are? A woman of my size should not be standing for so long. There are—" She took one look at Dana's face, then dropped her purse to the floor and held out her arms. "I'm sorry."

Dana brushed away tears, then stepped into her friend's embrace. "You don't know what's wrong."

"I haven't seen you cry in about fifteen years, so I know it's big."

"I'm fine. Or I will be."

"You're not very convincing. I take it this is about Garth?"

"I told him I loved him." Dana stifled a sob. She'd been one massive emotional bleed for nearly two days now and it was getting old. "I told him I loved him and then I walked away. And he let me."

"That bastard." Lexi took her arm and they walked over to the sofa. "When did this happen?"

"After we rescued Kathy."

"You didn't call me."

"I hurt too much."

Lexi took her hand. "I'm sorry you're hurting, but I don't understand how this happened. Garth cares about you. Why would he let you just walk away?"

Dana shook her head. She was willing to be a fool for love, but she drew the line at being played for one. "He doesn't love me, Lexi. I know he doesn't and you know it, too."

"But how... Oh." Lexi's blue eyes darkened. "You were there? I'm sorry. For what it's worth, I don't think he meant it."

"I think he did." Dana drew in a breath. "It's okay, or it will be. I did it. I fell in love. I gave my heart to someone. That's good, right? I'm growing as a person. Right now it feels like someone is ripping my chest apart, but that will get better."

"I don't know what to say," Lexi admitted.

"Another first."

"I'm sorry."

"I'm not. Isn't that the craziest thing ever? I'm not sorry. Loving him was the best."

"What happens now?"

"I go back to my regularly scheduled life. I heal. I continue to be a ray of sunshine in my friends' lives."

"Maybe he'll—"

Dana shook her head. "Don't. Don't pretend he could come back. Hoping would take the last ounce of strength I have. It's over. I've accepted that. Hoping would be too hard."

"THE THREE OF YOU are the most annoying women on the planet," Garth said, ready to start punching the wall. He'd never understood why a man would want to do that. At least he hadn't before. He got it now.

"It's a gift," Izzy said serenely, from her place on the chair next to the sofa where Lexi reclined, her hand on her huge belly.

"Poor Garth," Skye said, from the other chair. "Do you have a blood pressure problem? Should we be worried?"

"I didn't have one before today," he said, unclenching his teeth.

They were in Lexi's living room. He'd brought along a list of Titan assets with the foolish hope they would be able to easily divide them. There was plenty to go around. But would his sisters talk rationally about any of it? Of course not. They'd shifted the conversation every time he'd tried to steer it toward stocks, the racehorses or the house.

Defeated, he tossed down the papers he held and dropped his head to his hands. "I give up," he said. "You win. What do you want?"

"Magic words," Izzy said with a sigh.

"They are pretty," Skye agreed.

"Not pretty enough." Lexi groaned and shifted into a sitting position. "We want to talk about Dana."

His head snapped up. Every sense went on high alert. "Why?" he asked warily.

"She moved out," Skye told him.

"I know that. She said she wanted to go and she did." He hadn't liked her leaving, but she was an adult. He couldn't force her to stay.

"That's it?" Izzy demanded. "You don't have anything more to say?"

"I miss her?"

Izzy rolled her eyes.

"She's in love with you," Skye said quietly. "Do you know that, too?"

"She told me."

They all stared at him.

"And?" Lexi prompted.

"She probably doesn't mean it."

It was a weak response, he knew that. But it was the best he could come up with.

"Men are so stupid," Izzy grumbled. "Dana tells you she loves you and all you can come up with is she probably doesn't mean it? What if she does? What if she totally loves you and believes you're the one?"

His first thought was that his luck wasn't that good. His second was that she would expect him to love her back and that wasn't going to happen. "She doesn't."

Lexi glared at him. "Are you serious? Come on, Garth. Give us something to work with here."

"This isn't your problem."

"It is because we care about you both," Skye said. "Dana is our best friend and you're our brother. Let's walk through this together. She said she loved you and you said what?"

"Nothing."

All three of them stared at him.

"Nothing as in…" Izzy said.

"Nothing," he repeated. "She told me not to say anything."

"And you chose that moment to listen?" Izzy's voice was a shriek.

Lexi's annoyance turned to speculation. "You were totally freaked out," she said slowly.

"That's not how I would describe it."

"But you were. You don't want her to love you. After all, you stood in my office and said you weren't in love with her. I believe your exact words were 'I don't love Dana. I don't do love. Ever.'"

The sisters all exchanged a look. He knew exactly what they were thinking, but they were wrong.

"She wasn't there," he said.

"Yes, she was," Lexi told him. "She heard it all."

He swore silently. No way. He wouldn't have wanted that. Wouldn't have said anything if he'd known. "Are you sure?"

Lexi nodded.

"Talk about sucky timing," Izzy said. She pointed at Garth. "This is all your fault."

"Why? What did I do?"

"You hurt Dana."

"I never asked her to care about me," he said without thinking.

"There's a defense," Lexi snapped. "Dammit, Garth."

He stood. "No way. I'm not the bad guy here. I was minding my own business."

"You were coming after us," Skye reminded him.

"When out of nowhere, Dana appeared."

"You hurt us," Lexi said. "She was protecting us. Man, you so don't deserve her."

He agreed with that.

He hated that he'd hurt Dana. She didn't deserve that. She was…he didn't know what. Special for sure. But love? He wasn't the kind to fall in love. Out loud, he only said, "I don't believe in love."

Lexi nodded as if she thought that was perfectly understandable. "Yes, but the question is, do you believe in Dana?"

Garth was quiet. "What?" Izzy demanded. "What are you thinking?"

"Shh," Skye said. "Let him be. He's a guy. This isn't easy."

He ignored that and them.

He'd always told himself he didn't want to fall in love. That love was all risk and no benefit. He'd won—he had it all. And without Dana, what was it worth?

He wanted to be with her, to share his life with her.

He wanted to make her laugh, make her happy. He wanted her crabbiness and her humor, her stubborn determination and her tender heart.

"What the hell have I done?"

"Finally," Lexi said, and collapsed back on the sofa. "I'm exhausted."

Izzy tilted her head. "I could almost hear the rusty gears grinding in place. I wonder if Nick went through the same kind of thing. I'll have to ask him."

"There's a conversation designed to make him feel good," Skye murmured.

"What do I do?" Garth asked. "How do I fix this?"

"Not our problem," Lexi told him. She picked up the list he'd brought. "Back to dividing up the assets you bought. There are a few personal things I want from the house. A desk in the east guest room. One set of china."

"The one with the blue flowers?" Skye asked. "You always liked that pattern."

"That's the one."

"There's a great set of flatware that goes with it, and you should take some of the crystal."

"Okay."

"I want the racehorses," Izzy said. "When they retire, they can come live on the ranch. Rita will be thrilled." She turned to Garth. "Rita runs the stable."

"I don't care about who gets what," he said, frustrated again. "You have to help me."

"*A,* we don't have to do anything," Skye said, grinning. "*B,* you called this meeting to divide up assets. I'll take a few thousand shares of Titan World for Erin. I know you're going to sell off the company, so they'll be converted into something else, but that's fine. Mitch should get the cattle. I'm with Lexi on wanting a china set. Which leaves the house."

They weren't listening and he had a feeling it was on purpose.

"I'm thinking Garth," Izzy said.

"You should have it," Lexi told him. "You earned it."

"Plus we can have Christmas Day there," Skye said.

Wait a minute. "You said you were having Christmas at Cruz and Lexi's place."

"We changed our minds," Izzy told him. "Just as an FYI, you need a really big tree. I know where all the ornaments are, if that will help."

"It won't."

"I have the name of several caterers," Skye added. "I'm guessing you won't want to cook."

"We are not having Christmas at Glory's Gate."

"Of course we are," Lexi said. "Trust me. You'll love it."

He dropped his head to his hands again. "You're killing me."

"Then our work here is complete."

GARTH EASED HIS CAR up the long driveway.

"Where are we going?" Kathy asked anxiously from the passenger seat.

"It's a surprise."

The look she gave him told him that in her world a surprise wasn't a good thing. Something else Jed had done to her, he thought grimly.

"I have something I want to show you," he amended. Kathy didn't look reassured. He reached out and patted her arm. "It's right there."

He pointed to Glory's Gate.

The large house stood silhouetted against the blue Texas sky. It seemed larger than usual, with windows staring down like eyes and a white fence that rolled to the horizon.

"Who lives here?" Kathy asked as the car came to a stop.

"No one, right now. I want to show you the house."

It was something he'd been planning since he was fourteen and Jed had thrown him out of his office, he thought as he parked the car, then came around to the passenger's side and opened the door.

Kathy got out slowly, cautiously. He held out his hand and helped her out of his car. She stared up at the house.

"It's big."

"Yes, it is," he told her. "And very pretty inside."

She didn't look convinced.

"Jed used to live here," he said.

That got her attention. She smiled. "I know Jed." The smile faded. "He's very sad. He cried. But he'll be better soon."

Nothing Garth was hoping for.

"Is he here now?" she asked.

"No."

Jed was in jail. The judge had seized his passport and revoked bail. The list of charges grew every day. More people were coming forward with information to help the prosecution. It seemed that everyone Jed had ever screwed wanted payback.

"I knew him," Kathy said slowly. "A long time ago." She screwed up her face, as if trying to remember something, then shook her head.

Garth nodded, then released her hands. "Come see the house."

She followed him up the stairs, then through the wide front door. He'd been by earlier, to make sure the place was clean and there were fresh flowers. Now he led her from the entryway to the living room. He started toward the kitchen, but she came to a stop and shook her head.

"I don't like it," she whispered.

"It's my house, Kathy. I bought it for you."

She shook her head again. "No. It's too big." Tears filled her eyes. "I want to go home. Please take me home."

Anger filled him, quickly followed by helplessness. Why couldn't she see he'd done this for her? He wanted her to have everything….

And then he knew. In one of those blinding flashes of insight that were never comfortable, he got it.

All these years and all the effort that had gone into winning, into beating Jed into the ground, had one purpose. He'd always believed that if he could defeat the man who had let this happen to her, if he could just hand her Glory's Gate, then she would be healed. He'd allowed himself to think that simply stepping through the doors and knowing this was her home would be enough. That the magic of victory would replace the damaged cells in her brain.

He'd been wrong.

"Garth?" she whispered.

He crossed to her and put his arm around her shoulders. "It's all right," he whispered. "I'll take you home now."

"Do I have to come back here again?"

"Not if you don't want to."

GARTH RETURNED AT SUNSET. It had been the kind of day moviemakers dream about. Clear and bright with a brilliant sun. He stood in the middle of the house, where his mother had stood. He stared at the walls.

How many generations of Titans had lived here and died here? How many lives had been altered? What secrets existed that he would never know? Glory's Gate. After all this time and all the effort, it was just a house. Nothing more. He'd been the one giving it power it had never earned.

Kathy was back in her house, with her caretakers and her pet store. She was happy again, if still fighting the demons Jed had unleashed. The psychologists said it would take time. The one thing they all had.

He heard a car outside and crossed to the front porch. Dana parked her truck next to his BMW. The contrast made him smile, as did seeing her climb out.

She wore jeans and boots, a long-sleeved T-shirt. He couldn't tell from this distance, but he would bet she wasn't wearing any makeup. Which was just like her. Her gaze met his, then she started toward the house.

"You texted," she said when she was halfway up the stairs.

He'd sent her a message earlier, asking her to meet him here. He hadn't been sure she would show up, but he'd hoped.

He didn't know why he hadn't seen it before. He'd spent his whole life chasing justice, never realizing it couldn't replace what had been lost. He'd been searching for the wrong thing. He should have been looking for love and connection. But until today, he didn't think he would recognize love if it came up and bit him on the ass. He was hoping to change that.

Dana slowly crossed the porch. She didn't know what to think, what to expect. Garth's half smile was a little scary.

But seeing him was good. He was as tall and handsome as she remembered. He was the kind of man who made women look twice. The kind she never would have looked at even once, mostly out of fear. Now she stared hungrily, taking in all of him. Being without him had been harder than she would have thought. More painful. Being around him made everything easier... better.

She didn't know why he'd gotten in touch with her. In a few minutes she would ask, but for now it was enough to be close. Which made her one sick puppy, but it was a weakness she could live with. She wanted to hope, but she knew better. His text message could mean anything. It wasn't as if he'd sent her a message saying "meet me at Glory's Gate. I can't live without you." Life wasn't that tidy.

"I'm here," she said when she reached the front door.

"Thanks for coming. Tell me what you think of the house."

She looked at the place where she'd spent so much time growing up. "It's big and I'm sure it's a bitch to heat in the winter."

He led the way inside. She followed.

"I brought Kathy here," he told her. "I thought being here would fix her."

Pain sliced through her. "It didn't. I'm sorry."

"I've spent most of my life fighting ghosts," he said, staring at the large rooms around them. "I told myself if I won, if I could defeat Jed, then things would go back to the way they were before. I didn't even know that's what I believed until I brought her here. But she doesn't want this. The house only scared her. It's been a hell of a day."

"I'm sorry," she repeated. "Is she okay now?"

He looked at her. "Yes. I took her home."

"I know it's hard, but in the end, you got everything you wanted."

"Did I? I'm not so sure."

He stared into her eyes. She looked back, wanting to protect herself, but knowing there wasn't much point. She loved him and she'd already told him. There weren't any more secrets between them.

Then he smiled at her. "Damn, but I wasn't expecting you."

"You asked me to come."

"That's not what I meant. I wasn't expecting you to invade my life, my bed, my house, my soul. I'm doing this wrong, aren't I?"

As she didn't know what he was doing, she couldn't answer. Hope returned and even though she tried to squash it, she couldn't.

Then he did the most amazing thing…in the history of the universe. He dropped to one knee, took her hand in his and said, "Dana Birch, I love you. I'm sorry I didn't get it before. I never thought I would love anyone. I didn't believe in love. You're amazing and I'm so lucky to have found you. I love you. Marry me, please. Marry me."

The unexpected words stunned her. She couldn't breathe. Then, to her amazement and horror, she started to cry.

"Of all the times to turn into a girl," she muttered as he stood and pulled her close.

"It's okay."

"It's not. It's humiliating."

But it was hard to feel anything but good when his strong arms hugged her tight against him.

He kissed her, his mouth warm and sure.

"I love you," he whispered against her lips. "I love you."

Words she would never get tired of hearing.

"But I thought…" she began.

He drew back and stared into her eyes. "I panicked."

"You know I heard you?"

"Yes. Please forgive me. I'll do anything."

The kind of apology she liked best, she thought with a smile. "Maybe," she said. "Over time. If you convince me."

"Absolutely."

He kissed her again and she felt the familiar melting begin inside.

"You haven't said yes," he said. "Are you going to marry me and live with me here?"

She rested her head on his shoulder. "I'll marry you, but we're not living here. This house is from another time. I want us to plan our future. We'll find a new place in the suburbs."

"Seriously?" He sounded worried. "The suburbs?"

"Uh-huh. You can cut the lawn on weekends."

"Can I get a rider mower?"

"If it makes you happy."

"You make me happy." He pulled a diamond ring out

of his pocket and slid it onto her left ring finger. "I bought this, in case you were wondering. I have a receipt."

She laughed, then caught her breath. The diamond sparkled on her finger. She never would have thought of herself as a diamond kind of girl, but she totally got the appeal.

He pulled her close again. "I need you, Dana."

"Not as much as I need you."

Then his mouth was on hers and absolutely everything was exactly how it was supposed to be.

EPILOGUE

Christmas Eve

"I'M GOING TO THROW UP," Skye said dramatically. "And I can't breathe. What if Mitch changes his mind? What if he's not there? What if he's found someone else?"

Lexi looked at herself in the mirror. "I'm a whale."

"A beautiful whale," Dana said. "Skye, you need to start breathing. And where the hell is Izzy?"

"Probably having sex with Nick in the closet."

"The ceremony is in ten minutes," Dana said. "I refuse to be in charge."

"Too late," Izzy said, breezing into the downstairs study. "You are, by default. Which is kind of funny if you think about it."

"Am I laughing?" Dana asked. "Do you see me laughing?"

"Someone has to be and it's not me," Skye said, turning from the mirror, where she'd been pinning up her hair. "There are—" Her eyes widened. "Your dresses. They're so beautiful. And they match."

"We knew you really wanted bridesmaids, but didn't think you should," Lexi said, hugging her. "Surprise."

Skye's green eyes filled with tears. "I love you guys so much." She waved her hands in front of her face. "Help! I can't cry. I'll ruin my makeup."

"Crabby thoughts," Izzy said quickly. "Think crabby thoughts. The last time you were cut off in traffic. Or how some people don't recycle."

"That would be *my* annoyance," Lexi told her.

"Oh, right."

Skye sniffed. "I'm okay now. I'll be fine. I can't believe you did this for me." She sighed. "But we don't have flowers for you."

Dana rolled her eyes. "Seriously? You think we'd go to all this trouble to buy matching dresses and then not take care of the flowers? You've got to trust us."

"I do," Skye said earnestly. "I love you all so much. But we can't hug. We'll wrinkle."

"Sentimental to the end," Dana said.

Fidelia, Mitch's housekeeper, bustled into the room with Erin at her side. Skye's daughter was dressed in a satin plaid dress of black and Christmas-green and red. Her hair had been curled, she proudly wore lip gloss and carried a basket of flowers.

"Mommy, you look so beautiful."

"Thank you, Bunny Face. So do you."

Dana took in Skye's long ivory gown, the spray of flowers she'd pinned in her hair and the glow of happiness that made her even more stunning.

This day had been a long time coming. They'd been through so much together. First fighting Garth, then fighting Jed. But they'd clung to each other through all of it, and had survived to walk out the other side.

No, not survived, she told herself. They had thrived. Jed was in jail. Every day brought new charges, as more people came forward with information. He'd been the bad guy for a lot longer than anyone knew.

Lexi and Cruz had made a life for themselves and were expecting their baby in a few weeks. Lexi was determined not to know the sex of the baby until she was surprised at delivery, but Cruz had hinted he knew it was a boy. They were planning a wedding sometime in the late spring.

Izzy and Nick would spend most of the winter remodeling Glory's Gate. Garth had given it to them to use for the disadvantaged kids they hosted. They were going to turn Glory's Gate into a year-round facility.

Skye and Erin would stay with Mitch at his ranch, where they were now. They wanted to start a family right away. Erin was excited by the thought of a baby sister or brother, along with a puppy. Dana had a feeling the puppy would arrive first.

As for her and Garth, they were buying a house close to Lexi and Cruz. Dana had left the Titanville sheriff's office. Being engaged to a Titan made working there difficult at best. She was using her share of the stock sale to start a security business aimed at teaching single women how to stay safe in their lives.

In two days, right after Christmas, they were flying to Las Vegas to get married. It would be quiet and fuss-free. Exactly what they both wanted.

There was a knock on the study door. Dana went to answer it. Kathy stood there, looking pretty in a blue dress. She was smiling.

"The lady in charge asked me to say it was time," she whispered to Dana.

"Thank you."

"Garth said you're going away for a little while."

"Just five days," Dana told her. "Then we'll be back. We'll come see you."

"Good." Kathy beamed. "I found your puppy. He's a black Lab and his name is Jack."

Dana hugged her. "Thank you so much. I can't wait to meet him."

"You're going to be with Garth now, aren't you?"

"Yes, I am. We'll be a family together."

"You're the one I wanted for him," Kathy said. "I know you'll make each other very happy."

The words were spoken with an unusual clarity, as if for that moment, she was the way she'd been before. Then her expression softened and her eyes took on a dreamy quality. "Garth is always nice. He's a good man."

"Yes, he is."

Kathy waved and went to join the other guests.

Garth stepped into the hallway, looking sinfully handsome in a black suit. "We're ready."

"I heard. Your mom found us a puppy."

He looked worried. "You okay with a dog?"

"It seems inevitable. His name is Jack. We can pick him up when we get back."

He leaned in and kissed her. "Still want to marry me?"

"Absolutely."

"Good. Because I'm not letting you get away." He smiled. "I'll be the good-looking one at the other end of the aisle."

"Thanks for the hint."

She turned back to Skye and Lexi and Izzy. "They're ready."

"So are we," Izzy said, passing out glasses of sparkling cider. "But before we go, I'd like to propose a toast. To us. I love each of you."

"I love each of you, too," Skye, Lexi and Dana said. They clinked glasses.

Dana's heart was full. She didn't think she'd ever been so happy in her life. For years she'd been afraid to love too much, afraid to want to belong, for fear of getting lost in the need. It had taken women who were like sisters to her and a very special, very unlikely, hero to show her the power of believing, not only in herself, but in those around her.

"To the Titan sisters," Lexi said. "All four of us."

"To us."

* * * * *